W9-BLA-285

BROWSING COLLECTION
14-DAY CHECKOUT
No Holds • No Renewals

FLORES
AND
MISS
PAULA

ALSO BY MELISSA RIVERO

The Affairs of the Falcóns

FLORES AND MISS PAULA

A NOVEL

MELISSA RIVERO

ecco

An Imprint of HarperCollinsPublishers

This is a work of fiction. Names, characters, places, and incidents are products of the author's imagination or are used fictitiously and are not to be construed as real. Any resemblance to actual events, locales, organizations, or persons, living or dead, is entirely coincidental.

FLORES AND MISS PAULA. Copyright © 2023 by Melissa Rivero. All rights reserved. Printed in the United States of America. No part of this book may be used or reproduced in any manner whatsoever without written permission except in the case of brief quotations embodied in critical articles and reviews. For information, address HarperCollins Publishers, 195 Broadway, New York, NY 10007.

HarperCollins books may be purchased for educational, business, or sales promotional use. For information, please email the Special Markets Department at SPsales@harpercollins.com.

Ecco® and HarperCollins® are trademarks of HarperCollins Publishers.

FIRST EDITION

Designed by Alison Bloomer

Graphic by Rodina Olena/Shutterstock

Library of Congress Cataloging-in-Publication Data has been applied for.

ISBN 978-0-06-327249-1

23 24 25 26 27 LBC 5 4 3 2 1

For Seba, Gabo, and Bartosz

SPRING

1

FLORES

I FIND THE NOTE UNDER MY FATHER'S URN, ON THE MORNING THAT MARKS what would have been his sixty-third birthday. It has been rolled like a scroll and flattened under the weight of the wooden box that houses his ashes. The paper is white and unlined, its corners sharp enough to slice the skin on my hardened fingers. The ink is black and faded, but I recognize my mother's elongated loops descending toward the edge of the paper.

Perdóname si te fallé. Recuerda que siempre te quise.

My stomach drops. I reread the words, my thumb going over each one as I mouth them, just to make sure my eyes got them right. For nearly three years, my mother and I have tended to this altar and my father's urn, but this is the first time I've seen this note. My mother asking for forgiveness now when he is no longer here—it's almost appalling. Except that she's not one to recognize her failings. She has never once acknowledged when she's wronged me, and I can only recall my father ever asking *her* for forgiveness.

So what had she done that needed forgiving? And did it really take death for her to admit a wrong? Better late than never, I guess, but to do so here, on this sacred space, seems almost sacrilegious.

When my father was alive, my mother had devoted this shelf in the living room to la Virgen de Fátima. Her statue stood at the center, a pyrite cluster glittered at her feet. My mother offered her fresh flowers weekly and water in a wineglass daily. Sometimes she burned palo santo from Peru or candles affixed with images of Christ that she bought at C-Town. Occasionally, she held folded pieces of paper to her mouth and, with her eyes shut tightly, whispered to or even kissed them before tucking them under the pyrite cluster. Prayers and petitions, I assumed. Spells, certainly. Confessions, perhaps. Maybe even desires. I always knew better than to look and never dared to ask.

Now my father's urn is the altar's center. The items that were once at his bedside reside here too: his rosary, with its silver cross and red glass beads; the bell he rang to call us over when his voice became small; prayer cards for Saint Jude and Sarita Colonia; his statue of San Martín; and a seashell he had brought home from a beach long ago. His favorite picture, however—one of him, my mother, and my grandmother on a boat in Yarinacocha—is in my bedroom. My mother, superstitious as she is, forbade the image of any living person on an altar, especially her own.

Over the last three years, new additions have appeared. An amethyst has joined the pyrite. So has a glass rose I found at the Salvation Army and which my mother insisted be kept in the hallway until she was able to cleanse it. Right now there are the pink flowers, which I bring my father regularly, especially on important days like today. He favored peonies, for their rosy scent and fullness. It is spring; they are in bloom for only a little while longer.

This period—the three months that stretch from his birthday to his deathday—is the heaviest of the year. My mother says it is because he comes around during this time. I say it is because the memories do.

These days, I mostly tend to the altar, wiping the area with a mixture of my mother's agua Florida and tepid New York City tap water. Growing up, she had filled our Brooklyn apartment with its smell, setting water in a glass jar on the fire escape whenever the full moon rose, waking up before the sun to make sure its light never touched the water. Then she'd stuff the jar with orange and lemon peels, cloves, sticks of cinnamon, rum or vodka—whatever was cheaper—and let it sit until the next full moon, when she'd squeeze out the ocher extract, pour it into spray bottles and jars, and use the elixir to cleanse herself, us, our home. It's also what Ma used to wipe down this altar and all the ill bodies she cared for over the years. It's what I used on my father's body during the six weeks he was home from the hospital, before Death called. A kind of role reversal: How often had he rubbed an egg on my body as a child to take away susto or el mal de ojo? But there was no escaping the unseen force that lingered during his final days. When I clean the altar now, I repeat the same ritual and prayer I whispered then, a version of what I had seen both my parents do whenever they needed a reset. I rub the mixture behind my ears (*to open them*), press my fingers on the bone beneath my eyes (*that I may always see with clarity*), and dab the spot between my nose and lips, inhaling the tang of orange peels and cloves (*a reminder to breathe*).

But I never touch my father's urn. Not until a moment ago, when I replaced the old doily it sits on with a new one my mother brought home from work.

It's not unusual for my mother to leave notes under her crystals, often with a distinct offering: one red rose. Sometimes she'll even include incense or a splash of wine too. There's a note now, visible under the pyrite. Once the saints have done their work, she takes the petition to the fire escape, where she burns it and scatters the remains. The single red rose is discarded, replaced with a bouquet in all the colors imaginable.

But the petitions are always out in the open—never hidden, like this one. Had I not wiped the space clean and moved the urn itself, I might never have seen it.

I read it again.

Forgive me if I failed you. Remember that I always loved you.

What does she mean by putting it under my father's remains? How long has this note been here? What is it she wants him to forgive, even in death?

I roll the piece of paper back up and tuck it under the urn, just as I found it. I wonder if she'll ever burn it.

· · ·

IT'S THE TUESDAY after Memorial Day weekend, and of course I'm the only one at the Bowl. I'm usually the only person here before nine A.M. anyway, which is fine by me. The fewer people to talk to, the better. I can sip my quad Americano in peace, take a few deep breaths between emails and my to-do list—my *to-do* list—before the week ahead hits. Try to will away the latest headache induced by my mother, if I'm being honest.

Lately, though, the newbies have been coming in at this ungodly hour, eager to show their enthusiasm for working at our small but intrepid online fish and aquarium business. They arrive decked out in their collared shirts and khakis, unable to shake those corporate fatigues or that early morning start, as if trying to model some kind of behavior that the rest of us are supposed to emulate now that a new round of funding has hit. It always rubs us OGs the wrong way. The newbs catch on soon enough.

Today the office is still in a slumber, as is much of DUMBO; what you'd expect after a holiday weekend. The sun splits apart our open floor into slabs of shadow and light. Rows of black screens divide the white room into rows. Three massive television screens hang on the wall. Later they'll live stream the latest panda giving birth at a zoo, a gaming competition, or whatever else fascinates the head designer, the self-appointed controller of the TV screens. Cables twist and bulge like varicose veins beneath desks and along the gaps between the islands. Like other start-ups, our office is dog-friendly, and sometimes a paw or two gets tangled in the cables; human feet too, but how else do you fit eighty-plus people in here?

I head to my team's pod at the far end of the room. This means I have to make my way through the front end—or what some might call the "pretty" and "friendly" side of the business. Workstations are decorated in varying degrees of creativity—and toxic positivity, if you ask me. The creative services team with their Pokémon drawings taped to the backs of their monitors; marketing with their *Finding Dory* Happy Meal toys spread out on their desks like talismans; customer specialists with marquees that read THANK COD UR HERE and FISH UPON A STAR. Even wedding photos in personalized frames. Ludicrous to think they or we will be around long enough to settle in. This is a start-up, after all.

I glance at the marketing pod. There's no sign that Max Dorado, our vice president of marketing, is at his desk yet. He has a habit of coming in on the early side too, unable—unwilling, maybe—to adjust to our normal working hours, even though he's been here for over a year now.

My team—a trio soon to be a quartet—is spread out over two black tables tucked into a corner of the office, beside the accounting pod and near two of the four windows in the entire space. Unlike our other colleagues, our desks are sparse. They have only what we need to do our job: monitors, notebooks, a pair of calculators, a pencil holder, a drawer full of pain meds and Emergen-Cs that I've been hoarding from the first-aid cabinet in the pantry. The corner suits us—we are finance, after all, and need privacy to do our work with minimal distractions. Except for nosy newcomers curious about our "sales" after a marketing push, most folks come by only to peek at the world outside the windows (which we're thankful to face) or to adjust the blinds (which pisses us off), but otherwise we're left alone, and that's something of a relief. To have no one chatting you up or looking over your shoulder while you work. And at least we're not the engineers, who are siphoned off to an entirely separate room with a single window. Let's be real—what engineer likes to interact much with the outside world anyway?

I settle into my space. My boss, Jon, sits directly across from me, our monitors back to back, but neither he nor the rest of my team is in the office just yet. I take off my father's bomber jacket and hang it over my chair. It's summer, but once Jon comes in and turns on the AC, I'll need it. And unless it's thirty degrees out and I *really* need my North Face, I wear my father's jacket.

I pull my PC out of my JanSport, a beat-up teal bag like the one I carried back in eighth grade. At the bottom is the crushed letter from my landlord. I connect my laptop to the two monitors on my desk and power them up. All three chant, but that letter is louder.

This letter serves as official notice that your current lease
for the abovementioned unit will not be renewed. The last
day of tenancy will be September 30.

My head pounds. A couple of episodes of *The Handmaid's Tale*, a few glasses of wine, the letter, that note I found on the altar—yeah, I guess I should expect a hangover. I practically inhaled that tagliatelle last night just to make sure there was enough in my gut to suck up all that Cab. Guess it didn't work. Maybe it's age. Maybe I can't do at thirty-three what I did at twenty-three, but I need to be good today. Jon wants a closer look at the numbers so far this year. Numbers that he and Eric, our CEO, will eventually weave into a narrative. A certain kind of spell or prayer, not all that different from the ones my mother brings to her altar. In any case, whatever I conjure is never something that describes the actual state of the company, but more akin to an aspiration. No one wants to hear that we have just six months of cash left in the bank. We need the good stuff: how our acquisition of Fisk & Tanks will help us expand in the Midwest; how we're ramping up marketing activity on the West Coast; how the overpaid Ivy League grads we hired this past year have already started to turn things around. That's what I need to help Jon show Eric, and what Eric needs to tell the board. It's why I need to focus on these charts and the presentation, not on my messy home life.

But why am I making these damn presentations? Why am I still here?

Deep breaths. I've asked myself these questions since day one, if I'm being honest, when I worked well into the night, knowing I needed to pull the long hours. Even when I came back after Pa died, I didn't mind doing the grunt work and whatever else was asked of me. I needed to stay busy. I wanted to prove I was okay. I just didn't expect to still be doing it all these years later. I have an MBA, coño, and a couple of hundred thousand dollars in debt to prove just how overqualified I am for this job. It's fine. It's fine. I need to focus on the prize, which isn't a title or even a salary increase.

It's how much I'm gonna get once we sell this fucker.

My phone screen lights up.

Yoli me llamas

I give my mother's text a thumbs-up, but decide to call later. We should both be working.

I take off my Invisaligns, pop a couple of Advils for good measure, chug my lukewarm Americano, then turn on my headphones and let Benito's "Soy Peor" ease me into my inbox. Minutes later, a ChitChat notification slides across the bottom right-hand corner of my screen. It's from Max.

Estas?

2

PAULA

"COME, COME, MISS PAULA!" SHANTI WAVES AT ME FROM THE REGISTERS AS I walk down the center aisle to start my shift at DollaBills. Or *Doyabiys*, as I like to say to the other sales associates that speak Spanish, but Shanti speaks nothing but English. I had to explain the different ways you can pronounce the *ll* in Spanish for her to get the joke.

The wide center aisle, which has been assigned to me for a year now, is only partially filled with the summertime items that I re-stocked from the basement just yesterday. Beach towels and pails, flip-flops, inflatable flamingos, and straw hats so big they could shade a pair of D-cup breasts. I took two home. All the items are clearly selling well. I'll need to replenish our stock today.

Four registers sit on top of an elevated platform at the end of the aisle, though there's usually just two of us working them at any given time. Today it is me and Shanti.

"Come on, let's go!" she urges as she opens the side door that separates the platform from the rest of the floor. "You are so slow these days."

"What do you mean, *slow*? Have some respect for your elders," I say in my very best and sternest English, though she just laughs. It's not my age that slows me down today, although sometimes I wonder if people expect me to walk with a cane now that I'm sixty-three. But we're in the middle of a heat wave, and I walk the twelve blocks from the apartment to the store. That is obviously why I'm slow. That and the soreness in my thighs from last night's Total Body Workout class at the YMCA.

I set my purse inside one of the cubbies beneath the registers, and Shanti leads me to the back, all the way to Sandeep's office. "What are you doing?" I whisper. "We can't leave the registers."

"Don't worry, someone will cover." She whistles and waves over one of the other store workers. As we enter the office, Sandeep stands beside his desk, holding a bouquet of flowers from the grocery store down the block and a small box of Russell Stover chocolates from aisle 8.

Shanti shouts, "Happy anniversary, Miss Paula!" but it is Sandeep who startles me. He leans over and kisses me on the cheek. Twice. Who knew he wasn't afraid of touching.

"Happy anniversary!" A peppermint candy rolls around his mouth as he hands me the flowers. "Two years, Miss Paula. Who'd have ever guessed? Do you remember your interview? I did not think you'd last two days!"

"Neither did I!"

We laugh, but seriously, who'd believe I'd still be here?

• • •

TWO YEARS AGO, I sat in this very office while Sandeep looked over my application and "résumé." I had never needed one, but thankfully, I had a daughter who had written plenty. I had shopped at this store for decades, when it had a different name and when there were many discount and dollar stores in the neighborhood instead of the handful that remain. Shanti had started working here the year Martín got sick. Of course he started chatting her up immediately, Martín being Martín, always flirting and making jokes! I could never get *that* comfortable with people. I always believed that if someone laughed it was because they were laughing at me. If they wanted to be my friend, it was because they wanted something from me. Better to keep everyone at a distance. Besides, Shanti was just another store clerk, no different from all the others he'd been friendly with over the years.

But then she came to his memorial, as did so many of those people he chatted up and joked with in the neighborhood over the years. So many that when the organist played "El Pescador," their hum swelled like a river behind me long after the song ended.

For months after Martín died, Shanti and I chatted whenever I went into the store—about her boys, both now in elementary school, and her husband, a police officer in the Bronx. Back then, they lived with her parents in Ozone Park. Then one day, as the first anniversary of Martín's passing came closer, I went into the store for shower curtains. She must have seen the look on my face. Maybe she remembered the anniversary too. She told me they were looking for help.

"In case you want to stay busy, Miss Paula," she said.

Sandeep interviewed me. I had seen him in the store many times, racing down the aisles from one worker to the next in his polo shirts and pleated pants like he was hurrying to talk himself out of a parking ticket. And oh, those glasses! He always wore a different pair. Tortoiseshell one day, red another. I thought he was either losing them too frequently or making a lot of money from the store that he could afford so many pairs. Later I found out that his son happened to work at a popular online store for frames. I now have three pairs myself.

During my interview, Sandeep rolled a mint in his mouth, like he's doing now. He read my application and résumé, both of which, at the time, I thought only someone who spoke English all their life could fill out. I needed your help typing up how I had taken care of viejitas until they died of old age or Alzheimer's. I even mentioned how I cared for Martín when he was sick, which wasn't so different but much harder to say aloud, and probably just as hard for you to write.

But I was most nervous about the things we wrote that were not so true. I never worked in the men's shoe department at Saks, but I had practiced what to say many times over the phone with that friend of yours, Jasmine. Taking care of sick people wasn't enough, you said, and Jasmine had worked at that store for millonarios. I needed to pretend that I had worked there even if Dolla-Bills is not a store for millonarios. Sandeep even called Jasmine, right then and there, and when my reference "checked out," he offered me the job: twelve dollars an hour, minimum of thirty-five hours a week, and one day had to be a weekend day.

I took the job. It was the first time I worked since Martín's diagnosis. Since he died. Who knew saying yes to Sandeep's offer would bring me to the edge of tears. I did not know whether it was appropriate to hug him, so I shook his hand instead, thanking him and thanking him, though I couldn't explain why I had reacted this way. I gave Shanti two thumbs-ups as I left. She clasped her hands in prayer and looked up toward heaven. *Is God even listening?* I wanted to ask. Since your father got sick, I had started to wonder if my prayers were being ignored, but in that moment, I thought maybe God was finally paying attention.

The next day, Sandeep handed me my DollaBills smock. Green, with the logo just above my left breast, and a badge with my name on it in large black letters: PAULA. What would Martín say if he saw me now? "Que vergüenza," probably. Folding clothes, organizing trinkets, letting the world see I do such menial work for a living. But I'm not ashamed of it. I've worked hard enough that my pay is now three dollars more an hour, and Sandeep doesn't touch my Sundays unless it's an absolute emergency. It pays more than taking care of old sick people ever did. It's not as sad. I worry only about feeding myself and my child and cleaning myself and no one else. My back doesn't hurt as much. And the YMCA is just a few blocks away. I stop there three, sometimes four days out of the week to run on the treadmill or take a class. Me, doing Pilates! I've lost twenty pounds. I wear tight pants now when I exercise, the ones they sell in aisle 2, not the sweats, and always take advantage of my ten percent employee discount.

That night I got the job, you took me to Cardamone's to celebrate over an Italian dinner. We laughed, loudly and in spite of the stares. I can't remember when we last laughed like that. In some ways, it felt like a betrayal. In others, a small triumph. An old but familiar sensation arose within me, one I recall feeling when I first kissed Martín; then when I stepped onto the plane that brought me to him and to New York; and again when I first heard your cry. That night the joy and unease of the new job—of hearing our laughter, after so long—became one such moment. An instant of infinite and deliciously terrifying possibilities.

. . .

"I'M GLAD I hired you," Sandeep tells me now, "and even happier that you stayed these two years. I thought you might run back to Saks at any moment." He winked, and though he's never brought it up, I always suspected he knew that I had lied about the Saks job. Would a place like that ever really hire someone like me? ¿Una viuda, vieja y gorda? Even I have to laugh at how ridiculous it sounds. But he's never said anything about it, and this makes him good, I think, because the truth is, I had nowhere else to go and nothing else to occupy my time.

He lowers his voice and hands me an envelope. "I hope you stay for many more."

It is my bonus. Mi yapa. Now, the word *bonus* usually means money, but this is DollaBills, not Saks. And this is Sandeep, who is thoughtful but mindful of his money. On my first anniversary, I got the same show: the brightest sunflower from Bloom Corner Deli, a box of chocolates from aisle 8, and an envelope. I thought, *Yes! I can get new bedsheets, or paint the entire apartment, or even get on a bus to Atlantic City for the weekend!* But it was a twenty-dollar gift card to Dunkin' Donuts.

Perhaps today it is a thirty-dollar card. Except when I take the envelope, I don't feel a hard, rectangular gift card inside. The envelope is thin, and as I start to thumb the flap, he puts his hand up. "Maybe open it at home, Miss Paula."

I look at Shanti, who just shrugs. I thank him, grab a few mints from his desk, then head back to the registers. I slip the envelope inside the little pocket in my purse before sending you a text.

"It's money," Shanti whispers. "I know."

"How?"

"Because he gave me money this year too."

"How much?"

"Oh, Miss Paula." She laughs. "We can't talk about that. If we do, we may not be friends anymore."

3

FLORES

THE CHITCHAT MESSAGE IS FROM MAX. HE JOINED THE COMPANY OVER A YEAR ago to a bit of fanfare. In the weeks leading up to his first day, word had spread about this Harvard grad who'd join the ranks of middle management. The Bowl was a bit of a hit with investors in its early years, but by the time Max joined, it had lost some of its luster. Our growth had stalled, and Max was part of a newly refurbished marketing team that was supposed to restore some of that sheen.

A few folks caught glimpses of him during his interviews, which naturally caused a bit of a stir.

"He's really tall!" Starr had shouted to me from another bathroom stall. "And before you say I'm being racist for expecting him to be short because he's Mexican, I'm not. He's at least six-one or six-two. That's just *tall*."

Jasmine had been equally astonished, but in her case, it was by his choice of attire. He wore a suit to every round of interviews. A *real* suit, and she'd know. She used to work at Saks. Now she did double duty as the Bowl's office manager and receptionist and had the dubious pleasure of tending to candidates at each interview—fetching water, offering Cheez-Its and gummy fruit snacks, pointing out the restrooms. It was on his second interview, as she escorted him to Betta, the interview conference room, that his sleeve brushed against her bare forearm. "It was virgin wool, Flores," she whispered to me then. "No way are these guys ever gonna hire a pretentious fucker like that."

But Max was going to get the job no matter what he wore. Nik, our EVP of marketing, had been courting the guy for months. Before the Bowl, Nik had worked with major ad agencies and Fortune 500 companies. He had grown accustomed to limitless budgets and blamed his stunted creativity at the Bowl on our penchant for penny-pinching. There wasn't much he could do aside from having the occasional YouTuber stand on a random corner in Midtown and sign Bowl-branded fishbowls. He didn't have the budget for anything else, or so he said. Then, on his annual trip to the Maldives, where he reset, recharged, and refilled his creative well, there was a moment of clarity. He needed to hire a number two, specifically Max, especially if he wanted the promotion to chief marketing officer. Nik had met Max at one of these e-comm "disrupters" conferences. Max's presentation on distinct branding for millennials and Gen Z had bar graphs and tables, and the best part was that Nik didn't have to introduce himself to the guy. Max already knew who he was—that's how great Nik was at networking and ass-kissing. All Nik needed was someone who could do the analytical work he despised. Max was the perfect fit.

And although Max is supposed to report to Nik, he grabs coffee on the regular with Eric, or so Jasmine tells me. Presumably to discuss what's working and what isn't on the marketing front. But this is Eric's typical MO with Bowlers he values: regardless of who you report to, there's a dotted line to the CEO, and this is how the Bowl can get into trouble.

It's also why I don't totally write Max off as just another overpaid shiny hire. The other reason is that we're both hyphenated Americans, straddling our two cultures. He's Mexican; I'm Peruvian. In some ways, it's only natural that we'd be drawn to each other in the first place. Not that Jasmine felt the need to connect with him this way. To her, he was still an opportunistic white man. But he clung to his Mexican identity in a way that made me feel like I could claim my Peruvian one. It didn't matter that I hadn't been to Peru in years, or that I wasn't particularly close to my family there, or that I wasn't as familiar with its history and politics as I could be. None of that eroded my identity. Perhaps I needed his reassurance because I knew very few Peruvians outside my parents' circle, and certainly none in places like the Bowl.

· · ·

MAX HAD BEEN to all the places in Peru that were on my bucket list, in case I ever went back: Cusco, Arequipa, Trujillo, Iquitos. I had been to Peru only twice, I explained to him over coffee. The last time I was a teenager, and we visited my father's family in Lima. Pa had always wanted to visit other cities in Peru, but once you leave a country, you go back to see family, not to play tourist. And when he lived there, my father had only ever been to Pucallpa, the place where his mother was born, and incidentally, where mine was too, though my mother rarely talks about it or her family. What I do know is that they had moved to Lima when she was just a kid. The city was harsher than either of her parents imagined it would be, and years later, her mother left it with another man. My father told me this, his way of explaining why my mother walked out of the apartment or stepped out of the car whenever they argued. She'd come back, he'd tell me, don't worry; this is just how she learned to deal with tough stuff, but she's not her mother. Still, I wondered if she'd do the same to me and Pa. If she'd leave because it had gotten too hard or because she could find happiness with someone else. I always thought she'd leave first. I never expected it to be Pa.

I still don't know why I dropped all of that during my first conversation with Max. Maybe it was our connection to Peru. Maybe it was because I knew somehow that he had experienced a similar loss.

"But you still have your mother," he told me then. He confessed that he had neither parent. He never did say how they died, only that he lost his father when he was a child, his mother when he was a teenager, and what he remembers distinctly about her is the Chanel No. 5 she put on before she stepped out the door.

As the months passed, and we reviewed his team's key performance indicators and spend, he vented about the work, befuddled at how anyone could give fifty million dollars to a bunch of "cowboys," as he put it, just so they could sell high-end aquariums and exotic fish online. ("They're good salesmen," I told him.) He was utterly shocked at the suppressed elation of a small cohort of Bowlers just after the presidential election. ("They're from Virginia," I explained.) Venting quickly turned into "We have to do *something*." ("Do we?")

"Buenos días." He smiles now, blushing as he wrestles his foot from a cadre of cables. He wouldn't normally come to my desk to talk to me. We have a tacit understanding that no one should see us together to avoid gossip and any sort of perceived "alliance" that would make us vulnerable to office machinations. We usually meet outside, a few feet from the Bowl's back entrance. "Don't worry, no one's here yet," he says. He's in a pair of James Perse flannel pants, soft Ferragamo loafers, and Burberry frames. About as laid-back as he gets. "Como siempre, la primera en llegar."

His Spanish has a Mexican accent, and the ease with which he commands the language is both admirable and enviable. He doesn't pause to remember what the word in Spanish is for this or that. He always knows which article to use for which word. *El agua*, not *la agua*, he corrected me once, even though I knew that. He hadn't learned this in school, nor could he object to learning it by responding to his parents in another language, like I had. Then again, Spanish was not a language that marked him in Mexico, like it marks one here. It can make you an outsider. It's why some of my parents' friends never taught their kids to speak Spanish in the first place. Acclimation was paramount for them, but not for mine. They wanted me to learn the language as a way for their only child to keep some part of the identity they thought we might lose here. I used to think those other parents knew better because I never did feel confident in my Spanish, let alone in my Peruvianness, whatever that actually means.

Up until Max's arrival at the Bowl, I spoke Spanish only at home. Mostly with my father and always when he recounted memories: how his mother styled his hair for his monthly confession, where he mumbled his sins to the lattice panel and never actually faced a priest; how he slipped on the ice at Wollman Rink the very first time he and my mother put on skates; how he liked to walk along the Atlantic Ocean on cool gray dawns in the fall. Recollections that seemed more vivid in Spanish, especially toward the end. Maybe because it was his first language or because the memories were tender ones, or perhaps because the closer he approached the end, the more alive his life became.

In any case, I don't really speak Spanish to my mother anymore. I reply mostly in English, whenever it is that we actually speak.

Except that Max insists on it here and now.

"You really don't need to be in the office this early," I say in Spanish. When he first started, I told him the early bird mentality didn't exactly fly here, not when everyone's writing code or fretting over Oxford commas well past midnight. But he'd always throw shade. *Working late? You mean, emborrachandose*, he'd say, all because we had Cuervo and Ketel One in the kitchen cabinet, and the engineers had a few cans of soju in their mini-fridges, and the COO was never without a Bud Light. *That's practically water*, I'd argue.

"I'm here to do my job, just like you," he says.

"But I work with our numbers, Max. Confidential stuff. The fewer metiches around asking questions, the better."

He chuckles. "Except I don't need to ask questions because you tell me everything." He ignores the coffee cup on my desk and doesn't so much suggest as insist we go to Tazza. He's committed to their organic, ethically sourced, fair-trade Ethiopian coffee, openly rebuffing Pulso, with its South American blends and loyalty punch cards. More evidence of Max's snobbery, according to Jasmine. But there's a practical reason for his preference too. Tazza is a solid seven-minute walk away. Few Bowlers ever venture that far from the office.

Over the past year, the bulk of our talks happened on our strolls to Tazza. We'd catch up on what we did over the weekend, though he'd often tell me his plans beforehand and I filled in the rest by watching his Instagram stories. This past weekend was a typical one for him. On Saturday, he ventured into the galleries in Bushwick and bought a print from an artist he'd been following on social media. On Sunday, he trekked to Flushing Meadows Park from Nolita for a soccer match in Queens. Yesterday he went to the beach, naturally.

I stick to the highlights of my weekend: I too went to the beach with one of my homegirls yesterday, made it to a hot yoga class in the neighborhood on Sunday, had an omakase dinner with a friend in Chelsea on Saturday, and took a couple of sunset walks along the East River with my Canon. I mention this last part only because he'd seen my story on social media and hearted it, which prompted yet another request for a print. "I'll take any of your sunsets," he tells me, but not once have I taken his requests seriously because he's never actually fallen in love with any particular image.

I don't tell him that I stopped by a church to light a candle for my father, or that I made myself an egg white face mask to fend off these baby wrinkles, or that the omakase dinner was actually a date with a guy I was hoping to sleep with until he bragged about how many connections he had on LinkedIn. I stayed in bed that night scrolling through Feast looking for a hookup, with no luck.

He digs his hands into his pockets. "So . . . you wanted the weekend to think about it. Have you made a decision?"

Max has been pressing me about his proposition for days. At the next board meeting, he wants my help in crafting a different narrative for the Bowl, one that diverges from the usual spin about our financial situation.

I hesitate. "Let's talk when we have our coffees." For years now, the company has had the same modus operandi: "Be easy to work with." We simply follow orders. No rocking the boat. It also means we work like bankers without getting paid banker money, trusting that the leadership would get us to success before we went bust. If they were fucking it up, there wasn't anything I could do to change things—that was clear pretty early on. No one expected me to, anyway. Not my job to hold anyone in a position of power accountable, and there were simply too many egos involved to let the thing fail.

Besides, I'm mostly here for the steady paycheck. My bills need to get paid, after all, and I need to move soon, which means I need to stay employed. I'm not sure I even want children, but if I want to save my eggs, now's the time, and that too is a small fortune. My mother should retire instead of working back-to-back shifts at that store, going from the treadmill to a Punk Rope class to yoga when she's not at work, like she's trying to prove her body isn't aging. She doesn't get that I *need* her to slow down.

Yet I can't shake this unease that Max has stirred up with his proposition. The company has had its few bad days; sometimes, a few bad weeks. But this particular string of bad weeks is longer than any other stretch. We'd pumped so much money into local TV spots and targeted social media ads, highway billboards, and trade magazines geared to doctors and dentists—all in an attempt to build brand awareness. We spent millions before Max came on board, and although he's managed to rein in some of that spending, we bleed green. If I look at the numbers one way, you could say we'd plateaued. Another, and it's clear we're shrinking. Either way, it's not good.

"It's just one chart, Flores," he whispers to me now as we settle into a corner table.

I do my usual scan of the coffee shop to make sure no one from the Bowl is here before saying, "It's more than one chart. You're asking me to tell *your* version of things. To the board!"

"It's not *my* version. I'm asking you to tell the *truth*."

"I've never lied."

And I hadn't. There are mounds of data and countless ways to spin numbers. My team tracks them daily. So does the leadership. You watch something that closely, a narrative starts to form—first in your own mind, then in the collective. Before you even sit down to work on a deck, you already know what kind of story you're going to tell investors, one that guarantees there's still a shot at hitting our ultimate goal: to sell the company. Grow it quickly by being nimble—sprout some gray hair in the process, sure— and sell it. To a national pet supply chain, perhaps, or an internet megastore, where we could fill out their pet capabilities, or an office supply and furniture retailer, though that might be a long shot, but hopefully—and actually, most important of all—to a place that valued my $0.49 stock options at $10, $20, $50! I'd make the spread, a sizable chunk of money, in exchange for my time and personal life.

Imagine what I could do with that money. Pay off my loans, or at the very least the one I took out when Pa got sick. A vacation. Maybe make that trip to Peru or Paris. I've always wanted to see the Louvre. I'd set aside money for Ma. She's lucky she has me to look out for her. Who do I got? Me, and that's fine, but I sometimes wish she'd see that.

I've been at this for years, though, and let me tell you, start-up years drag like dog years. So the plan for the next board meeting, per my boss's instructions, is to tell a very clear and succinct story: We need another round of funding. Eighteen months of runway that will help us entice a buyer.

Max disagrees. He wants the board to make its own conclusions on what the next best steps are based on the numbers. In other words, he wants *me* to change the narrative. But self-preservation has always been at the core of our story. Of every story, really. Why change that now? And what story ever told the whole truth anyway?

"You want me to say something that could totally backfire," I whisper.

"I want you to show sales numbers and where the money is going."

"It went to buy Fisk & Tanks."

"And we bought that company just for the hospital deal? We both know there's more to it than that."

Not that I'd admit it. Last year, we inked a deal to install aquariums in a Detroit hospital. It seemed reasonable to buy Fisk & Tanks, a small midwestern manufacturer that could make it easier to service the hospital and other businesses in the area. The problem is that the hospital is funding the project with grant money, and we can't start until it comes through. Maybe we jumped the gun on the acquisition (legal didn't think we looked at their operations closely enough), but it did take the spotlight off some of our other questionable expenditures, like those highway ads, the influencer videos on TikTok, and our inflated salaries, including Max's. So yeah, there was more to the acquisition than simply trying to better service a single client or even a region.

So what?

"They've got to know," he insists.

"Don't you think they already do? They're investors, not idiots."

"They invest in dozens of companies. They can't keep track of everything. They focus on the plans and the press, and that's all smoke and mirrors."

"It's what's going to make our options count for something. And look, I know you don't need to worry about money, but I do."

"That's exactly why you *should* say something. We can turn this place around, Flores. Change the game plan. Eric won't be able to raise more money, and even if he does, he doesn't know how to manage it. Now Nik—"

"—is a narcissist. Easily distracted. A good talker with absolutely zero substance."

"He's experienced, energetic, charming."

"Flirtatious. With women, that is."

"Flirtatious, period. And sometimes you need to be all those things if you're going to succeed in the world."

"Oh, give me a break! He's an idiot who knows how to fall forward."

"He's not as dumb as you think. And yes, some of it is luck, but with his connections and vision, Nik can turn this place around. And we'd both be by his side helping him. He'd be taking guidance from *you*, Flores, not your frat boy of a boss."

I chew the inside of my cheek. "So you'd get rid of Jon?"

"We'd clean up the dead weight. We have more people than we need as it is, yet there's another Welcome Breakfast next week. Why are we even hiring at this point?"

"Because we need the help. I'm getting a junior analyst and you're getting a full-time designer, not just an intern. Besides, we budgeted for those roles months ago."

"You may need the help, but I wouldn't have made Starr a full-time designer. I know she's your friend, but her work is . . . uninspired. She needs to mature. As an adult and as an artist."

"Wow, that is not at all patronizing," I say. "Look, clearly, she's good. Otherwise Nik and his predecessors wouldn't have made all the promises they made to her."

"It just means he keeps his word. Honestly, I don't understand how you can be so hard on him, but not Jon. They're not all that different, except that Nik isn't the CEO's best friend."

He wasn't wrong. Like Nik, Jon also has his charm. His enthusiasm for the place is the fuel that keeps my team going, even when things look dire. Nik has that too, a certain flair that perks everyone up whenever he walks into a room.

But Jon is also Eric's closest confidant. Eric prefers to surround himself with people he trusts—people who are hungry. And when Jon first got on Eric's payroll, he *was* hungry. His first marriage had just ended; his shitty sales job in magazine publishing gnawed at whatever was left of his spirit. All the while, Eric's wide smile and carefree face appeared on cable business shows and in some of the very same magazines Jon pitched to ad agencies. So when Eric asked Jon to join him, Jon didn't think twice, even though he got paid a fraction of his previous salary. It worked out—Eric's last start-up got Jon closer to being a millionaire. He proceeded to give his ex a massive fuck-you by marrying her best friend, the woman who'd been the maid of honor at *their* wedding (quite scandalous).

To Max's point, would Jon even have the job and title if he weren't so close to Eric? Or if he hadn't been so down on his luck just as Eric reached a high point in his own life?

Would *I*?

When we first met back in college, Eric and I were in such similar situations that being around him was almost like viewing a reflection. He understood the hustle of schoolwork and real work, that silent pressure to succeed that served as the undercurrent for everything we did—every internship we secured, every move up our class rankings, every dollar we earned. But he wasn't all business-minded, either. By our sophomore year, he knew me well enough to guess who I was crushing on without my saying a word. He looked out for me then and never really stopped.

After my breakup with Vasily and my layoff, Eric offered me a job here—no questions asked. He was actually the first person to call me by my last name. There had been other Monicas, including two ex-Bowlers and a sales rep, so it was easier to just call me Flores. And I didn't mind. It was better than being known as Finance Monica. My last name felt more formal too. It separated Monica the Employee from Monica the Friend.

But even then, Eric's role as the company's leader didn't become real to me until more and more people mounted the employee pyramid, each one vying for his attention and praise. He got up every week to address the multitude he had assembled over the years, performing to a crowd that adulated him. I too became infatuated with who he had become and how he made me feel.

"This could save us, Flores," Max whispers. "This company, our options. You can finally get what you should've had all along."

"With you and Nik in charge?"

"Until someone else steps in, yes." He lets out a labored breath, as if even the prospect of the task is exhausting. He's a terrible actor. He's not afraid of hard work, especially when the payoff is the spotlight. And that is something he and Eric have in common.

Is he playing me? I want to believe we're friends. That for all the spoken and unspoken schemes playing out in his mind, he's looking out for me too. The long coffee breaks, the lunches on the stoops on sunny summer days, the walks around the block for fresh air, his dead parents and mine—I want to believe that the past year couldn't have been something I made up. That it's not all part of some chess game. But maybe it is. Maybe that's all it has ever been—with him, Jon, and Eric. Maybe I've been getting played by everyone all along.

"I need more time," I say.

He nods. "We've got until the next board meeting, but that's our only real shot. Otherwise, we're going to run out of money by Valentine's Day." His eyes flicker with concern. "Promise me you'll really think about it, Flores. If not for me, then for you. Your mother. All the sacrifices our parents made."

My parents. They're always there, in the back of my mind, propelling just about every move I make. The trope about the first-gen kid who must succeed because of all the sacrifices her parents made. Like I ever asked for that debt in the first place, but yeah, that's me, and that is a debt I'm not sure I'll ever be able to repay.

There's also that fear of running out of money, not just the company's but mine. It takes up more headspace than I care to admit. Truth is, he's not exaggerating with his timeline; the company has only a few months of cash left in the bank. That's better than me—my savings amount to a two-week vacation, something I haven't taken in years. The grind is starting to chip away at a layer I've armed myself with over the years. I'm not quite ready to see what's beneath it.

But I'm not going to tell Max this. He's too much of a worrier, and he wears that worry much like his collared shirt and flannel pants. It's something else that's conspicuous and out of place at the Bowl.

• • •

HERE'S THE TRUTH of it: I need money. Hundreds of thousands of dollars of it. That's how deep I am in debt. The bulk of it was for school and Pa's care after he got sick. That education my parents wanted for me—the degrees and the promise of a certain kind of job with a certain salary and supposed job security—none of it came cheap, even with financial aid. The salaries I expected never materialized, either. I always knew I'd have to take care of my parents at some point, but I didn't expect it to be this soon.

By the time Pa was diagnosed with cancer, I'd accumulated so much school debt that another $30,000 loan to cover his rent, medical bills, and credit cards would hardly make a difference on my monthly payments. Not that any of it mattered. What was an extra hundred dollars a month plus interest if it meant I had more time with my father?

4

PAULA

IT IS FIVE HUNDRED DOLLARS. MY BONUS. FIVE HUNDRED! IT'S A CHECK AND not cash, but still a little more than a week's paycheck. It's not the bonuses that I'm sure people who work in offices get, but I had expected coffee dollars. I couldn't wait to get home to peek into the envelope, so I checked in the DollaBills bathroom during my lunch break. I squealed and had to immediately cover my mouth. Even when I wrote down my prayer for abundance and slipped the piece of paper underneath the pyrite on Martín's altar, I wasn't sure it'd work. But it did! I don't quite know what to do except text you. I have to thank Sandeep, of course, but he had already left for his store in Jackson Heights. I'll thank him tomorrow.

Six hours after my text, you called.

"So you finally remembered your mother," I say.

"I was busy," you mumble. "¿Qué pasó? ¿Estás bien?"

Not an *hola* or a *¿Cómo estás, Mamá?* You always assume there's something wrong.

"Don't be so pessimistic, Yoli, I'm fine. I have good news." I cup my mouth against the phone and whisper, "I got a bonus. An entire week's salary!"

"That's great, Ma! It's about time too. You've given so much to that place these past few years."

"I want to celebrate. What time will you be home?"

"Seven. Actually, probably closer to eight."

"Yoli, this is why you're alone. You spend all your good hours in that office when you should be out with a new guy every night. Or with whomever—at this point, I don't care."

"Ma!"

"I worry about you."

"Just don't, okay? Are you going home now?"

"First the gym. I ate too much chocolate today."

"The gym, sure." I can feel those eyes of yours rolling. "Alone?"

"Yes, alone. Why do you ask?"

"Never mind. I'll see you tonight," you say, and I'm glad to hang up without having to answer any more of your questions.

• • •

I STOP BY the bank to deposit my bonus check. I can't remember when I last felt this sense of pride for something I accomplished on my own. I take a picture of the front and back with my phone for whenever I need to remember this feeling. Martín would be proud too, I think. We would've gone to Atlantic City with this money. A night at the Showboat or the Taj Mahal, just the two of us, like we did every year on our anniversary, before he got sick. We'd play the slot machines until we ran out of quarters, and then after a cocktail or two, find ourselves dancing in our hotel room. Swaying just like we used to do back in his parents' store in Jesús María, after he closed it for the day and blasted the radio. Except in our hotel room, we'd dance to whatever música criolla mix we could find on YouTube. I always imagined that one day we'd get back there. But that store is no longer mine to dream of; never truly was mine in the first place.

I'm at the ATM, slipping my check inside its thin mouth, when I hear two taps on the window. I know who it is, even before I turn. Vicente waves, his mouth hugged by lines that show up only when he smiles. My lines don't do that. They hug my lips all the time! He just has a few lines of gray in his hair too, like someone decided to draw them in with a pencil. They took a paintbrush to mine. It's why I go between Wella Koleston 61 and L'Oréal number 6 every month.

He holds a leash, and though I don't see her, I hear ChaCha's scratchy bark. He pulls her close, and his plaid short-sleeved shirt hangs loosely. He's lost weight since last summer. He needed to. His triglycerides, his doctor said. "Ensaladas," he told me one afternoon when we stopped by the Coster Diner for a late lunch. "Leaves and grilled chicken," he complained. "That's it. I can't even have a drizzle of olive oil." On a bad day, though, he'll crave pizza and we'll get a few slices to go at PrinciPizza. Sometimes he'll even get one with pepperoni.

I wave back, excited to tell him about my check. I make my deposit, print a copy of the receipt with the check image in case I need to prove it is real, and meet him by the door.

"I'm surprised to see you here," he says. He doesn't kiss my cheek. We see each other so often now that the formality seems unnecessary. But he can't *really* be surprised to see me. He always asks about my hours. When it's a later shift, he'll come around the block just as the gates come down. On a day like today, when my shift ends in the early afternoon, he'll take ChaCha out for her midday walk, or simply buy something at the store and ask if I'm leaving soon; he'll just be outside. Sometimes he'll walk me to the YMCA. Other times, he'll walk me to the corner of our block, but only to the corner. The days are warmer. Those chismosas with nothing to do will be sitting on their stoops or peering out their window ledges. Better to avoid them and their lingering gaze. It makes him feel better, I think, to pretend that these coincidental collisions are between friends. It makes me feel better about them too.

So I go along with the lie. "I'm surprised to see *you*," I say. "You'll never believe this. I got a bonus!"

"That's fantastic!" He puts a hand on my arm. My arm is bare. His fingers rest there for several seconds, his cold skin on my sticky one. A few seconds, I know, but that touch has the same effect as a spoon-tip of ají on my tongue. My body rises. My mouth is afire.

. . .

IT HAD NOT always been this way between me and Vicente. He came to the United States not long before me and Martín, but unlike us, he had a brother here who installed wooden floors in monstrous houses out on Long Island and needed help keeping up with the work. Vicente was single then, and for a couple of years had the typical life of a single man. He lived with his brother and two other Peruvians in a two-bedroom apartment in the neighborhood, paid $500 a month (which probably paid for part of his brother's rent too), and spent every weekend playing soccer or watching matches at bars in Queens, ultimately ending the night at a club. He met Renata at the Copacabana. They got married at City Hall six months later.

By the time she gave birth to Daniela, every Peruvian in New York knew of Vicente. He was, after all, the young man from Iquitos—el chico de los pisos—who was on an Atlantic City bus that crashed on the highway, injuring his leg so badly that he still walks with a bit of a limp. He got a lawyer, and the lawyer got him money from the bus company. He spent that money on one property, and that multiplied into more: the three-floor, six-unit building he lives in right here in the neighborhood, the two-family house he rents out in Forest Hills, and the house in Bayamón, where Renata grew up.

He has money, and because of that, he has no problem talking about it.

. . .

"ARE YOU HAPPY with it?" he asks of the bonus. *Ecstatic!* I want to say, and how I wish we could celebrate over a drink and a game of bingo, that's how happy I am! But his own success—or maybe simply his luck—tempers mine. He'd laugh at my few hundred dollars.

Still, I tell him yes, I am happy with it, even though it's not much.

"How much doesn't matter," he says. "It's the recognition. The fact that people notice our work and appreciate it. That they notice us at all!"

"Oh, Yoli wouldn't say that. She'd say the amount *does* matter. Too little and it's an insult. Too much and they're just going to make you earn it, so it's not really recognition, but more like an expectation."

"It's different for her. Your daughter is a professional. They measure their worth by money and titles. Besides, you've worked hard. I've seen it. All these late nights where you're closing the store and then opening it before the sun's even out. In snow or rain, doesn't matter. And you're happy working there. Few of us can actually say we like what we do for a living."

"It's a distraction," I clarify, though a part of me does enjoy being at the store and the work itself. But there are days when standing for two, three, four hours at a time is unbearable. My feet swell into tamales; my back stiffens to a cutting board. I have no illusions about what I do. Unpack boxes; arrange shampoo bottles; check expiration dates on potato chips; collect payments for plastic shower curtains, slightly irregular panties, and soap bars my neighbors buy. It's not special or glamorous, but when I first took the job, it felt better than putting a spoon into another ailing mouth, and much better than being home, in silence and surrounded by Martín's absence. Back then, even stepping into our bedroom felt like falling into a void. I kept only a handful of his shirts, but they were like boulders placed in our closet. So were the leather shoes you bought him at Macy's and the white

Nike sneakers I bought at VIM, all lined up and rooted under my bed, next to my chancletas. I was grateful that the IV pole was gone; the medicine pouches, the pill bottles, and the basin too. The statues and pictures of the saints had also moved out and into the living room, beside his urn, with the glass rose you found at that Salvation Army. "Esta pesada," I remember saying, and so I burned palo santo to try to break up the heavy energy the glass rose carried. In the bathroom, his toothbrush still leaned against mine inside a glass jar I'd saved after we finished the marmalade you bought at the farmers' market. I'd look at myself in the spotted mirror above the bathroom sink, unable to recognize the reflection. It wasn't just the glass rose that felt heavy.

And now I sell the very same men's shirts I used to buy for Martín; even jars of marmalade, though they aren't organic. Shoes too. And mirrors. All new. Somehow, every time I step into that store, a small part of me feels like I could be new again. Like I can break apart the load.

We walk a few more blocks, and I pick up a bouquet from the flower shop with the twenty dollars I took from my bonus money. Vicente wanted to pay, but I refused his money. The flowers had to be paid for with the bonus money, a thank-you to La Virgen. Instead, he can pay for the coffees we'll have with a strawberry cheesecake.

His eyes widen. "Not a croissant?"

"That's for everyday Paula. Today, I am rich Paula."

And so we head to Caramelo Café. A man sits inside, reading a newspaper. Two women sip tea and share a chocolate cake. I catch the words scribbled on the chalkboard near the entrance:

GARDEN IS OPEN, 8 A.M. TO 7 P.M.

"We can sit in the yard," I say. We've been here before, without ChaCha: me, for their cappuccino and croissant; Vicente for their black coffee and biscotti. Lately, he's been bringing ChaCha out more, forcing us to just walk around the neighborhood instead of sitting down for a proper break. Maybe it's because the weather has improved so much; maybe it's because both Vicente's doctors and ChaCha's vet have told them they needed to lose weight. Or maybe it's for all to see just how friendly—and how *just friends*—we both are. Not that I mind being seen with him, but there is something soothing about keeping our time together just between the two of us. "You can tell me what it is you're planning for the Fiestas Patrias celebration."

"One cheesecake wouldn't be enough for that." He smiles. "But I can tell you about the dance performances we've got planned. I know your daughter loves them."

"She does!" and my enthusiasm convinces him because he bends down and places a shaking ChaCha inside my bag, her head poking out.

"Adelante," he says, holding the door as I amble in like a queen.

• • •

YOU COME HOME that night a little before eight, sweating. Your hair wrapped in a bun. Several tight-lipped pink and red peonies are tucked under your arm. I am not prepared for the hug, a gesture so foreign that my own arms tense and my feet fuse to the floor.

"I'm sorry," you say, springing loose. "I had to walk over the bridge." It's not your body that offends me, but the shock from this burst of joy, directed at me, that catches me by surprise. My mouth cannot form the words to explain this, and so instead I take the flowers as you announce that you need five minutes to change your shirt, and that we're going to Sage to celebrate. You notice the flowers on the altar. "You bought more?"

"Prayers were answered," I say. "Besides, your father loved them."

I wash the stems of the peonies you brought, cut their ends, pull out two vases from under the sink, and begin to separate the pinks from the reds. After all, pink flowers have their place here, as do the reds. I barely finish splitting them up when you tell me to hurry, it's late, and I abandon the flowers on the kitchen counter.

Halfway down the block, we run into Manuelito. He just finished the last class of the semester, he tells us, and is running to the last yoga class at the studio. He asks if you'd come again to hot yoga, and instead of giving him a firm answer, which I'm curious to hear, you announce that we're going to dinner to celebrate me—*me!* I stand a little taller when he offers his congratulations. He asks if you got his text about the museum, and you both stammer when you see my reaction, but what did you expect! First yoga and then a museum of all things. He warns us to walk quickly when we pass the old willow, languishing just across from our buildings. It's dead, but no one's come to remove it yet.

At Sage, we order shrimp pad Thai, chicken red curry, two beers, and also a Thai iced tea, and "Bring it all out together," you say, a feast! Even though it is quite late and we'll both complain about acid reflux later. Even though we should not be eating out, not with how you watch the money, but then again, when do we ever indulge like this?

"To you, Ma," you say as we raise our beers. "I see how hard you work, and I'm glad that your boss finally noticed it too. ¡Salud!"

For a moment, I hesitate before drinking. Martín had always thought it odd, how parents here drink alcohol with their children. He would never. *Never.* It signaled igualdad: permission for the child to be insubordinate, with no respect or deference to their parent, when parent and child were never equals. If they were, it would mean a breakdown in the order of things.

This is *a breakdown*, I think. So I accept your cheer, sip, and make a confession.

"I prayed for it. The bonus. Well, I prayed for abundance. We'll need it if we want to stay in the apartment."

"Ma, we can't stay. It's not like Janusz is raising our rent. He's not renewing the lease."

"Did he tell you that?"

"In person, on the phone, in his letter. His son had a baby. He wants the apartment. Besides, I thought you wanted to move out."

When you first mentioned leaving the apartment, I flung the idea of living separately out of anger. How could I leave my home of twenty years? You insisted it was never really ours to begin with because we didn't own it. All these years, we were merely borrowing space. If you didn't think that we made a home, then did it matter if we lived together now? We could go our own ways, I said, I'm sure Vicente could give me a deal on an apartment in his building, and that seemed to offend you. But the truth is, I'm not sure where or how to begin anew or if I can do it alone.

"I don't want to have this conversation now, Yoli."

"Fine, but at some point, we need to. Anyway, what you really need is a raise or at the very least a promotion. Have you talked to Sandeep about that? You can certainly run that store if you wanted to."

"That's very ambitious, but I'm too old," I say, though it sounds more like a question. I admit I've thought about it. I've had two years of setting up displays, arranging aisles, even managing inventory and the schedules of the seasonal workers Sandeep hires. But this is hardly how I imagined I'd spend the last third of my life. At least not how I imagined it when Martín was alive.

No, no. La tercera edad, as we call it, was supposed to be different. I had imagined myself with Martín, dining out every Friday night, sitting on the couch and watching movies on Telemundo, splitting our time between New York and Lima to avoid each city's winter. I didn't think about growing old necessarily or what that meant until menopause hit. The insomnia, the heat bursts, sitting in the dark kitchen in the middle of the night, crying. Even though I didn't feel it, I was entering a new stage in my life, that of the crone. My doctor at the time suggested exercise for both my physical and mental health, and movement did give me some relief. The treadmill, the barre class, and just being at the YMCA kept me from thinking of the end—*my* end—and all the lives I did not live and the one I had, and how frightening the future seemed. At the time, Martín thought it was silly—to act as if my body were twenty-one when I was fifty-one! But I wasn't going to spend that last third of my life aching, limited by my own thoughts. Not if I could avoid it, and no matter what Martín said. Certainly not after he died.

And when he did die, whatever illusions I had about my future did too. I needed more than the gym to get out of my head. At the store, I could escape the suffocation that lingered in every corner of our apartment, and I'd have people to talk to. After losing so many friends over the years—to illness, greedy landlords, and even their grandkids—it would be nice to have some again. This explanation softened the puzzled look on your face when I first asked you for help with the job application. I wanted to make money too, not just depend on the couple of hundred dollars a week that came into my bank account straight from your paycheck. Even though that is what children should do, no? Take care of their parents? With this job, I could put some money away for retirement, even though you chuckled at the idea. I understand how ridiculous it might have sounded. That I was thinking about how I'd support myself in retirement when I had just started putting money into a 401(k) a few years before Martín died. But I was proud to set money aside for myself and my future, even if that felt silly in some ways—the idea that I'd make it to sixty-five at all when Martín didn't. That sounded ambitious too.

And the store *did* help me approach my own pain differently. I promised myself that no matter how low I was feeling on any particular day, I would greet every customer with a smile, even if they didn't offer one back and even if my eyes betrayed me. The other associates always had stories to tell, especially Shanti, who shared whatever clever thing her children had said at breakfast or recounted the latest movie or television show she'd watched on her phone. Sorting the items in the right aisle became a game for me. I made sure all the product logos faced out, and if a customer purchased large quantities of the same item, I immediately told Sandeep because it was, after all, his responsibility to make sure we were always in stock and never lost a sale. I got a charge with each exchange, something that fortified my resolve at home and made my own future feel less ominous.

"You should talk to Sandeep anyway," you say. "It's better to make more money an hour than to get a bonus whenever he decides to be generous."

"I just got this check, Yoli. I can't demand more money now."

"Not demand. Let him know that you know your worth."

"I'm not one to ask for things."

"You pray for them! No way is anyone up there or out here gonna listen to you unless you help yourself first. Believe me, you'll never get what you want if you *don't* ask."

"You ask, and it doesn't get you far."

"Thanks, Ma."

I don't mean it as an insult, but to make a point: a woman with more education than me, more power in her position, at least from where I stand, and she is still largely ignored. What chance do I have of succeeding where my own child has failed?

We forgo dessert because you have that Thai iced tea and I had that cheesecake with Vicente. "He's married," you point out, "which is also why you shouldn't even think about asking him for help."

"I haven't told him about our situation."

"What, you think it'll hurt his feelings if we move away? Honestly, Ma, I can't even remember you ever sharing a drink with Pa, let alone cake. And he was your *actual* husband!"

"Mónica Yolanda, me estás faltando el respeto. No seas tan

malcriada." If you were still a child, I might have reached over and tugged that hair of yours, but all I can do now is reprimand you in a whisper. "We were celebrating my good news, like we're doing now. We're both trying to cut down on sugar. And he's an old friend. It made sense to share."

"Old friend, right. Did you hold hands too?"

My own turn into fists on the table. It's been decades since that happened, and still it haunts us. I wonder if you'll ever let it go.

"I need friends, Yoli. People who understand. Just like you have your Mexican friend. The orphan. You know, the one with the *fiancée*. You've told him about your father, I'm sure. Over coffee or maybe drinks when you're out late. That's even more dangerous."

You scoff. "That I have coffee with my coworker?"

"That you trust your coworker. You've opened up to him. You've shown him your heart."

"Oh, come on, Ma. I'm not into the guy like that."

"You've made yourself vulnerable, Yoli. You do that with friends, not the people you work with. It complicates things. Just remember, he will always, *always*, think of himself first."

"Don't try to make this about me." You push away the glass of iced tea. I could never quite get you to listen, and certainly not after . . . well. Not that I blame you. It was Martín who always got through to you. Not that I blame you for that, either. He was mostly a righteous man. Even when he confessed to me that he was falling in love with another woman, I was more surprised by his decision to tell me than by the betrayal itself. By then, I had known, for some time, that his mind and heart were elsewhere.

"Look, I get it, you're lonely," you say. "You miss Pa. Vicente is familiar and that's comforting. But maybe it's still too soon to be, you know, sharing a cheesecake? Especially with a married man. Especially Dani's dad."

"Exactly, Dani's dad. Someone who understands," I say, and this ends the conversation.

We hurry home, eager to avoid the rats feasting on the garbage bags that line the street, brought on by the construction on our block and the restaurants that opened in the last year, like Sage. We speed past the willow tree. You head straight to the vase of pink peonies on the kitchen counter and place it beside the urn. We had ordered the matted wooden box from Mexico. The ones that the crematorium tried to sell us—oof! We were not going to let thieves prey on our grief. Martín's full name and the years that mark the beginning and end of his life are etched in gold. On his birthday, I refilled the wineglass with water blessed by the moon. I wiped down the santitos, the amethyst Shanti gave me for my birthday, and the pyrite I brought with me from Peru, a talisman for good fortune. Now you light the palo santo and place it on your father's seashell. When I am alone, I burn it too. The smoke always reminds me of la curandera in Pucallpa, the one and only time Martín and I got a limpia in the market.

There is no photograph of Martín, even though this is what a true altar should have. Images of those souls that have passed, of spirits we call on for guidance and protection. It is one thing to see his image in my mind, in a picture album, in my own daughter's face, but oh! It is another to see eyes once filled with wonder, lips I have kissed, a face I have loved sitting beside a box where his ashes now lie. I can barely contemplate the note sitting under the urn and the longing it stirs in me, for all the moments he and I shared and all those we never got to have. No—I cannot see his face there. It is enough to simply know he is dead.

You touch his urn and make the sign of the cross as I walk by with my flowers. I set the vase on the nightstand in my bedroom. The peonies hum, a vivid red that pulsates.

5

FLORES

JON AND I WAIT PATIENTLY AT OUR DESKS THIS MORNING FOR THE CALL TO THE Welcome Breakfast. Jasmine usually sends the office-wide message over ChitChat around ten A.M., which is the only reason most Bowlers arrive early today. The Welcome Breakfast is a chance to informally meet our new colleagues, although one of the two people joining the Bowl isn't exactly "new." Starr's been an intern for more than a year, but her position has just now been converted to that of a full-time designer. Carl Aguirre is the real new hire. He's joining our team as a junior analyst, which, Jon expects, will somehow help me "get a life."

"What do you mean by that exactly?" I ask because I enjoy making my boss squirm. The two of us are alone in our corner of the office, and he's already got the air conditioner on full blast. I wrap Pa's jacket around my shoulders. Steve is on the other side of the room, chatting with the folks in the legal pod, who were mercifully moved to the opposite corner of the office when they needed more space for their growing team (not that we need more lawyers).

"I'm just saying, you and Steve work hard, but he's got his stand-up and basketball. He's dating."

"I date."

"You hated that dermatologist because he's on TikTok!"

"How are you going to make videos about Botox for an audience that clearly doesn't need it?"

"So poor marketing strategy, really? That's why you won't go out with him again. Okay, what about the accountant?"

"He wasn't a fan of one of the greatest actors of all time."

"Not Swayze again."

"He didn't even like *Dirty Dancing*. If he doesn't know a good movie, no way can he be my man."

"Damn, well, I guess you gotta draw the line somewhere. But if you want to get married, have kids, then you need to stop being so picky."

I should be offended, but the truth is, I *did* expect to have these things by now. Specifically, a quiet life in the suburbs—with two kids, because I think I would have liked to have had a sibling, but more than two didn't seem practical, especially when I had to care for and support my parents. Plus we're killing the planet. I had imagined myself working at one of those large companies just off the Garden State Parkway, where certain titles give you preferential parking spots, and after my decades of service, said company would throw me a retirement party in recognition of all the years I devoted to it. I'd retreat to an even quieter life of teaching yoga at the community center, organizing a book club for my neighbors, and volunteering as a docent at the Cloisters, just to make sure I get my art and city fix.

But I haven't had these cookie-cutter aspirations since before Pa got sick, when I was still with Vasily. That steady life I dreamed of, filled with achievable markers of success, seemed possible only with my ex, before he became my ex, and when both my parents were still alive. It seems ridiculous to me now that I'd ever had such confidence in this vision. I hadn't considered the most fundamental factor in any plan: life happens.

"No offense, but maybe I don't want your life."

"It's not a bad one." He smirks, and it certainly isn't. Except for a few minor blemishes in his past (namely, his divorce), Jon has achieved what I imagine most parents dream of for their child, and then some. He has settled into a steady marriage with a supportive partner, is raising a pair of bilingual children, and lives in a four-bedroom colonial on a cul-de-sac in Montclair. He surprised his mom with a trip to Hawaii one Christmas, and bought his dad a cobalt Porsche for his sixtieth birthday. What better ways to show your Chinese Jamaican immigrant parents they made it? I sometimes think I would have done the same for mine if I had the chance.

"Then again," he goes on, leaning back in his chair the way he always does when he goes into contemplative mode, "it's not easy. I mean, don't get me wrong, I'm grateful for my wife, my kids, this job, all that. It's just that sometimes . . ." He looks past me, pauses. "Sometimes I wonder if this is it, you know? Like, where do I go from here?"

"Cry me a river," I say, and of course he laughs. "It's too early in the day for this shit."

"All I'm saying is that sometimes, in dating and in life, you just gotta shoot your shot."

It's this sentiment that defines Jon, and why I sometimes resent him. There was no pay bump or promotion for me this year, although he claims he tried to get me one. There was, however, a title change for him. For months, he had been quite vocal about wanting the promotion. The announcement, made at an All Hands and without his mentioning it to me beforehand, had only added to my bitterness.

Even so, I have a hard time separating Jon the Boss from Jon the Friend, which is what I think we have become. He treats me to monthly lunches at Samantha's Dumplings; brings me a rose every Valentine's Day; and always wonders aloud if a newly divorced friend might be the right guy for me. We don't exactly socialize outside of work. In the office, he gravitates toward his own group of friends, made up mostly of Bowlers in their twenties, like Starr. His way of staying young, I guess. After all, he *is* on his second marriage now, second mortgage, first pair of reading glasses, two kids with another on the way, still clinging to a full head of hair, even though it's mostly gray now. And while he no doubt advocates more for himself than for me, the guy does work. Doesn't matter if it's a weeknight or a weekend or if he's on vacation. And he worked for virtually no pay during the Bowl's first year while Eric raised money. Few people would take that leap of faith or be that reckless. It's something I can't help but admire.

What I do know is that sometimes he muses aloud about his own life, and I wonder if any of us will ever really be satisfied with what we have. If we truly wanted what we have in the first place.

• • •

AS SOON AS Jasmine messages that breakfast is ready, I hustle toward the cafeteria on the other side of the office, what feels like a borough away, hoping to get to the kitchen counter before the others ravage the food. The coffee grinder whirs as the scent of coffee beans coats the air. Trios and quartets of Bowlers dot the room, mostly in subgroups of their own departments or cliques: marketing, data science, the Eastern European pack from Queens, the Asian American crew that grew up in Jersey. Two lines queue on either side of the kitchen counter, topped with trays of bagels, butter, and three types of cream cheese—a generous but standard spread for the interns and low-level engineers fresh out of college that we typically hire.

The music pounds as Max comes up behind me. "I didn't get Drake for my Welcome Breakfast," he jokes. He picks up a bagel and scowls. "Sign of the times." The previous breakfast had been more plentiful by comparison, with bacon and sausage egg sandwiches, cinnamon rolls, and gluten-free blueberry muffins, like the one we had for him. Back then, there had also been more recruits. Some lasted only days, promptly replaced with the second-best candidate or, more likely, an investor's kid. But when Max joined, there was also excitement, curiosity, a certain kind of optimism. There he was on that first day, dripping in the look of success; on that, we all agreed. Tall, like Starr had said, with sardine eyes and burnt-sugar hair parted to the side, a shoo-in for the role of el galán on a Televisa telenovela. His collared shirt was a touch too small, underscoring his very vocal commitment to CrossFit and the Mediterranean diet. During his first few weeks, every one of his jokes got a laugh, every manicured hand stole a touch to his forearm, each fleshy palm double-tapped his back before heading to their desk. He was charismatic, a necessary skill for the job he'd been hired to do. After all, what successful marketer couldn't make love to you with his words? *His* because only cis-het men typically rose through the ranks, from what I could tell. Of course, I tend to loathe the sales and marketing variety, so my initial inclination was to hate the guy. But besides Jasmine and me, he was the only other Latino at the Bowl, and that granted him something of a pass. The more we spoke, the more complex I realized he was.

I grab the only cup of vanilla parfait—which I know was ordered specifically for me—before he catches sight of it, then head to the coffee keg, where Jasmine is pouring cups of cold brew.

"Happy hump day!" she says, smiling. "You're welcome for the yogurt, by the way." For the last three years, she sneaks vanilla parfaits onto breakfast orders for me, even though they sometimes put her over budget. I've gotten so used to the gesture that I almost take it for granted.

"This is the highlight of my day, so thank you." I scan the room and find Starr and Carl standing beside Jon and someone from HR. "How long do you think my new analyst will last?"

"With your bubbly personality and penchant for optimism, four months." She laughs. "But since he's probably drinking the Eric juice, one year. Then again, he might fit right into the circle jerk, so maybe two? Unless he really sucks, in which case, you guys will cut him just before he earns that second paycheck."

"He's got to last longer than that," I say. "Steve's been here almost a year and I'm still getting crushed. Maybe I can start passing some of the more sensitive shit off to Steve and we can give Carl the *less* sensitive shit. Anyway, he's my consolation prize, so I'd like to keep him around for as long as I can."

She snorts. "I guess it's too much to ask for the help you need *and* get the raise you deserve. Let me guess. Jon gave you that 'take one for the team' bullshit we've all been served?"

"No point in getting salty about it now," I say. "Besides, I want to enjoy my breakfast and high vibe for this guy. Jon had nothing but good things to say about him."

"You didn't interview him?"

"You know how it is. He's a friend of a friend's younger brother or something. I'm lucky I got to meet him before he actually started." Not that I have a right to complain. Jon never interviewed me. Eric simply offered me the job.

"It's crap. I swear, if they weren't paying for my degree . . ." Jasmine is a year away from getting her bachelor's in interior design at the Fashion Institute of Technology and not at all quiet about the fact that she's only here for that reason. "They never have money and yet we got your boy making more than both of us combined. And then Nik, who probably gets a bonus just for showing up to this breakfast."

"Well, he needs to be here. He *is* Starr's boss now, officially."

"Took them long enough. Eighteen months! Don't get me wrong, the girl says some ignorant shit sometimes." She holds her hand up as I begin to protest. "And I know she doesn't mean it! But I do admire her tenacity and commitment to this place. So if she wants Drake on repeat all morning, she's gonna get it."

"Definitely. And Max is not my boy, just so we're clear. We're not friends like that."

"Just so we're clear, you're lying. And you need to ask him when exactly he's going to turn marketing around so we can get our J.Lo money and get the hell outta here."

"We're not getting J.Lo money." I laugh, but I've always had to temper Jasmine's expectations of the place.

"Well, more money than I can get anywhere else," she says. "After all the years we've put in, I'm not leaving without getting what I'm due. Though as far as I can tell, your boy's nothing but a suck-up with no actual results, which you correctly predicted. 'He's gonna be so far up Nik's ass, he might as well be a hemorrhoid,' remember? Well, you were right. Except he's like that with Nik *and* the investors." She leans in as other Bowlers show up for their morning kick-starter. "He went out with Ethan last week. Just the two of them. Wasn't even on his calendar or anything."

"Ethan Blue?" I ask. Silver Blue Ventures is our largest investor to date, and Ethan is one of two siblings who manages the family-run venture capital firm. His sister, Nina, has had nothing but a passing interest in the Bowl, which is how it should be. Most investors just give us their money and go away. They have other investments, some much more lucrative than this one and requiring closer attention. But Ethan is the all-in, hands-on, surprise-visit type of investor. Unlike the other board members, he has what some (me included) believe is too friendly of a relationship with Eric. That friendship shields the Bowl from some of the other investors' more prying questions, but it also gives Ethan the kind of access to the company that the others don't have.

It doesn't shock me that Max had coffee with him. Max is, after all, one of our most notable hires. What bugs me is that Max hasn't mentioned it to me at all.

"The barista at Pulso told me he was there in the back room, all secretive," Jasmine whispers. "That's covered by the FrieNDA, by the way." Not everything we share is a secret, but if it is, it falls under what she likes to call our "FrieNDA." It's every bit as binding as the nondisclosure agreements our paranoid lawyers (is that repetitive?) make every Bowler sign, in case they end up stealing our supersecret fish and spy technology.

"You guys!" Starr shouts as she makes her way to us. She tends to curl her hair into soft waves on special occasions, and today is no exception. She's not one to bare her teeth when she smiles, but her imperfect incisors beam behind her All Fired Up lipstick. Her lash extensions rapidly pat the smooth pale skin beneath her ocean-black eyes. "It's official!"

I grab a cold brew and raise it. "Congrats, friend! You more than deserve it. Though I can't say this place deserves you."

"Does it deserve any of us?" says Jasmine. "I swear, if Eric wasn't such a great human . . ."

"Well, I'm glad he is," says Starr, "and I'm glad Nik finally put a ring on it, so to speak." She laughs, then nudges me. "Flores, who is your new guy?"

"His name is Carl. Recently graduated from NYU. He's a very junior analyst, but I could really use the help. And of course, your boss is already chatting him up."

"Flores!" Nik shouts, and Jon waves us over. My cue to greet our new teammate, even though I'd rather leave it to Jon and Steve to make up the entirety of the welcome party. Nik puts his arm around my shoulder as I join the group, giving me a shake. "I was just telling your new hire that he's lucky to have a real OG for a boss!"

"Thanks," I mutter as I take his arm off me.

"Flores's been here from the start. Shit, even before the start! She and Eric go way back. She knows everything you could possibly know about the place. How to get the good snacks—hint, hint, be friends with Jasmine—where the best lunch and coffee shops are, or bubble tea now that it's summer." He puts his arms around me again, but this time he grabs Carl too, bringing us into a huddle, and audibly whispers, "She knows where we're hiding all the bodies. She might tell you after a few drinks! Just don't tell legal."

I shrug him off. "Don't believe everything that comes out of this guy's mouth," I tell Carl. Jon laughs and mutters an *Oh, shit.* Nik chuckles nervously but shuts up. "Jasmine orders the snacks, but this isn't a restaurant. We get what we get. And you can find the good coffee and bubble tea spots on Yelp. Anyway, welcome."

Starr and another designer excuse themselves just as Max joins the group. Nik is much better at introducing him than he was at introducing me, dropping Max's title, listing the places he's worked, and as always, layering the Harvard MBA on a bit thick.

"You worked at Canto?" Carl asks with genuine excitement. "I was at Spin. Way better UX and music library. And I'm not just saying that because I used to work there!"

"Whoa!" exclaims Jon. "You're lucky Starr didn't hear you say that. She interned at Canto ages ago. Hates Spin. She's probably the only twenty-something here that still uses Canto, am I right?"

"It's terrible when people think they can be deejays," says Nik. "Playing the right music takes skill. Otherwise you end up listening to a lot of the same shit. Probably why this garbage is on loop." I expect him to confess to his onetime aspiration of becoming a professional deejay, but it's too early in the day for that.

"Aguirre . . ." says Max, and by his squint, I know the question that's coming. The same one he asked me when he first started. I cringe, because there was no indication anywhere on his résumé, his LinkedIn profile, or even his social media that hinted at Carl owning that last name. "Does that mean you're not *from* from here?"

"I am," he says. "Well, not Brooklyn. Queens. Forest Hills."

"¿Entonces hablas español?"

"No, not at all." He snickers. "My grandpa on my dad's side is

Uruguayan, so that's where Aguirre comes from. My mom's Irish American. But nothing beyond high school Spanish for me."

"That's too bad," says Max. "I thought maybe Flores and I had someone else here to speak our language. Jasmine's mother is from Puerto Rico. She understands Spanish but doesn't really speak it, either."

She actually speaks Spanish pretty well, just not with him. Still, the *our* in his declaration grabs me—it implies belonging. I never quite felt that here. Not just at the Bowl, but in all these in-between spaces. I am, after all, a child of immigrants, but the wrong type of immigrant. And even though I don't look like Salma or Selena or however this place wants me to look, I can't say I really care. I like that I have my mother's warm skin, my father's gaze and cheekbones, my grandmother's hooked nose, though I sometimes do long for fewer strands of gray in my curls and a bronzier glow in the winter. I cringe every time a form attempts to reduce me to a simple category. How easy would it be if I could just put myself into a box? Black or white, they say. American Indian. Hispanic or Latino. But my Spanish is not great. I check "other," and sometimes in that empty space, I write in *Brooklyn*.

It's moments like this one—Max injecting that *our* into my morning—that I don't know I need until it manifests itself.

"I still consider myself Latino," says Carl. "Where are you guys *from* from?"

"Mexico," says Max. "I grew up in Monterrey and Mexico City, which is why I have this accent. I came here for college." He blushes, then goes on to explain, "My grandfather is from Wisconsin, which is why I *could* come here." The funny thing about Max is that he feels the need to explain his Mexican-ness because people always seem perplexed by it. That ignorance is their problem. We're not a monolith, no matter where we're from. And Max might touch on his background, but avoids going deep on what makes him different: his purely European ancestry, his elitist American education, the wealth his family has accumulated from their Central American trucking company. He's outraged by what the current White House resident said about Mexicans, as we all should be, even though Max isn't who this person had in mind when those comments were made. Max, after all, is rich, educated, and white. He'd get the red carpet into the country.

"Flores is from Peru," Max goes on, and I feel myself getting hot.

"My parents," I say. "I was born in Brooklyn."

"Oh, sweet!" says Carl. "I was in Cusco a couple of years ago. Did the Inca Trail. Even tried the cuy. Are your parents from Lima?"

"They grew up there, but their parents were from different places. Pucallpa. Chincha. My father was not the kind to say he was Limeño."

"*Was*," he repeats. "Sorry for your loss."

I shrug. "It's not your fault."

I've gotten used to the offers of condolences whenever I mention Pa. I wish I hadn't now. I think of what Ma said, about showing my heart at work. Carl is my subordinate, after all. I don't want his pity, though the condolence hits like a gut punch. My father's absence strikes like that sometimes, coming at me out of nowhere. Sharp, quick, a pang that erupts in tears on a subway car or a tea-lit table at a restaurant or, like now, in an uncomfortable silence. Other times, it wells up, rips at a seam I thought I'd stitched up good, a slow bleed that plunges me into an abyss. His death was the ultimate wound. I thought the breakup with Vasily would undo me, but those cuts were nowhere near as deep. When his absence strikes and the memories of those end days reemerge, I lie in the loss until I am forced back here, to the Bowl, to a place that, in its own way, saved me.

And so, I head back to my desk, to the work that waits for me. My anchor these last three years.

SUMMER

6

PAULA

I TOOK THE MORNING OFF FROM WORK TO BE WITH VICENTE. WE WALK IN silence to the park. The peony in my hand is in full bloom; the half-dozen purple roses in his still have a day or two to flower. We head toward a bench not far from an area where, long ago, we had lived what seems like another life.

These walks would have never happened in those early years. Certainly not between a couple unless they were husband and wife, and even that was an oddity. Back then, the days were about raising our kids and making our dollars. Working in factories, cleaning homes, tending to someone else's children or sick parent, all while trying to care for our own families. Life had started to unfold for us then, not just because we were here, in this new place, but because this is what starts to happen in your twenties and thirties. Parents become ill; they die. Grandparents and other elders too. Painful, yes, but one accepted that this was the natural course of life. Older people died; they had lived lives. Their absence was not of the unfulfilled kind, and that offered some consolation to those of us left behind.

Friendships were usually formed as a consequence of one's family, work, community. Maybe you chatted with the mother waiting for her child at dismissal or you ran into another at McDonald's after church because she also promised her kids Happy

Meals. *If you just keep quiet during the homily,* we'd whisper, gently tugging on a sideburn to make our point. Or maybe you met someone on a Sunday afternoon in the summer, where you turned your child over to the sun and parched grass and, in the exchange, found your own breath.

I savored those summers at the park. Back then, we called it all El Parque, one name that included the actual park in our neighborhood, but also its baseball field, track, and swimming pool. There were more immigrants from Europe then too. Rarely did we mix with them or the younger Americans that were just moving in. The separation made you feel visible to your own people, invisible to the others, and in that way, safe. On Sundays, we claimed a corner of the park, a section that was home to two giant trees that offered their shade, and the soccer field just across the path. A path lined with gardens, birdsong, and red-tailed squirrels. For almost twenty years, a bench has also lined the path, one dedicated to the person that had sparked all those Sunday outings.

It is where Vicente and I head to now.

· · ·

VICENTE'S BUS ACCIDENT made him a man with a metal hip, a slight limp, and plenty of time and money, most of which he spent on his properties. He took pride in renovating them, replacing carpets with hardwood floors, upgrading radiators, paying closer attention to cabinet colors and wall paint. He became a churchgoing man after the accident, though he told me once he was always a man of God—just too busy with work to make it to Sunday mass. After the bus accident, he headed to church every morning, right after he dropped his children off at school. He'd sit at McDonald's or Dunkin' Donuts, reading *El Diario* at a stool by the window while he sipped his black coffee and ate hash browns or glazed donuts. Everyone knew his name—the women at the registers, the men who prepared the food. Once, he paid for our family's breakfast after Sunday mass. Three Big Breakfasts with a couple of apple pies. I thanked him, but Martín hollered, "Mira este, se cree un rey." Not that Vicente thought of himself as royalty. He was simply a generous man.

On Saturdays, he coached Daniela and her soccer team, right here in this very park. He saw the joy it brought her and longed to bring the community closer together. And once he started organizing adult soccer matches, he did become kind of a king. Well, among other Peruvians, that is.

He and I walk in silence now toward the bench. It's not too far from the picnic tables where we—the women—had spent many Sundays eating anticuchos, drinking Budweiser, playing bingo, giving ourselves permission to ignore, at least for a little while, the small hands tugging on our shirts and the shrieks from hungry mouths. Vicente and I have taken this walk every week for the last few years, but it feels different on the anniversary. Twenty-one years now since his loss. Soon it will be three years since mine.

"I started it for us," he tells me as we take our place on the bench, always maintaining the space between us to honor Daniela's plaque emblazoned in its center. Its golden sheen reflects the sun, the dandelion carved beside her name and the nearly fifteen years that were the span of her life. We've sat on this bench before, in silence, watching the runners, the bicyclists, the parents trailing children as they stumble through the grass. We were those people once. I wonder if he thinks of Daniela whenever he sees such a child, the way I think of Martín whenever I see such a parent. It was never me doing the chasing.

"I don't mean just my family," he goes on, "but *all* of us. All the Peruvians that were here."

Including Martín. For two summers, he was the goalie for the Guerreros, though he was not a very good one. Anyone who played against them—the Colombianos, Salvadoreños, Chilenos—knew they were almost guaranteed to get the ball past Martín if they could just get through Los Salcedo, three cousins who grew up playing soccer on the streets of El Callao. The Guerreros' opponents were not necessarily better players, not at all. Sometimes they were younger or newly arrived, still in awe of the sky towers, the underground tunnels that connected one island to another, the pace with which they were now expected to move. They didn't know their hearts could reach such speeds. Mostly, though, the opponents of the Guerreros were like us, nearing middle age, waffling between the city's intoxicating charge and the wear of its rhythm.

For us, the charge and the wear met on the field.

"Oye, huevón, ¿sigues vivo?" Martín would call out to no one in particular on the opposite team, just to see who he got a reaction out of. He'd taunt that player for the rest of the match.

While he played, and you were off with Daniela, I sat with the women. Renata had placed folding chairs on the left side of the field, several meters from where Vicente sat at his own gray table, keeping score. After all, it was Vicente who ran the league; Vicente who collected the fees, took bets, paid out money to whoever eventually won the championship at the end of the season. We mostly sat, the wives that is: gossiping, cheering whenever we bothered to pay attention to the game or noticed Cabezón Salcedo adjusting his shorts. Not all the men played soccer, and those who preferred to eat instead usually gathered near us, but far enough away that we women could talk without having to whisper.

Lunch was a combination of a juane and a can of Inca Kola that Norma sold back then for $8, un robo, but that was the price one paid for an afternoon in community. Once the matches were done, we played bingo on the picnic tables until either the moon took ahold of the summer sky or we ran out of singles. Martín only grumbled the first time I held out my hand for more cash to play; by the end of the night, he was at least three pilsners in and just gave me his wallet.

It was in between the soccer and bingo matches that Vicente and I first began to talk. I can't recall how it started, exactly. He sat at his table, under a blue-and-white beach umbrella, the notebooks where he kept track of the matches spread out before him. A single chair was beside his, meant for Renata, only she was so preoccupied running after little Samuel, their youngest, and managing the food vendors that it mostly sat empty. Vicente drank nothing but water, bottled and stocked in the cooler, still partially frozen. Sometimes I'd take him one and sit beside him, not thinking about his wife because she could see us. Everyone could. There was nothing to hide.

"These idiots are going to lose," he'd say about the Guerreros. He always betted for his team, sometimes begrudgingly, and I often teased that he was better off betting on the other.

"They won't, and not because of my husband. It's those three," I'd say pointing to Los Salcedo. "They know how to play, especially that Cabezón."

"So you've been watching him too? I thought only Renata found him handsome."

"Everyone does, but he's made some spectacular goals."

"It's the size of that head."

I laugh. "But that's why they'll win."

Often the Guerreros *did* win. And one night after one of those victories, Vicente joined us for bingo, the only man ever allowed to do so. Not because he was El Rey, no, but because he threw in five-dollar bills, sometimes ten, while we were putting in quarters and singles. Maybe a man with money is king, I don't know. But even if you were watching your money all week, you'd find a few extra bills when Vicente played. That first time, he sat next to me and bought me an extra bingo card as a thank-you for being so optimistic about the game. He ended up winning—twice. He sat with us every Sunday after that. Sometimes he'd squeeze next to me even when Renata was there, declaring that I brought him luck, and whenever he won, he'd slide a few bills under the table for me to top off my own winnings. La yapa.

On those Sundays, Vicente made a place that was never meant to be ours, *ours*. And while everyone knew him on this level, he was familiar to me on a more personal one. We had daughters who were about the same age—you were a couple of years younger than Daniela, but close enough that you became friends. For three summers, the two of you circled the park on your bicycles, disappeared behind the handball courts, and lined up by the Mister Softee truck for ice cream. Swam in the public pool behind us. Daniela was eleven years old when Vicente started the league; fourteen when she left us. We would have celebrated her quinceañera that year, had she lived.

"Dani did love it here," Vicente says. "We had the backyard, but it wasn't like being with other kids. Kids like her. Like Yoli. Dani would ride her bike out here just to sit with the dandelions. Sneak up on the butterflies. She liked the white ones. I think she found them soothing."

He never mentions Samuel, the only child he has now, or Renata, unless I bring them up. You see, after Samuel left for college, Renata made more and more trips to Puerto Rico. To see her mother or attend this niece's quinceañera or that nephew's wedding, then to rebuild their family home after a hurricane, or so Vicente said. He'd visit once a year, that's it. *It's too hot and every meal's got plantains*, he'd complain. I can never get enough of the sun or tostones.

I rarely see Renata now. The last time I saw her, months ago, she was still slim, her flat black hair parted in the middle, like when we were younger, in the days when she watched Samuel compulsively. *Tu nuera no te va a querer*, we'd shout from the picnic tables, teasing her about a future daughter-in-law who wouldn't appreciate Renata hovering over her son. She'd laugh, but never took her eyes off that boy. She didn't seem to worry much about

Daniela, but then neither did Vicente. Not even when she'd fall on the field or complain of a head injury. The older Dani got, the less attention Renata paid her, or so Vicente would say. It was the boy she watched, he insisted; the son she had waited for all those years. Not his Daniela.

"Water soothed Martín," I hear myself say, and for a moment, I forget my own unspoken rule. *Never talk about water around Vicente.* Even though water is what reminds me of your father. The first time he took me to the beach, it was to Punta Hermosa. By then I'd been infatuated with him for more than a year, making all those morning trips to his parents' store for milk and eggs before he finally asked me out. Then there we were alone, the sand coating our toes, the sea at our noses. The Pacific air was cool; its dark water, frigid. We ran back to the shore whenever the ocean gathered under our bare feet, but at one point, he rolled up his pants and walked in as far as he could, and I watched him still the sea. Back in the car, he wiped off the sand on our feet with his sweater. We watched the clouds descend on that August night. They did not completely block out the sun, like they usually do in Lima's Augusts. The sky settled on violet as Lucha Reyes came on the radio. We kissed, and her forceful plea swelled inside me. "Regresa." In that moment, I could not imagine ever kissing another man, never mind letting him go.

And every time he did leave me, for work or an errand, I'd whisper a prayer, and when he left me for this country, I wrote that prayer down and left the piece of paper at San Martincito's feet. I prayed that Martín would come back, never really believing there'd come a time when he wouldn't. When he'd go off into that sea.

"It's okay, Paula," Vicente tells me. He puts his hand on my back. I clear my throat to avoid crying. He can't see me do that. Now, I may not know when or how to say things sometimes, but like you said, words are a way to let go. A way to breathe.

"Martín had a complicated relationship with water. He'd never fully go into the ocean or a lake. Just let the water get right above his ankles. His knees if he felt brave enough. But he loved it. He'd stand there quietly. Have this moment of reconciliation with whatever he both loved and feared. And whenever he was afraid or had a nightmare or a negative thought, he'd open up the faucet and tell it to the running water so that it'd carry it away."

I had watched him do this over the years, and finally tried it when we decided we wanted children. Each time a pregnancy test came back positive, I asked the water to take away my fear of miscarrying, even though that fear never went away. And then the only time I did carry to term—with you—I whispered to the water, whether it was trickling from the faucet or the agua Florida your father rubbed on my face and hair, hoping to wash away the fear and pain of labor. I cannot separate that ache from what Martín endured. Can you believe that? The pain of death sounded to me like that of birth. I held him each time he bent over his hospital bed in agony, like he had once done for me. He clung to my hand and to each breath as I yelled for the nurses and kept pressing on that button for more morphine or whatever it was that they were pumping into him. It never seemed to work. When the episode passed, I'd cry in the bathroom, into the running water, even though I knew this wasn't going to pass. There was nothing on the other side of it but more pain, and in those moments when Martín dug into my grip and could barely hold on to his breath, when I labored for mine, I prayed for death. I prayed for it in a way that first made me feel ashamed, then hopeful, because perhaps this was it, this was the end, and San Martincito, the Virgin, or God himself would have mercy on this man I loved and take him as I held him.

But then his pain would subside, and the cycle repeated. Maybe not that day or the next, but it would, eventually. The water had listened—some form of the suffering had passed. Until the day the doctors said there was nothing more they could do.

This, I don't bring up to Vicente. He never heard his daughter's breath again. Never held her hand. Daniela was alive one minute; lifeless the next. His memories of her are of the days she lived; my memories of Martín are mostly of his end days.

"Does it get easier?" I ask, knowing there is no real answer to that.

"It comes in waves. But twenty-one years, and I can't say it's gotten much better. It's different. There are days I miss her so much that I'd be fine not waking up the next. Sometimes she seems so close, like the way I'm sitting next to you right now. And then there are times where I don't feel her at all and I'm afraid I'm starting to forget. I will say, if there's one good thing about time passing, it's that I'm getting closer to seeing her again. At least that's my hope. That she'll be there, ready to take my hand when it's my time to walk into the next life."

His profile is sharp; his eyes cut the sun. A part of me envies him, the comfort he must find on this bench, under these trees, with the sound of the air brushing the grass. Am I too supposed to settle for the water now? To find Martín's touch when the sea rushes to my feet, or his gaze whenever lilac light breaks through an overcast sky? Am I supposed to simply wait and hope to see him again when my time comes?

I place my hand on Vicente's thigh for just a moment. We've never tried to console each other with words. There's nothing one parent can say to another over the loss of a child. I'm not sure he can really say anything to me about my loss. But we both know the other has a void, and that we're each trying to navigate it in our own way.

We walk a little more around the path before he heads home and I to the gym. When we part ways, we do so quietly, mumbling a *cuídate* and *tu también* before we go. But each time, almost as soon as I turn away, I ask a God I'm not sure I know anymore to please, at the very least, let our beloveds lie in peace.

7

FLORES

MY THREE MONITORS ARE WINDOWS INTO MY WORK. ENDLESS ROWS, CELLS fattened with numbers, tab after tab of information that is distilled into bars and lines pasted onto PowerPoint slides. The company's work reduced to electronic scribbles. These are the building blocks I use to craft the story of the Bowl. The monitors act as a partition too, a necessary barrier against the rest of the company, and even from my own team, particularly Jon. His energy borders on the nauseously optimistic, especially when there's a new Bowler around. It's probably why he's better suited to be CFO than I am.

This morning he stands at his desk, candy-cane coffee mug in hand, rambling to Steve and Carl about his eldest son's fourth birthday party. With his stories of late-night diaper blowouts, dislocated elbows from the monkey bars, and random tumbles down the stairs, I sometimes wonder if Jon and his kids will make it to kindergarten intact. Today's cautionary tale on parenting is about his brother-in-law, a bounce house, a concussion, and how the guy should've known better than to go in there in the first place.

Then he taps the top of my middle monitor. I slide one of my headphones off.

"Is that deck ready yet?" he asks.

"It's ten-thirty," I point out. "You got here ten minutes ago. We're not meeting until this afternoon."

"It's a simple yes or no."

"Finish up that coffee and then we'll talk."

His head snaps. He glances at Carl. Great, so now he cares what the new guy thinks. "Girl, we don't need to have a conversation about it. Just answer the question." He calls me *girl* even though he's only a few years older than me. Even though he's my boss and should know better. He'd never call Steve or Carl *boy*, but that's the patriarchy for you. Maybe he calls me that to remind me he *is* my boss. He can tell I'm pissed because he leans over and whispers, "Look, everyone's going away for the Fourth. We gotta make sure these idiots have their story straight before they all bounce to the Hamptons."

The presentation that has him so anxious is our quarterly sales deck, which he first presents to the department heads for their input, and we then build out for the board. Now, let's be real, it's never anything grim. My job's not to tell the absolute truth. Just a version of it, something that makes our investors feel comfortable (even if not confident) about the direction we're headed. In other words, what they *need* to hear and what we *want* them to hear.

I have somehow become the default PowerPoint deck preparer and slide swiper for all our meetings. Probably because I manipulate data, graph charts, and don't need someone to interpret the information for me. That's the point of getting everyone together beforehand, so that they understand what kind of narrative we want to create with the numbers. At the actual board meetings, all I really do is take notes and click from slide to slide as the others review the past quarter and explain their strategy for the next one. Jon presents my work, of course, and the guy can talk circles around numbers, dodge questions like a boxer, fake it in the boardroom like one might in the bedroom, except he is actually believable. My mandate is to make the decks easily digestible so he can fake it well. Otherwise I'm not doing my job. How do I make it easy? Color. Vibrant charts with visible milestones clearly highlighted. Of course, I have my go-to Excel shades: Flora for up-swings, Spindrift for emphasis, Blueberry for dips. Red tones are a no-no, except for the occasional circle to point out a number, and even then, it can only be Cayenne.

I focus on all the numbers our investors need to hear. If the return on investment of a particular advertising campaign isn't great, I'll concentrate on the overall gross merchandise volume, just to avoid putting the spotlight on money not well spent. In other words, whatever metric tells them, "Hey, our business is doing great!" and not "Fuck—we're *fucked*," because that could be the message we inadvertently send if we're not all on the same page. Even if some numbers look funky, we can find others to give the overall state of the company a positive spin. A look-on-the-bright-side angle. That's my job. I remind myself that it's my job even as I look to Jon for some acknowledgment during these meetings— a shout-out, a thank-you, a "let's give it up for Flores." It's something I admit I still crave, even after years of zero praise and as Max mutters mutiny, because the truth is that in the last two quarters, faking it has gotten harder. But I'm good at it, and it's mine. It's why my skin prickles when Jon turns to Steve and asks if he can work on the numbers instead.

"I'll have it to you in an hour," I say.

. . .

THE AFTERNOON WE meet in Bio, short for Bioluminescence, our larg-est conference room. It's tucked away at the opposite end of the floor behind the reception area, far from curious eyes and ears. Except Jasmine's, who naturally took decorating this particular room to heart. The floor here is the only one in the office that is carpeted. The plush blue rug tempts you to walk on it barefoot. Three of the rooms four walls are pewter, the only ones in the of-fice that are not pearly white. They're painted with bursts of neon orange sand, lime green seaweed, and fuchsia corals. The single black wall is bare, except for the massive screen mounted on it. The table at the center of the room is the color of sand, its edges shimmering like a rainbow, with nooks and craters that give it the feel of an ammonite. Twenty white mesh chairs surround the table. They look like they belong in a medical office and totally throw off the underwater theme we were aiming for, but I don't ever tell Jasmine this.

Jon and I are the first to arrive, but hints of life at the Bowl are scattered throughout the room. A sports channel is muted on the screen. Three empty bottles of IPA sit on the table. Several bite-size Milky Way wrappers are piled near the phone. We clean up quickly, and he mumbles something about people not doing their jobs. I remind him that cleaning up after others isn't in Jasmine's job description.

Eric arrives with Nik and the other department heads. Each one is a friend of Eric's from some point in the past, before he became a serial entrepreneur and everyone was eager to give him their money in the hopes of making a quick buck. He displayed a bit of a savior complex when it came to hiring from within his circle of friends and acquaintances. Each one of us had some sob story to tell when we were recruited. The need to be saved from emotional or financial turmoil is almost a prerequisite for working with Eric.

And he knew how to channel our pain into something everyone wanted in on. Growth was exponential that first year at the Bowl, and Eric had the kind of story that people wanted to hear: a family guy, once down on his luck, who wanted to share with the world the comfort and beauty that fish and aquariums brought him as a child and now as a successful businessman. He hit the local morning news shows, then cable networks, propelled by the prosperous runs of his previous companies and all the promise of this one. He was humble about his success, always ending interviews with gratitude toward his immigrant parents, who modeled hard work, and his wife, who put her nursing career on hold to be the primary caregiver for their children. And us, the employees, the company's backbone. All things that Americans eat up and that investors write checks for.

But broken souls and telegenic charm could go only so far in selling aquatic creations. When our sales began to decline, he sought help from people with track records and marketable degrees instead of just reliable friends. And because Max was one such recruit, Eric made an exception for him to join the board meetings. This vexed Jon, and for good reason. Nik was already present. Why did we need his second-in-command there too?

Jon's resentment of Max, however, was only an extension of his rivalry with Nik. In that way, his animosity toward Max was predestined. Jon had interviewed him, but that was merely a formality. Nik had already made it clear that he was going to hire him. The day of the interview, Jon stood over my desk as we looked up Max's LinkedIn profile. It read much like the profiles of the other Ivy League grads that had joined the Bowl over the years, each one deluded into thinking they could cut it at a start-up because they had stints at blue-chip companies or consulting firms, near-perfect GPAs, and top class rankings. Each had a smattering of details on their profiles that made them seem more human—an interest in a sport (usually golf, basketball, squash) or mentoring underprivileged kids. Occasionally you'd find an affinity group listed on the profile, meant to show that this person really did identify with this or that marginalized group and wasn't just a box checker. Few had actual e-commerce experience, which was the only kind of experience that mattered. And of course they were almost always guys.

But Max was different. Another Ivy League grad, but thrice over. A polyglot who worked in Singapore for six months, played college basketball, and even now played in a soccer league in Queens with men who were decidedly not Ivy League grads. His profile included a news clip where he talked about how he placed thirty California king beds in the middle of Times Square to promote an online mattress company. The award he got for the stunt was listed there too. Peppered throughout were words of praise from his former bosses, who marveled at his ability to negotiate complex transactions and bring internal teams together to plan, strategize, and successfully execute campaigns—all within or below budget.

When the interview was over, Jon pointed out that Max's profile picture was outdated. His hair was fuller in the pic, his face thinner. Did he still look good? I joked. Maybe he's deceptive, Jon suggested. Maybe he has better things to do than updating a profile on a stupid professional social network, I replied. I didn't even have a picture on my LinkedIn page. I don't care if you crush on the guy, Jon said, but we just don't need another asshole.

On that point, we agreed. The company didn't need any more alphas, especially ones with the credentials to believe they were actually superior to the rest of us. He'd never admit it, but Jon and the other men ate that shit up. Bring in someone who could swing dick, Jasmine would say, and the others sway along with him. That was true of Max, at least for a little while. He restored our mojo with a couple of back-to-back marketing campaigns that upped our sales. Soon enough, he was presenting to the entire company at our weekly All Hands, calling marketing team meetings without Nik (who was off at some conference or another), and participating in these board meetings, his face in front of the leadership and investors. And while some seemed to despise him now, including Jon, I couldn't.

When Max walks into Bio, he takes the seat across from me. I bring the presentation up on the screen. He and Nik tag-team the board meetings, highlighting their wins, places they see opportunities for improvement, and plans for the next quarter. But at our internal meetings, Nik mostly nods at the slides I've prepared, largely preoccupied with his phone or watch, responding to comments on his latest LinkedIn post or announcing whatever news alert popped up. Occasionally, he takes his eyes off his "rings" to make sure a slide "feels" right. Not that he hides his disdain for these meetings ("a waste of time" is a common complaint).

He munches on a handful of trail mix now as he crosses his ankles on the conference room table. His eyes roll as my slide shows the lackluster performance of his team's most recent radio campaign. He'd been credited with turning all the other companies he's ever worked for into gold mines. Places that made shit you'd never find me peddling (diet supplements, fast food, big pharma). He's not particularly analytical, but he talks a good game and smells like sex on a fur rug near a crisp fireplace in a snowed-in cabin. Anyway, his ideas always border on the ridiculous. He once ran a contest on Facebook where people had to guess how many Skittles were piled on a table. The prize: a Skittles sculpture of the winner made by one of his famous "artist" friends. It got a lot of reposts, which is his marker for success. The winner opted for a sculpture of his dog—made up of only yellow Skittles—instead of himself.

A man like Nik is never good with criticism, so when Eric tells him that Nina Blue will join her brother at the next board meeting, he jerks his gleaming white sneakers off the table. "Why is she even in the room?"

"Because she's an investor," says Eric.

"No, no. Her daddy's *firm* is an investor, not her, and the seat belongs to her brother. She can't just show up. Besides, remember what happened after the last board meeting? She crashed our dinner. Grilled us on every single campaign we did this year, all the while smiling and stuffing her face with a fucking crème brûlée."

"That's why I'm giving you the heads-up—"

"She tried to make me look ineffective," he goes on. "Someone with zero marketing experience."

"She has an MBA!" I blurt out. After Jasmine told me and Starr, between cackles, about that dinner, I looked Nina up. She didn't seem to exist on any social networks, not even LinkedIn. Most of what I learned was from her company website and news articles. A managing partner at the firm, she was a Brown grad with a JD from Yale and an MBA from Wharton. The eldest child and only daughter of Harrison Blue, she'd had stints at a consulting firm and a national retail chain, even clerked for a federal judge before taking the reins at Silver Blue Ventures alongside her younger brother. Her picture on the firm's website was the kind of image you'd find on Shutterstock if you searched for "woman" and "office": a cuarentona in a white room filled with natural light, wearing a pair of black-framed glasses, a sharp-cut bob parted in the middle, and a thin gold necklace over a black V-neck sweater. It was fun to imagine her getting Nik all riled up.

"So do I," he claps back. "And I've been doing this work for twenty years. Granted my MBA is from Stanford, not Wharton, but it's also not from my daddy's alma mater. And when I graduated, I didn't go into 'consulting' before going to work for Daddy. I actually had a *real* job." He throws his hands up, looks around the room. "Can someone remind Flores what it is I do around here? Or at least why someone who doesn't know anything about marketing shouldn't tell me how to do my job?"

"She can," says Eric, and then as if to both clarify what he is saying and remind me of my place, "*Nina* absolutely can. She and Ethan practically run their dad's business and they gave us a shit-ton of money. That buys her an opinion."

Nik points his finger. "*She's* the one. I'm telling you. She's talking shit about us to Ethan and God knows who else. He always lets us do what we need to do. Ideate, experiment. But now he's meddling. I get it, subway ads aren't exactly innovative, but he suddenly thinks they're a waste of money?"

"They cost hundreds of thousands of dollars," Jon points out.

"It was never just about numbers for Ethan. It was about the company's mission. *Your* mission, Eric. And that's what we were doing. We were getting our name out there. To everyone! Lawyers, doctors, bankers. People with stressful jobs and stressful lives. Isn't that what you wanted when you first started this company? To help people build better homes, better workplaces? Better lives. A way to relax and hit the reset button. That's something you can't quantify." He turns to me and Jon. "Or maybe we could if you all didn't cut our budget."

"Oh, here we go again," says Jon.

"Does anyone on the 6 train even bother to look at the ads?" I say. "They're probably just playing Candy Crush on their phone."

Nik snorts. "First off, junior marketer, we need people to know our brand. If no one knows who we are or what we do, we can't get sales, and everyone in New York rides the subway. The Erics of the world, but also the Jasmines, and they're the ones doing all the buying for the offices they manage. Second, all New Yorkers are stressed. They need *something* to take them down a few notches. It can't just be weed, wine, or CBD gummies."

"But we already have a strong user base," I say.

He rattles his head, dismissing me, and spins his chair around to face the rest of the room. "What we need are more eyeballs."

"Nik is right," Max concurs. Jon tenses beside me; my own face goes hot. "If Nina wants to see numbers, then we need to focus on growth. That means acquiring new customers and, like Flores points out, retargeting our users. They're totally engaged in our chat rooms. We know they're on Facebook and not TikTok—yet. They like home renovation shows and are really passionate about self-care and the environment. We can invest more money on targeted TV ads, influencers, more social media. We obviously can't do that if we're going to spend it buying glass businesses."

Jon snorts. "Fisk & Tanks isn't just a glass business. It's going to help us bring down our costs overall."

Eric holds up his hand, shutting down the argument. "That acquisition is going to increase our reach in the Midwest. I don't need to rehash why I decided to buy it. It's a strategic move and a done deal." The room goes silent, and he lets out a slow, even breath, like he's in between oms. "Nina hasn't been happy with us for a while," he acknowledges. His eyes grow distant before he looks straight at me, and suddenly I feel seen, bare to the bone. Is he actually pissed that I challenged Nik? Did any of it have a ring of truth? Or does he know about my conversations with Max and how we doubt him?

I wonder if he doubts himself too.

"I'm working on Ethan," he goes on, scanning the room and making eye contact with everyone in it. "I just need the rest of you to do your jobs."

8

PAULA

THE FOURTH OF JULY WAS NEVER A HOLIDAY I ENJOYED, BUT SINCE WE LIVE SO close to the river, and Macy's usually sets off the fireworks there, we can't avoid celebrating it. It's not just our block that turns into a party; the entire neighborhood becomes one. And each year, the party gets louder. More and more young people from Manhattan make their way onto our streets and rooftops. Children chase one another on the street, tossing party snaps at their feet as if they're simply discarding chicle, unaware that a single pop can give someone over fifty a heart attack. On their stoops or by the trunks of their cars, our neighbors grill every animal part: burger patties, hot dogs, chicken thighs covered in Sazón con Culantro y Achiote, that thick salty sausage they sell at Krakowski Meats. It's the smell of summer, rubbing its way into your nose and onto your tongue. Absolute torture as you wait for someone to offer you a bite.

Then there's the music, which no one can agree on. You walk a few feet, and there's Phil Collins blaring from Chito's station wag. A few more steps and you'll hear Tito Rojas belting away from Miriam's window. Then right in front of the building next door is that obnoxious perreo coming from Manuelito's car. He flips strips of meat on his grandmother's grill while his cousins dance to this barbarity. It's impossible to look at them without imagining what must happen in their bedrooms.

Then again, they *are* dancing. On the sidewalk and in the street, and it's hard not to feel so very alive.

I wait for Shanti and her kids on my stoop. The two beach chairs I bought at DollaBills with my employee discount are set against the chain-link fence that separates the building from the sidewalk. Shanti texted that she and her boys were just a few blocks away, so here I am. We won't have to walk far to see the fireworks. I can certainly do without the deafening blasts and the smell of gunpowder on my clothes, but Shanti's children are still awed by the spectacle. How fortunate and fragile that is—to be so young and protected that one can find magic in something others find terrifying.

"Tía, ¿usted quiere un hot dog?" Manuelito asks as he makes a plate for his own son. He flips over what looks like steak, and I wish he'd offer me that instead, but I settle for the hot dog. His black T-shirt and gym shorts are streaked with grease. Beneath the tattoos on his arms, there's muscle. He complains about how expensive everything is now that the neighborhood's gotten popular with these blanquitos with family money. Then again, he told me once that he prefers that fancy gym near the train station because it has more machines than the YMCA. He pays monthly for un-limited classes at the yoga studio near the McDonald's too, and carries that mat around like a status symbol.

"What I want is for you to change that music," I say. "Can't you play something with more energy? Like Olga Tañón or Los Herma-nos Rosario?"

"You don't like Shakira and Nicky Jam?" He laughs. "Yoli loves them. Where is she anyway?"

Of course he asks about you. He's had a crush on you since he was a skinny, pigeon-toed boy hopping on that yellow school bus. He's a grown man now, not quite hecho y derecho, but getting there. I admit, after he got that girl pregnant, I didn't have much hope he'd get his life in order. He dropped out of high school, and then his grandmother got sick. He didn't marry the girl, and that was probably for the best. If he had, he might not have gotten his GED, let alone be working on a master's now. And the boy seems happy. He's a smaller version of his father, with spiky black hair and a crooked smile.

"De chamba," I say. "Can you believe she went to work today?"

"I believe it. Yoli's always setting the bar real high. You know, I got one more year of juggling school and teaching. Then I can just teach." I wonder what parent would want a man with tattooed arms teaching their child, even if those tattoos are of a condor in the colors of the Colombian flag and the face of Jesucristo. *Especially* if it's Jesucristo, but I don't say anything. He points to the chairs. "Are you two going to the pier?"

"No, I'm going with a friend. Yoli's probably going to watch from home."

"Like on the TV or the roof? You can't really see much from the fire escape anymore, with all the buildings." He takes out his phone. "I'll text her. Maybe I should make her a burger or something."

"She's on a diet," I say, but his thumbs race across his screen anyway.

I spot Shanti halfway down the block, her two little ones skipping a few feet ahead of her. She's not the same Shanti I see every day at the store. Her shiny leatherlike hair is tied in a half ponytail, like a schoolgirl's, and not wound like thread on a spool on top of her head. Her lips are painted violet, not the usual tangerine gloss she puts on and on because she keeps chewing it off. Her jeans stop just above her knees and are dotted with silver studs all along the seams. I recognize them from aisle 13. Her top is fitted and solid yellow, like the sticky notes we sell. I remind myself that she is only thirty years old, younger than my own child, and more than deserving of Manuelito's glances.

"It's like one huge block party!" she shouts as we kiss each other hello.

"All day and all night," I say. "It's the one day everyone can eat outside, listen to this garbage music as loud as they want, and the police won't bother us. Not even if the blanquitos call them."

. . .

THE FIREWORKS DON'T start until after nine P.M., but it's already seven, and by the time we reach the pier, it's packed. The patterns in the sky will be the same all along the river. We'll be able to see it no matter where we are, but the police barricades and vans have already divided the streets. It's clear where we can and cannot go. An officer points us to the playground, where we set our chairs down near an already crowded bench. Shanti gives her children a few dollars for neon glow sticks that a woman is selling from a laundry cart, and as they head off to the sprinklers, she lets out a long breath, the kind I used to release when I was a young parent. She pulls two cans of Coors Light from her bag and hands me one.

Across the river, the top of the Empire State Building glows red, white, and blue. Marc Anthony's "Vivir Mi Vida" plays somewhere behind us, and ahead of us, music from what Shanti tells me is Bruce Springsteen. The smell of charcoal still lingers, carried by the lullaby of a Mister Softee ice cream truck.

"Are you all right, Miss Paula?" she asks. "You seem so pensive." I remind myself that Shanti is still my coworker; I cannot cry. She touches my arm but doesn't seem to notice when I recoil. Her lower lip pouts. "Are you thinking of Mr. Martin?"

I want to pretend that all is well, that everything is fine. Some days are easier than others. This day isn't. "He used to love this holiday," I admit. "When we were younger, we'd get together with other Peruvian families. In the park, every Sunday. And then every

July, we celebrated Peruvian Independence Day. Not with fireworks, but with music and dancing. And eating, of course. That was my favorite holiday. But my husband loved the Fourth of July. He liked the show this country put on. I never understood it. All the lights and noise—they just mask all the bad things about it. I used to tell him it's a trick! But he didn't care. Not on this day, at least."

He never did want to see things for what they were. For Martín, everything had an explanation, even if it wasn't one that he liked or agreed with. If there was an immigration raid, he didn't think much of the children left behind; it was undoubtedly sad, but that was the risk one took when coming to this country. Easy for someone with a green card to say. Whenever the police pulled him over, he spoke to them as if they were old friends while he thumbed through his wallet for his license. As if they had not killed immigrants like him. Dark-skinned men, like him. Shot one forty-one times for holding a wallet; killed another for simply selling a cigarette.

"What choice do we have?" Shanti says. "This country's far from great, Miss Paula, but there are worse places in the world. At least if there's an injustice, you can say something—*do* something—without being killed or thrown in jail." She snickers. "Well, most of the time. Besides, sometimes we need to believe the lie because the alternative is worse."

"That is true of most things," I say. "When I had Yoli, I thought we would go back to Peru, but Martín was convinced this was the best way to help ourselves and our family back home. I kept telling myself that my daughter had better opportunities here than she had there. And having a child is like stepping onto new land altogether. I wasn't sure if I was doing anything right. But Martín had a good job cleaning an office. Our landlady at the time offered to help me with Yoli, so I went back to sewing curtains a month after I had her. A month!"

"Well, who needs to spend time with their baby after it's born? Certainly not its mother! And it's not like you needed time to heal. She didn't blow your vagina to smithereens!"

"Don't be vulgar," I say. "But really, who has time to think about healing when you have a mouth to feed? We didn't have enough money for me to stay home. I had help and a chance to work. And when I think about *that*, well. What would I do back home? What would my Yoli do? We had to stay."

"Didn't Mr. Martín own a store back in Peru?"

"His family used to own a bodega. It became very complicated when he left. His sister took it over after my mother-in-law died, but Martín and I thought we'd go back to run it once Yoli was married and settled here." For years, we treated the store as if it was meant to be ours. We took out loans to redo the interior, replace the roof, pay the taxes that were due, but that didn't make it ours. All those years we were away, your grandmother and then your aunt took care of the store, but we invested so much into it that we let ourselves believe they were merely safeguarding it for us. Looking back now, I realize it was never truly ours. I still resent your aunt for doing what she did behind our backs. "Then Martín got sick, and my greedy sister-in-law ended up selling it. I'm not sure I can ever forgive her for that."

"Is that why you like working at DollaBills?" she asks. I hadn't thought of it until now, and it sends a shiver through my spine. She laughs. "Or maybe you just like working, Miss Paula. I don't. I'm going to save my money and build a nice home in Guyana with a beautiful garden and a guesthouse so you can come visit me anytime. As soon as my children are grown, I will go back and show everyone what a woman can do. Married or not." Shanti's husband used to shove her, scream at her, until two summers ago, when her eldest refused to stay in the other room and instead hit his father with the baseball bat he got for his birthday. She and the boys live with her parents now. Her husband is still her husband, on paper. He blamed his outburst on the stress of being a cop. He's seeing a therapist. I think she still loves him, though she would never admit it.

"I don't think about going back," I say. "Yoli used to, just to visit. She wanted to see Cusco and Arequipa. Even Pucallpa. That's the last place her father and I visited before he came here. It's where our mothers are from. He loved it there. Bugs and sun. None of it bothered him. But she forgot about it when he got sick. I don't ever bring it up. It might be too much for her. To go back to a place that reminds her of her father."

"I guess that's why she's not here, either. Because of Mr. Martin."

I tell something of a lie to protect you because Shanti is right. His memory is what brings me here; it's also what keeps you away. But that is your truth. It is not mine to share. "She's never really liked the noise and the crowds," I say, which is true, or was. The way these explosions pound the air, the smell and glow of the light—it would make any child cover her ears and dig her face into her mother's belly, and so you did. Eventually, Martín would come out to this pier alone, even though year after year, he asked that we join him. He stopped asking after September 11. The television screen was a good enough substitute for the real fireworks, and we could still feel the building tremble all around us. If the night was brisk and we could bear the smell, we went to the fire escape. I'd grip its steel limbs, praying it wouldn't collapse under our feet. Glitter exploded into the night sky. On rooftops, shadows whooped, and on the ground, it was the children who went "Wow!" The "everything is possible" kind of *wow*.

And this is what Martín loved about this day and this place. He used to claim that his only goal in coming to this country was to find steady work, but what truly brought him here was the promise of an adventure, of sparks, even when things were uncertain. When money and work were scarce, he preferred to ignore the bills and the phone calls. *We'll find a way or the way will find us*, he liked to say, while I wrote my pleas down on paper.

And just when the rent came due or when the electricity was about to get shut off or right when his sister was about to lose the store, there was that spark! A job, a second job, a tax refund, someone who owed us money was finally able to pay us back. We found a way or the way found us, and that was enough confirmation for Martín that he need not worry. God, the saints, our guardian angels were looking over us.

And the sparks surrounded him, in all the moments one might think are small. In every meal he made because they seemed so plentiful compared to what we ate back home. And whenever he managed to block a soccer ball from entering the net, what fire ignited then! He glowed when he saw you flow onto that stage at your graduation, in your cap and gown, and shouted your name—*his* name. ¡Flores! If he had any ambitions beyond these moments, we never discussed them. These sparks were enough to sustain him when things were hard and uncertain.

I didn't always share his excitement. What I mostly felt was relief that there was food on the table; that the game was over; that you had a degree. Maybe the relief overshadowed the pride I felt, or you sensed my fear and doubt, and that is what pushed you closer to your father's light. Relief, after all, is a temporary sensation. Unlike Martín, I couldn't bring myself to trust the good moments. They felt like tricks. I wonder how long he lived with the pain of his cancer before finally seeing a doctor, all the while hopeful that he'd find a way out of that pain. Even when he got chemotherapy, he didn't seem to accept how sick it made him feel or how much time he had left. It let him live another day, and there would be that spark again. For a little while, at least, but it was there; and for a little while, I allowed myself to be tricked.

This is how he lived. I did not have that same sense of wonderment, of carelessness even, that he had, but oh! what wouldn't I do to be close to it? To him. On nights like this, when the sky ignites and the ground swells, I let myself remember the warmth of his body standing next to mine; his arms around me as we danced under the moon in Miraflores, and how we curled our toes in the sand even in the winter. How we walked along Oak Street in the spring and summer mornings to catch the rosebushes in bloom, hand in hand. If I close my eyes, I can almost feel his fingers between mine and hear his voice just outside my ear. The sound swirls at the back of my throat, and for a moment, I accept the trick. I accept that the exchange for this ache of losing him are all the moments I was able to love him.

9

FLORES

THE MOMENT I LEAVE WORK, I BRACE MYSELF FOR THE NIGHT AHEAD. I WON'T sleep tonight. Truth is, I have a hard time sleeping. Mostly from the stress at work, even though it distracts me from the real shit, and that's fine during the day. When night rolls around, and I can't sleep, I search for other distractions. I rely on reality TV and wannabe actors pretending to fall in love in a gaudy mansion or wealthy women trying to outdo each other in the Hamptons. If those fail, *Dateline* reruns are always a good backup. Then there's the porn on my iPad, or if I'm in the mood, I'll sext with a match on Feast. And wine, if my stomach can tolerate it.

Today I won't need any of that. It's not just the sparklers and smoke and music that will keep me up, but the *day* itself. For some people, it's a birthday or an anniversary that hits hard. That's when the absence no longer lingers on the periphery but claims you. You'll begin to wonder about the possibilities; so will others. *He'd be a grandfather by now* or *She'd be married* or some other milestone a dead loved one might have reached were they not dead. You naturally wonder about your own life: where you'd be if they were still alive; why you are where you are; what's changed and what hasn't. What needs to. Basically, sucker-punch days.

Except it's not just a single day for me, but most of the summer. I feel it especially today—my father's favorite holiday—and because of where we were three years ago, when they told us there was nothing more they could do.

Not that the news came as a surprise—there were daily omens. Drains that stretched out from his abdomen. Sacks that hung on the pole at his bedside. Doctors who upped the dosages of his fentanyl and morphine. Surgeries meant only to relieve his pain, not end it. My mother never grasped that his condition was terminal, not when he was first diagnosed, not even when Dr. Mehta and half a dozen doctors took us into a hospital conference room and told us it was over.

"Pero la cirugía," my mother pleaded, tightening her grip on my forearm. "La quimio." She had counted on science as much as she had on her prayers and her belief that my father would somehow come out of this. In the face of death, my mother had chosen to cling to hope instead of fear, a rare choice for her, and one that I wish she would not have made because it forced me to say what I had only seldomly whispered over the past year. Whispered it because a part of me didn't want to believe; didn't want to put it out in the world. But this time, I said it: the surgeries and chemo were meant only to give him a little more time. They couldn't anymore.

Dr. Mehta handed me a pamphlet. The images—of another hospital with rosebushes in the foreground—blurred as I wept over the conference room table. Her voice seemed far and muffled; my mother's sob was the only sound I could hear. My eyes focused on a single word on that pamphlet, the same one that Dr. Mehta kept repeating. I managed to tell her, "He's not going to hospice. He's coming home."

Her lips thinned. She pushed a box of tissues toward me. "Even if he goes home, there are people at Divine Cup that can help."

When we got back to my father's hospital room, his eyes were shut. I gasped, fearful that he'd passed alone. He woke before I reached the bed. I took his hand, kissed his forehead. *Don't cry*, I reminded myself even as my voice cracked. "Pa, nos vamos a casa."

He shut his eyes and let out a cavernous breath. Until that moment, I did not know how much he'd been holding on to; how much he wanted to let go.

The doctors surrounded us, and he reached out for Dr. Mehta's hand. She said nothing as he muttered a *thank-you* in English and whispered to her, "I am ready to go home." This doctor, whom I had come to fear, began to sob. Silently, restrained for the sake of the others. I envied her—she was free to cry for him, unbound by a promise not to, like the one I had made.

My mother, meanwhile, stayed in the hallway.

That night, we took him home. My mother laid out a fresh set of flower-patterned sheets for their bed. He kept to his side of the mattress, close to the edge to make sure there was plenty of room for her, but most nights, I found my mother asleep beside me.

My father's rustling would wake me, and I'd wander across the hall in an old NKOTB shirt and sweats just to see if he was still breathing. Those last nights, my father resembled a young man. His skin was taut, his mouth full and pointed, as if he'd wake at any moment and say that he'd slept off whatever this was that plagued him, like a bad cold or a nuisance cough. Even now, when sleep does find me, I sometimes wake in the middle of the night and head across the hall, only to find my mother in their bed and in a deep slumber, no longer saving space for him.

• • •

ON MY WALK home, sparklers light up the block. La pompa pours frigid New York City water onto the street. Someone dares to play eighties music in the distance on Canto, ad-full. Manny shouts as I pass his building, asks if I want something to eat, even though I'd already texted no. "I got chicken breasts and ribs!" he offers, none of which are tempting. I have no appetite. "Tía said you were on a diet, but you don't need it."

A cousin of his snickers. I smack Manny's arm and laugh. "You don't have to tell the whole block!" I see Bobby by the pump, holding a water gun and dodging a couple of kids with theirs. "He's so big. Is he a teenager now?"

"Not yet, but he's already taller than his moms." He smiles, his perfect teeth making me wish I'd gotten braces as a kid. "So, what do you say about Kusama in November? We missed out on Carrington earlier. Don't want to make the same mistake."

He's been trying to get me to an art exhibition ever since he saw me with my camera, which is cool and all, but I just don't want to lead him on. Not that there's anything wrong with Manuel Sandoval. He clearly pays attention—he'll text me links or images of photographs or paintings he saw online or in museums with notes like *dope* or *thought of you*. He once sent me an image of an Os Gêmeos painting, two kids riding a graffitied subway car, when he was at a conference in Austin. *Back in the day!*

And he's one of the few kids that stuck around the neighborhood as an adult. Not that he had much of a choice. He could've married his high school girlfriend, I guess, moved in with her parents and all. Maybe they would have if his abuelita hadn't had that stroke. He's been taking care of her ever since. He gets it; the taking care part.

But he *is* four years younger than me, still in school, and just a couple of inches taller than me. Superficial shit, I know, but I've also known him for as long as I can remember, even seen him play in his underwear with the water blasting from that pump across the street. And he does have a kid. Not that I'm jumping to marriage or anything like that. I'm just not sure I can be someone's stepmom, or that I even want to get close enough to being one. Why complicate my life? Still, I find myself saying, "Maybe," and laughing. "It's weird!"

"*You* make it weird!" He smiles. "But if you're up for it, I am too. No pressure, though."

By the time I make my way to my bedroom, the flamingo sky had turned indigo. I throw on a T-shirt and a pair of shorts, then grab my Canon. It sits beside my father's picture, what made me pick up a camera in the first place. Pa called it his mother's picture, even though he and my mother are in it too. He's in the foreground, half smiling, standing on a motorboat at the edge of Lake Yarinacocha, north of Pucallpa. He is a young man in the picture, younger than I am now, with the same umber skin and black curls, even the same fleshy mole beneath his left eye.

My mother sits beside him, her eyes sealed by sunlight, her naturally straight black hair dyed copper, curled, and cut short to frame her face. They are both in a pair of pants and button-down shirts, conspicuously urban and unfit for the trip they are about to take, their last before Pa came to New York.

My grandmother sits across from my parents, the camera catching her mouth in mid-movement. She had left her hometown nearly thirty years before this picture was taken, and while my parents seem more relaxed, my grandmother feels distant. By then, my father explained, she belonged to Lima. Necessity and violence had forced her to make a home elsewhere. What choice did she have but to surrender to it? She is still quite young here, about fifty. Her black hair is tied back, emphasizing her sharp cheeks and sharper eyebrows. Her muted pink dress fails to soften her armor.

My grandfather had given her that dress a year before he died. I never met the man, and knew him only through my own father's recollection of him. He had been a dockworker who supplemented his income with donations from neighbors and travelers alike who sought him out to connect with their dead. He distrusted "everything that happened in Lima," meaning the government, because they simply wanted to hold on to power instead of helping people get access to food, water, electricity—necessities we take for granted here, Pa reminded me. My grandfather wanted to leave something to his children, which is why he and my grandmother worked tirelessly, saved their coins, and finally opened their store. All those years, my grandfather never lost faith, not even when the dock work was physically exhausting or when the spirits refused his invitation to connect. To him, nothing was impossible. His very existence, my father would say, was an act of defiance. He was a Black man who had *lived* his life. He had married a woman who had also escaped the violence intended to erase her. They owned a business; they had children. They loved. They were happy.

My father had wanted the same for me, though I'm not sure I know where or how to begin. When he died, this photograph came under my care, a picture that captured a multitude of cross-roads—a magical and frightening thing.

I can tell that my mother has already visited my father's urn tonight. A single pink rose stands in a narrow-necked glass bottle beside San Martín and La Virgen. Between the two statues, there's a folded-up piece of paper, where my mother had written down what I assume is another prayer. The rose is an offering. She will set out a bouquet for the saints only when the prayer is answered.

I lift the urn. The note I found on my father's birthday is still there, where I left it. With work and the lease being up, I've tried not to think about it. Not that my mother would tell me the truth if I asked her about it. She would get defensive or make me feel as if I'm intruding on something between her and Pa. Besides, I can guess what it is she wants forgiveness for. Something that couldn't have happened when Pa was alive, but did, in a small way. All these years, I've known deep down that there was something be-tween her and Vicente. Maybe it's not quite what I imagine it was. Maybe it didn't go further than what I saw that one Sunday after-noon, all those years ago. Pa probably forgave her long ago. He *did* always love her. Still, a part of me cannot help but resent how she deceived him and betrayed me too.

On the other side of the urn is the wineglass filled with the water my mother leaves out in the fire escape every month, under the full moon. She pours it into mason jars for us to drink, bathe in, clean with, give as an offering. I never ask about her rituals, either; there seems to be no logic to them, except maybe that she puts all the prayers on one side near the saints, and the items that represent the elements on the other. My father always played a part in them too, reminding her when the moon was full or when a feast day was approaching. He prayed, but never at her altar. I often caught him with his eyes closed, mumbling under his breath as he sat in the driver's seat of the car or stood over herbs, potatoes, and rice before turning them into dinner. I understood, even as a child, that these were private affairs, never to be disturbed. So sometimes, when my mother is not here, I light the palo santo for myself. My parents had always said it reminded them of Peru, but it's a Peru I do not know. I can sense it, though, in the exchange between my touch and the palo santo's etched lines and coarse spirals; in my breath as it mingles with the wood's familiar minty scent. I burn it now, make the sign of the cross over my father's urn and circle my body with its smoke.

In the kitchen, I pour my mother's water and several lemon slices into a mug. A cool breath enters through the window. I tighten the strings on my shorts, open the window wider, and slip onto the fire escape. Barefoot, I step onto its pockmarked black railing, carrying my camera and mug.

My father usually went to the pier on the Fourth of July, but the last year he saw the fireworks, before his diagnosis, we sat on this makeshift balcony. We watched the multitude of colors explode in the sky, its embers sprinkle onto the river. I worried aloud about whatever marine life existed in those waters. The light from several stars still reached us, despite the brilliance of all the buildings that illuminated Manhattan.

Tonight no stars dot the warm July night. Instead, the clouds sit atop the repurposed warehouses and new condo towers that climb above the modest four-unit building where we live. Few trees remain in the backyards below, but they susurrate as fireflies punctuate the smoky night. Underneath the notes of charcoal, fire, and singed meat is the scent of the river. A river much closer and more familiar than the one my father, mother, and grandmother once crossed, but which still feels foreign to me. And while I never cared for the smell of the Fourth, its burning, or the cacophonous booms—certainly not after 9/11—my father did. So here I am.

The familiar whistle of the first firework pierces the night as it races above the river and rooftops. A collective *ah!*, a cheer, makes my skin prickle, and I find myself breathing aloud, open-mouthed, as if I had been holding my breath all the while. The lemon water diffuses the sob that lays in wait inside my throat. The rain begins, a cascade of stars and stripes that sears the sky. My eyes narrow as my fingers adjust the lens, as the camera clicks, capturing the shimmer and its cinders, the taste of the river sitting on my tongue.

10

FLORES

THE BACK OF THE RECEPTION AREA IS STACKED WITH BROWN BOXES. I MAKE sure all my purchases are mailed to work, ever since my mother freaked out when I cut cable TV and reduced our Spanish-language channels to just Univision and Telemundo. Camera lenses, wearable gadgets, sneakers—I pick them all up here so I don't have to explain myself, though I think she'd forgive me for this pair of patriotic kicks.

"Your stuff's over there," says Jasmine, motioning behind her. She's fixated on her computer screen, her shoulders hunched over and her fingers rubbing her forehead.

I spot the one box with the Nike logo and am reorganizing the others like Jenga pieces when I venture to ask, "Are you coming to dance class tonight?"

She shakes her head no. Her phone buzzes. "Angel can't figure out dinner and Benny's being a pain in the ass—again."

"Aren't *all* teenagers pains in the asses? Like *all* the time?"

"So are women in their thirties."

"Speak for yourself and Angel," I joke, but this doesn't coax a smile out of her. "What's wrong?"

She looks around to see if anyone's coming. I lean in as she swings her laptop around and slides out the privacy screen. The

browser is open to a page labeled COURSES on the FIT website, and
only one is listed: History of Twentieth-Century Textile Design.

"That sounds cool!" I say.

"I was trying to take two classes," she whispers. "But then this
morning, HR tells me that they can't reimburse me for two because they're 'revisiting the employee career advancement program.' We both know what that means."

"They're cutting it?" I ask, and she side-eyes me. "I swear, Jaz,
I didn't know."

"Bullshit! Your team holds the purse strings around here. How
are you gonna tell me there's no money for one extra class when
I'm here planning this stupid summer party that's already costing
more than last year's!"

"No one's said anything to me about changing the program.
Are they totally killing it or do they just want you to cut your course
load? I would've given you a heads-up if I knew, you know that."

She turns the laptop around and slides the privacy screen back
in. "They didn't say they were killing it, just that they could only
cover the one class. They reassured me that I was welcome to take
as many classes as I want, take whatever time I needed, and in no
way would it impact my performance review." She rolls her eyes,
incredulous. "But those classes would be coming out of my pocket.
And then they'd see about reimbursing me once the class is over.
See, code for 'good luck getting your money back.'" She leans over
the desk and grunts. "I came into this shit-show because Eric said I
could finish up school and the company would help pay for it. That
was the deal. I wanted to be out of here by next year, and now it
doesn't look like that's gonna happen."

"Maybe try being less vocal about your plans to leave," I mumble. "Let me talk to Jon. I'm sure we can make an exception for
you."

"You think I was gonna talk to anyone but Eric about this? Hell
no. I get he's trying to respect people's roles or whatever, but he

didn't have to send some HR gnome to tell me this. He should've told me himself. Anyway, he said I could take extra weeks off over the holidays and just take another class then. One of the few times I actually get to spend with my kid. But whatever. I guess I should just feel lucky that this place is paying for my education at all, right?"

She straightens as the elevator door pings open. A couple steps out. A squat chatterbox of a man with sunflower-seeded hair moves nimbly toward us in his steel-colored suit. By now, Ethan is a familiar face at the Bowl, but the woman behind him isn't. Nor is she as formally dressed. Her white shirt has Stevie Nicks's face on it. The sleeves on her black blazer are rolled up to her elbows. And her distressed jeans are fitted enough that they are likely tailored. A diamond stud sparkles on her left nostril. A treble clef is tattooed on one wrist, a bass clef on the other. Not someone you'd expect beside Ethan.

"Good afternoon!" says Jasmine, beaming her brightest smile.

"Hello, Jaz," Ethan replies, his capped teeth whiter than our walls. He nods my way. "María, right?"

"Flores," I say, feigning a smile. "Finance," as if mentioning my function here might jog his memory. I've seen this man at enough board meetings over the years that he *should* know my name by now.

"I didn't know you'd be here today," says Jasmine. "I must've missed it on Eric's calendar."

"No, not at all. Just one of my surprise visits. Surprise! There's a special guest in town." He nods to the woman beside him. "Figured it'd be nice to swing by and say hello. Is Eric around? I texted him, but radio silence. The guy's always jet-setting to one place or another. I never seem to find him in the office anymore."

Ethan's visits had become more frequent, even though Eric is usually not here. When that happens, Ethan asks to speak to Nik or another member of the C-staff. Once it was Max who kept him company. Sometimes he simply asks for an empty conference room to work in, and Jasmine scrambles to move around meetings just to accommodate him.

"Because he's working," I say.

"Eric's in a meeting," says Jasmine, ignoring me. "But I'll let him know right away that you and Ms. Blue are here."

"Nina's fine." The woman smiles, and I might have taken a step back because of the shock. *This* is Nina Blue? What happened to the woman on the Silver Blue website? Is she a venture capitalist by day and rock-band front woman by night? My guess is she'd be totally fine with me fist-bumping her for making Nik sweat at that dinner.

Jasmine types quickly. "Great, he'll be right out." She turns to me, one massive stupid smile on her face. "Flores, would you be kind enough to show these lovely folks to Bioluminescence?"

Not that they need an escort, but I begrudgingly lead the pair into the conference room. This time, there are empty bottles of Evian and a couple of coffee-stained mugs on the table. Images of fish as bright as highlighters swim across Bio's massive television screen.

"This is an interesting room," says Nina as I toss the empty bottles into the recycling bin.

"We try to have an aquarium theme throughout," I say. "This one's named after our top-selling fish."

"How strange that people love genetically altered creatures," she replies. She takes a seat at the head of the table, spinning in the chair. "You've certainly had some strange ventures, E," she says to her brother, "but this one might top them all."

I catch myself doing that stupid thing people do whenever they meet siblings or parents and their kids: search for any resemblance between the two. She's taller, leaner. The features on her face are more angular. His are rounder. He has the kind of upturned nose that some of my tías in Peru saved up years for a surgeon to carve out.

He points to the neon fish on the screen. "The best sellers are those pink ones up there. Doctors really love those, right?" He looks at me for confirmation on this bit of insight. "I bet their patients find them interesting."

"Their patients must be children," says Nina.

"Could be, or maybe they just think it's, I don't know, cool."

Nina sighs. "Aquariums?"

"Yes, aquariums," I blurt out. "I mean, I don't have one, but when you have what *we* have, it's not surprising that people love them so much."

She extends her arm toward the chair across from her, offering me a seat at the table. Can you imagine? This stranger offering me a seat in my own home? In any case, I sit down and explain that the company has one of the most fluid user experiences of any comparable site. Certainly the most social and user-friendly mobile app in its category—just look at the number of daily engagements. Entire communities of fish and aquarium aficionados thrive on the Bowl's platform; chat rooms coalesce around the love of angelfish or a genuine admiration for moon jellies. Discussion threads debate the pros and cons of going from a twenty-gallon tank to a fifty-gallon tank; the challenges of breeding German blue rams; and which is the best showpiece fish (pugnax bettas are a favorite). There's always a flurry of convos over the latest piscine protagonist blowing up box office records.

"People have had a thing for clown fish ever since Nemo." I chuckle. "Too bad there's not a Jason Momoa fish."

She leans over and clasps her hands, the muscles on her forearms tensing. I feel my body brace itself. "I get it. You've created a social network for hobbyists and enthusiasts. With easy navigation and none of that inherent competitiveness that fuels other social networks. Whenever one thinks of a pet, a dog or cat usually comes to mind, not variations of Nemo. Or Aquaman. And yet you've provided a place for this community to thrive. That is commendable. But it isn't why we invested in this company."

Her tone is condescending, and I mentally kick myself for not having an even-keeled response at the ready. If this is a taste of what Nik experienced, then I'm less inclined to celebrate that takedown.

"You know more about these people than just their favorite aquarium showpiece," she goes on. "And *that* info is more valuable than any glowing fish or oversize tank you might sell. It's why my brother thought this was a good place to put our money. But you're several years in, eighty people deep and still piling on, and now you bought a fish tank manufacturer?" She sits back in her seat. "I don't care about the front you all put on. I just want to know why your growth has stalled and when we'll see a return on our money."

I swallow hard and channel my inner Jasmine to force a smile. "That's something I'm sure Eric can address."

"He can," she says, "but you're in finance, aren't you? You're close to the numbers. And your heart seems to be in this, with how you talk about the place. What do you think? What does your gut say?"

My gut says to run away from what feels like an interrogation. And so I'm relieved when Eric enters the room, dimples on deck.

"My man!" he shouts, pulling Ethan in for an embrace. He greets Nina less enthusiastically, with a gentle handshake. "Nina! You brought some of that California weather with you, huh?"

"It's much hotter here." She grins.

"I believe it! So what brings you by? Do you need a place to crash for your next conference call?" he says jokingly.

"I might take a call or two," says Ethan. "But I was at the Innovators Conference yesterday, and man, did you kill that speech!

So did Nik! I told Nina all about it. And since she's in town, we figured, why not come by?"

Eric's hands are on his hips, seemingly up for the challenge, but then a dodge. "Well, Nik is traveling, but you know, Max helped him with that presentation. I'll have him come by if you wanna pick his brain." He pulls out his phone, ChitChats Max, I presume, then turns to me, and asks, "Did you bring them water?" My face goes hot, and I stand, suddenly realizing I've been sitting at the conference room table the entire time. When was it, exactly, that I became the help? "Do you guys want water or coffee? A beer?" He laughs. Ethan smiles uncomfortably. "I'm only sorta kidding. We have cold brew, or we can make a run to Pulso."

"In that case, I'll take a decaf Americano," Nina tells him.

"Right on, and Ethan a cortado." Eric turns to me. "Nothing for me. Could you tell Jasmine? And bring the waters if you don't mind."

"Sure," I mumble as I leave the room.

"Did you see his suit?" Jasmine whispers as I walk by with the water bottles. "That's a real Valentino. And her perfume! I smelled bergamot and pepper notes. Probably Annick Goutal."

"That is *not* what I expected Nina Blue to look like," I whisper.

"What do you expect money to look like?" she asks.

When I return to the reception desk, I tell her they want coffee. "I'll text you the order," I say as I motion for her to move. She glowers at me and nearly crashes into Starr on the way to the elevator. Starr's eyes widen as I settle into Jasmine's seat and tell her we have investors in Bio.

"*Again?*" she whispers. "Didn't that Ethan guy meet up with Max, like, a few weeks ago? It's kinda strange that investors are always here. Is everything okay? Are we running out of money?"

"Don't worry," I tell her. "His sister's in town, that's all."

"That Nina lady?"

I nod. Silver Blue Ventures isn't our only investor, but certainly the most visible one, and even though Ethan and Eric are, by most accounts, friends, he still asks tough questions about margins, whether it made sense for the company to develop its own brand of aquarium accessories, or if the most recent investment in an out-of-home marketing campaign in New York made sense. Still, having Nina around isn't something we're used to, so I can understand Starr's concern. Normally I would brush this visit off, but Nina did call us an odd venture just now. Maybe Nik is right. Maybe it's her talking when her brother asks all those questions.

"I'm supposed to meet HR now," Starr whispers as Max comes by.

"Finally!" I say to him. "I'm sure Eric will be relieved to see you."

"Because of Nina?" He chuckles.

"Yes, but Starr's supposed to meet HR in there," I say.

"Is everything okay?" he asks, his eyes dashing between her and me.

"Yes, great!" Starr stammers. "I mean, I just officially got this job, so, you know, we're supposed to go over health insurance and commuter benefits. That sort of thing."

"I thought you did your HR onboarding with Carl," I say. He had asked me about my own pricy but deficient health plan soon after they started.

"I've just been so busy with this new campaign," she explains. "We've had to reschedule."

"But you don't need a conference room to talk about FSA and MetroCards," says Max. "It's not confidential or anything. Conference rooms are scarce as it is. I'm sure you can discuss it at your desk."

She giggles. "Yes, yes, of course!" She touches her hair, looks around, sways. I can't tell if he's making her nervous, uncomfortable, or if this is just Starr's awkward way of flirting. He doesn't move, and Starr finally realizes that he's waiting for her to go. "I'll just"—she holds up her phone—"let HR know we don't have that room, right?"

"Please," he says, as if Starr is doing him a favor, but I've come to realize that Max never asks for anything, especially not of someone on a lower ring of the corporate ladder. Starr's smile grows inexplicably wider as she retreats to the belly of the Bowl. So does his as he heads into Bio, but that's something I expect. His job is, after all, to charm.

11

PAULA

TONIGHT, LIKE MOST NIGHTS, I AM ALONE. I'VE GROWN ACCUSTOMED TO THE solitude. After Martín died, I thought to myself, *Well, you still have a daughter to keep you company.* Instead, it's mostly the television that does. In some ways, I thought his death might bring us closer, but there's still a distance. You surround yourself with this force field, a form of protection, even when you're with me. Maybe that's why you spend so much time at work, and when you are home, you stay mostly in your room. I never ask for an explanation when you are out late or don't come home, but you offer one every so often. Dance class, you say sometimes, or taking pictures, though I can't always say I believe you. Not that a mother needs to know every detail of her adult child's life. But I admit, I do peek inside that bedroom whenever the door is ajar.

It's strange how I worry more about you now than I did in the early years. Probably more so than Martín used to. He was always restless when you weren't home. *Ya regresa,* I'd reassure him, but that never satisfied him. *Where did she go?* he demanded to know. *And when?* He was only ever at ease when we were together, at home and within his reach. Everything outside our walls was a threat. Strangers, cars, loose bricks on top of buildings. Viruses, in particular, because they landed us in the ER with 103-degree fevers more times than I care to remember. It didn't matter how much oxtail soup Martín made or how many Pastillas McCoy we took, from pre-K through third grade, we were no match for a classroom virus. He'd stay home to care for you, run into that pink bedroom in the middle of the night to prop up your congested head or tilt your aching body sideways to help your breath flow a little easier. But no matter how many times we survived an infection, Martín always expected the worst with the next one. Every illness threatened to take our child. When the teenage years came, and you didn't want anything to do with us, oh! Then there was a bright side to our daughter getting sick. The child that mostly avoided us now needed us. What a funny thing that is, the desire to feel needed by someone you love.

Who knew the roles would be reversed so soon? That it'd be the child running across the hallway, keeping vigil over the parent? Shifting him, elevating his head to help the air into his body.

Some nights, almost always in the middle of the week, I sit here waiting as the hours stretch. *When will she be home?* I wonder. To think I once guarded you in my womb, under the thick coat of my skin, protected you in a way no one else could, not even Martín, and now I am at the mercy of your text messages to reassure me that everything is okay. That the only person I have left now will return to me.

· · ·

"TAN TARDE," I say. "I know you are not a child anymore, but you should have the courtesy—the *respect*—to at least let me know you're going to be home late."

Your backpack hits the floor with a thud, then those bright white, gold-streaked sneakers. Sweat glistens on your face; your mascara has run. I wonder if you've been drinking.

"I had to work late," you say. The same explanation as every other night. You pull off the hair tie holding your bun, then the second holding the ponytail, and slip both onto your wrists like bracelets. Several strands fall off. Grays have started to streak your hair too, and they've come on so gradually, I can't remember when it was that they first sprouted.

I move the spaghetti I prepared for dinner, now gone cold, from the pot to the Tupperware. The letters *YOLI* are scribbled on its side in black Sharpie, a tactic I resorted to after all those tales of grown men at the office taking whatever was in the refrigerator, even if it wasn't theirs. I detest cooking as it is. The measuring, the sorting, the mess—the labor and all those hours for only minutes of pleasure. If I'm going to do it at all, it'll be for my child, not for some Don Nadie. I wonder if you even notice.

"Does your boss work this late?" I ask, and there's that familiar lopsided face you make whenever I say anything about that job.

You disappear into the bathroom, leave the door wide open. "He has a family," you shout.

"So he doesn't have to worry about *starting* one," I shout back as you urinate. I've heard enough about this sinvergüenza boss that I know exactly the kind of man he is. He flirts with the interns. He sleeps on the office couch on nights he's out drinking with his coworkers and can't make it home. A grown man shouting Madonna songs into a microphone in a windowless room a few blocks from Macy's—how pathetic. He has a "night out" with friends in Manhattan every month because he's somehow convinced his wife that he needs this to be a better husband and father. There's so much stress, apparently, with this job and his life. Tonterías.

"Who better than a smart single girl to make him money? You realize you're wasting some of the best years of your life working for that clown."

"There are worse jobs," you say when you walk back into the kitchen. I hand you a glass of water. I can smell the mint from the mouthwash, but there's no masking the gloss in those eyes.

"I know," I say. "I've worked those jobs. It's one thing to be out this late because you're with a nice boy or your friends. But it's always that job."

"I'm sorry to disappoint you, Ma, but someone's gotta pay the bills."

"I *work!*"

Igualante. Children forget sometimes that they're still children, no matter their age. I forget too that they cannot hide their resentment over things that can no longer be changed. This has been a sore spot since you were a child, but even more so when I decided to stop working and stay home with your father. What did you expect me to do after he got sick? Did you think I could take care of other sick people when my own husband needed that same care?

Now, maybe I should have known more about the ins and outs of our money, but that was always something Martín handled, and I was happy to let him. Whatever we earned went into the same pot every week. He never told me I could not spend it, and if he did—well, I wouldn't have listened anyway. Every time we were short or late on payments, I worried, and for a little while I would watch my spending, but things had gotten better for us over the years.

When we got his diagnosis, we sat down as a family to talk about how we'd manage our money now that he was sick. I couldn't help but laugh at your questions (did you not *see* how we lived?), but mostly because I was embarrassed by our answers.

Savings? Save how? Separate bank accounts, retirement accounts—those are all luxuries. We were never savers anyway.

Health care? Well, we were lucky to be in New York, where we could go to a city hospital, see doctors, and get whatever medication we needed, even if we had to wait a little longer than you ever did for your care. Up until Martín got sick, we never had to navigate the system for something as serious as cancer, and what it meant to not have the right people for the right treatment.

A *budget?* I'd never had one of those.

We had credit cards. Four, to be exact. Two at their limit.

We had loans. We got one after the school shut down and Martín lost his job there. Another to help his sister pay the taxes and mortgage on the store, not for her sake, but because that was where he and I had first met, where his parents had built a life, and where I hoped we would wind down ours. I hope that is something you can understand. I needed to keep that store then, and more so as his death neared. Had I known his sister would sell it, I would've given it up long ago.

This was when you uttered the word *bankruptcy*, explaining what it meant and how the process worked. It felt like an open palm against my face. I was convinced you wanted to punish me, embarrass me for not managing my own money better. I walked out of the room.

I resist the urge to do so now. "I don't do what you do, and I may not make what you make, but I work. I pay my part of the rent. I keep the apartment clean. I cook! All your special diets. Meat only, 'clean' only, 'eating between noon and the six o'clock news' only. All that money that goes into 'organic' everything because you don't want to die like your father did. I hate to tell you, but you grew up with nothing organic, so whatever damage that does, it's already been done! You're doing more harm working at that place, drinking at your desk."

"It's bar cart Wednesday! I had two drinks."

"And I never complain about the things you've kept for yourself and taken from me."

"You mean beef and cable?"

"Yes, beef and cable! I kept a roof over your head for most of your life, Mónica Yolanda. It wasn't just your father. And while he was working, who cleaned your room and washed your clothes? Who helped you with your homework?"

"You never helped me with my home—"

"Me! I was the one who did all that, not your father. And I still do some of those things, but for what? So you can work at that toxic job and treat me like I'm just your roommate?"

"I'm sorry I didn't text." You roll your eyes.

"I worry about you, and maybe . . ." My stomach plummets. "Maybe I'd worry less if we didn't live together."

You scoff. "Well, we won't have to once the lease is up."

"Exactly. I could find a room. Jagoda rented her son's old bedroom to Rita when he moved out, and they're both happy! I might have the same luck."

"You might. Honestly, Ma, we should have moved out of this apartment and gone our separate ways after Pa died. You just never wanted to leave."

"Why would I? My friends are here, my job is here. Some of the best years of my life . . ." My words stop in my throat. This apartment is where I've lived for nearly thirty years now. Where we celebrated birthdays, your communion and confirmation, anniversaries, graduations—from kindergarten to that master's. Where Martín used to stand in this kitchen, cooking or cleaning, as Charlie Zaa or Lucha Reyes sang to their lovers. How I used to wrap my arms around him when he did so, press my cheek against his back, shut my eyes and sway as I felt his body against mine. Protecting him, in my own way. What a stupid thing to cry about. Not the thought of leaving, but the gratitude I have for what this place has given me.

"Papi's here," you say.

"And he's not," I shout, crashing the pot into the sink. I admit, when there was nothing more the doctors could do, I wanted your father in hospice. I did not want Death here. I had seen it, all those years caring for people weakened by illness and age. That smell of sweet earth—I did not want it in our home. But he wanted to be here, to transition in a place where he had done so much of his living, where he'd spend hours trying a new recipe or sobbing with you after watching *Ghost* for the twentieth time, and where he and I sometimes woke to the songs of birds or to construction workers arguing over parking outside our window at five A.M. We eavesdropped and laughed and curled into each other before making love quietly. Here was where he and I had danced, whenever and wherever the music called. You see, hija, I wanted to bring *my husband* home, not a dying man. I see now that this came with loving him. The losing him.

"Sometimes it's better for me not to come home," you say, and I cannot pretend I don't understand why. All those months that Martín was in and out of the hospital, it was mostly me changing his IV fluids, emptying his bag of bile, wiping him down with moist towels. By the time we brought him home, it was you, and in my mind, those were all the things a daughter *should* do. I tended to the apartment, making sure it smelled like pine, that his clothes and sheets were clean and always soft on his skin, that the air smelled of caldo de res and cinnamon rice even though we barely ate. I looked for a reason to leave the house. Sometimes I'd walk all the way to Rey's bodega to pick up those silly Condorito comics Martín found so amusing; then I'd read them to him. We left a bell on the nightstand in case we weren't by his side. You always sprinted when that bell sang, and a small part of me—the part that knew it should be me sprinting too—was grateful for the reprieve.

We hadn't even decided what to do with his ashes when you first brought up moving. First, you suggested leaving the borough entirely for Astoria or Woodside, or, if I insisted on staying in Brooklyn, then we could consider Bed-Stuy or Bushwick. They're still affordable, you'd say. Maybe even Bay Ridge. Bay Ridge, all the way on the other side of the borough! For that, we might as well move to Jersey.

But I have no choice now. Maybe it's for the best to live apart. When you lived with Vasily, it was easier to understand our distance because you were not physically with me. We no longer shared the same space. Now we share both space and grief. I wish I could protect you from that. I wish you'd want my comfort, because I long to kiss you, to hold you. To say, *You'll be okay, hija. We are going to be okay.* That's what a mother is supposed to do, I think. That's also what I want to hear.

• • •

IN THE MORNING, I meet Vicente for the Total Body Workout at the YMCA. It didn't take much to convince him to join me. For weeks, I talked about how strong the class made me feel. "You look better than you did when we were younger," he told me one night when he came by the store at the end of my shift. I knew he *looked* at me. He always commented on a new top or pointed out when I wore wedges instead of sneakers. It's one thing for him to notice; another for him to make a compliment. "Not that you didn't look great then. There's just something different now. You look . . . proud."

That may be. I can't say I carried myself with any kind of pride all those years ago. Pregnancy, miscarriages, and the long hours I worked left me physically and emotionally wrecked. Sometimes I didn't recognize my own body. My wrinkled navel, flattened breasts, dimpled thighs, hunched back—todo se te va al piso. Thirty-four years later and I still can't jump rope without a panty liner.

I was drained mentally too. By work. By parenting. Being a mother didn't come easily to me, no matter how I tried. Anytime I asked you to do chores, homework, or anything you didn't want to do, you'd talk back, and in front of people too! I'd take extra breaths, walk out of rooms, reach for my chancleta but never actually hit you with it. I resisted the urge to strike you. That's one thing I didn't want to do—become my mother. And every time it almost happened, I felt shame. You were just a child. But when you had the audacity to slap my arm after I took away a toy or turned off a television show or snatched your Game Boy, something had to be done. I'd tug at your sideburns or the hair on your forearms and mumble a command, just to remind you who you were talking to.

But then once, I used a belt on you. Only once, when that teacher called to say she caught you cheating on a science test. When I confronted you, you cried. Daniela was dead, you said, and seventh grade was horrible in its own way too because the other children teased you for the bottle of Malta and yellow rice Martín packed for lunch and the five-dollar rhinestone tees from Rainbow you wore on dress-down Fridays, and that teacher, well, she's a bitch and a liar. *And so are you!*

I was too stunned to speak, but you continued, shouting that I hid things from Pa and maybe, if he's going to know about the test, then he should know about that time you saw me holding Vicente's hand at the park too.

I grabbed one of Martín's belts and put all I had into two, maybe three whacks, and in that moment, I felt that you deserved each one. For trying to blackmail me; for seeing things you should not have seen.

When Martín came home that night, exhausted and already distant, you stood next to him, weeping, and told him only of the beating. Not that I could hide it.

He shoved me, so hard and quick that I had no time to brace myself. You yelped, and I hit the floor, shocked, because even though he wasn't the first man to put his hands on me, it was the first and only time *he* ever had. By then, his own confession had festered inside me. For months, I had wanted a reason to ram my fists against his chest and demand to know why his heart was elsewhere. I'm not sure I can talk about that yet.

But instead of hitting back, I got up off the floor and stepped closer. He was not much taller than me; our eyes were level. *Touch me again*, I dared. I remember hearing you shout, *Stop*. His eyes softened, and he took a step back before grabbing me, asking for forgiveness over and over. I pushed him off and walked out, thought of taking the train or the bus somewhere, anywhere, just to show you all what it's like to be without me. I wanted so much to feel like I was fine alone. But where would I go? What would I do? You were all I had.

I went only as far as our stoop. I sat there, refusing to cry, watching the new neighbors smoke out of their window, and giving anyone whose dog had just relieved itself a hard stare to make sure the owner cleaned up after it.

For weeks after that, Martín found ways to appease us both. He woke early to pack our lunches—a very American and "normal" peanut butter and jelly sandwich and pouches of grape juice. He made dinners on Sundays that were meant to last us several nights so neither of us would have to cook. He even wiped down the bathroom daily. But I was still on the outside of this two-person club made up of father and child. There were inside jokes at dinner, morning walks to the subway station, secrets he'd always keep for the daughter who whispered them into his ear. Even now, I think, you'd rather whisper them to his urn than say them aloud to me.

The soccer games had ended too, and though I didn't know it then, I wasn't going to see Vicente with any real frequency for a long, long while. He lived in Puerto Rico for a time, then moved into a house he'd purchased in Queens. Back then, I regretted simply not telling Martín why it was I had hit you in the first place: that I needed comfort, and holding a friend's hand was the only thing that provided it back then. After Daniela died, what I really should've done was held Vicente. Considering the circumstances, what friend wouldn't? I wish I could have told you this too instead of reacting the way I did, but you wouldn't have understood. I doubt you would now.

"I don't know how you do this class every day," Vicente tells me now, handing me my water bottle. He doesn't work out regularly and forgot to bring his own. His fingers graze mine. The bottle's mouth is wet from his lips. I take a gulp from the spout and cannot remember when I was this intimate with anyone.

"Not every day," I say. "But I try to work it out with Shanti and the others so that I can take this class at least once a week. The other days I do yoga, swimming. Sometimes I just run on the treadmill."

"That's what I should do," he says, breathless. "At least I can start at a slower pace." His black shorts are a bit too short; his red T-shirt snug around his pancita. Nothing too pronounced, just a little pouch. You wouldn't think he has cholesterol issues. At first he kept pulling up his black dress socks, but the sweat on his thin legs wins. He finally folds the socks over his red-and-white sneakers. "We should try it." The thought of Vicente as a gym partner is appealing. I've seen others come in pairs—they take turns on the machines, adjust each other's positions, yell out "one more rep" when they've seemed to give their last grunt. And it's not just *couples* couples, but *friend* couples too. I could use the encouragement, and he needs the accountability.

We decide to shower at home—not together, of course, and in our *respective* homes—instead of at the YMCA. We agree to meet again here tomorrow morning, before my shift. I get a flutter—una sensación tonta—in my core at the thought of seeing him twice in one day: at the gym for our workout and maybe in the evening for ChaCha's walk.

That sensación tonta is a vaguely familiar feeling. One I sensed whenever I caught your father humming "Alma, Corazon y Vida" as he swept the sunny floor of your grandparents' store back when we first met. He'd pause to hold the top of the broom close, his eyes shut tight, his mouth wide as he tipped his head back and belted a few lyrics. I'd watch him from the door until he finally noticed me, laughed, and eventually reached out his hand, drawing me in with that smile. I envied the curl in his lashes, his hair, how his skin devoured the sun; how I wished he would consume me.

That feeling didn't go away when we settled here or after I had you. All that time Martín and I were together, I tried to preserve what we had in the early years of our marriage. Our bedroom was our sanctuary, a place that belonged only to the two of us, and which I always kept alive and inviting with curtains and bedsheets that marked the seasons. In the winter, there were festive snow-flakes and massive red hearts; shimmering marigolds and sunflow-ers in the spring; soothing ocean waves and sand in the summer; copper trees and fiery achiote leaves in the fall. The leaves were my favorite—the sun would set them ablaze, and us in turn. Christ-mas began in November for me, and for two months Martín and I would make love on Papá Noel's face. Each year, he'd make sure there was a Santa or Mrs. Claus or Rudolph pillow, which I found shameful and he found comical. I'd flip over the pillows to avoid the stares of those cheery chubby faces, but I feel no shame in tell-ing you this now because you are a woman, and these are things you can understand. That *I* am a woman too.

I have not touched a man since your father passed, nor have any touched me, and it is not for a lack of access to them. There's Sandeep, and Rey from the bodega. The men at the YMCA, many younger, but some around my age, married or otherwise committed, but that doesn't make them or me undesirable. Except that I've had no desire for any of them. An unfamiliar touch on my body—my skin retracts just thinking about it. Not that I don't miss a man's touch, I do, but my mind immediately wants something more permanent to go along with that touch. It's never anything pasajero. Maybe it's because Martín and I were together for so long that I can't imagine a relationship that isn't as intense. I can't imagine falling in love again, much less looking for it like young people do now with the apps and the dates. It had all been like a flow for me and Martín; nothing was orchestrated. We weren't searching when we had found each other.

I am not in search of anyone now, yet that sensation has found its way back to me. I recognize that I may not awaken in Vicente what he has awoken in me. Even the anticipation of seeing him gives my day a boost. I am careful, though, with how much I allow myself to feel, mindful of all the ways he is still very much a married man; that his wife still touches him, makes love to him, and that even if none of that were true, I may not be ready for any of it yet.

. . .

MORNING COMES, AND Vicente is not at the YMCA. I check Messenger, but there is nothing from him. His status says he was last active eight hours ago. I send him a message anyway, then head into class, keeping an eye on the door, expecting to see him running in wearing those black shorts, carrying a mat and a set of fifteen-pound dumbbells.

It's not until hours later, when I'm at the store ringing up place mats for the church's choir leader, that Vicente replies to my messages. He apologizes—something happened that morning, but he was going to walk ChaCha later. *Hablamos después*.

After my shift, I wait for him by the lamppost. The humid night coats my skin in gelatin. My hair is in a butterfly clip, and I've put on just a couple of pumps of the hair spray from aisle 9 to keep the rest of my strands in place. I pull out the fuchsia lipstick I got for free with my points from CVS. He catches me mid-swipe, ChaCha barking at a dog across the street.

I don't ask why he didn't show up to the class that morning; only if everything is okay. I mean with us, but he thinks I mean in general: *Is everything okay?*

So what am I supposed to say when he tells me Renata has left him?

12

FLORES

NO MATTER HOW BAD THINGS ARE HERE, EVERYTHING IS ALWAYS FINE. SO what if sales are down this month? We had more people download the app in the last thirty days than in any other thirty-day period— great opportunity for the marketers to convert those email ad- dresses into sales! So what if fewer people on a fish's description page click the buy button? Those who do buy spend about thirty seconds on the page—that's down from forty-five seconds, so they're making purchasing decisions faster! If someone lingers on the discus fish page, then an ad for ten percent off Amazonian fish will pop up the next time they log onto Facebook or Instagram. Discounts kill us, but a sale is a sale.

That's Eric's approach; there's always an upside. Sure, we can focus on what didn't work, but that just means we're feeding negativity instead of taking what we learn and applying it to the myriad ways we can improve. And there is *always* a way to improve. Not just at work, but here—pointing to his chest—inside. We have to be courageous enough to check our ego and move into a space of growth and change, even if it's hard, even if it makes us uncomfortable.

And that, he tells us as he stands on a makeshift stage in the cafeteria, is exactly what we're going to do.

It's his annual State of the Bowl address to employees, which began half an hour later than originally planned. He'd been gone most of the morning, with Ethan and Nina, who'd come by again, and this made Jasmine nervous. A July rain had delayed the lunch delivery, so when it arrived, I helped her set up the Fatty Patty burgers and milkshakes, using the French fries to separate the beef and chicken sandwiches from the mushroom ones. Most Bowlers had already started to line up when she messaged that lunch was ready. That message lured Eric back into the office—with Ethan and Nina.

Jasmine sends out another company-wide ChitChat, reminding folks to leave their laptops at their desks, put away their phones, and save questions for the end of the presentations. I manage to snag a seat while others settle for the floor or lean against the wall as they eat. Some already had beers, including Ethan.

Why are they here? I text Jasmine.

Apparently they want to hear his speech :shrug:

But they're investors . . . :eye roll: Having them here is like having your parents at the club. You're going to watch what you say, how you act.

Onstage, Eric looks flushed, the sweat underneath his armpits visible whenever he gestures to the crowd or the screen. If it had been anyone else, I'd think they were nervous, but Eric doesn't know what it is to be stressed or anxious, or at least he knows how to mask it well. This is what he looks like after he's had a couple of old-fashioneds.

He presents the company's strategy the way he does every year, with his own story. Images of little Eric in a Super Mario Bros. sweatshirt and Lloyd Christmas haircut pop onto the screen; of teenage Eric carrying a tray of piña coladas at his cousin's barbecue restaurant; and finally, Eric just a few years back, in front of his parents' house in Queens. *When I had no job and had to move back home, I never dreamed . . .* The room sparkles as he speaks.

He brings the speech back to his opening: he embraced change. Transformation.

And this is when he takes us through a slide that sets out last year's goals, what we accomplished and what we only came close to. The room is enraptured, laughing at all the right moments, even the ones that belie the problems at our very core. He gets tee-hees when he compares the cost of getting someone to make a purchase on our website to the cost of day care; ha-has when he says the most expensive acquisition this year wasn't Fisk & Tanks but all the new folks on the marketing team.

I grab a beer from the cooler, not far from where Ethan and Nina sit. He's all smiles, but her countenance is exactly what I'd expect after our conversation in Bio: observant, her eyes narrowing behind mauve-framed glasses as Eric clicks through the slides. Every now and then, she scans the audience; then her eyes rest on me. She nods; I smile back, my face burning. I wonder if I'm giving anything away by *not* laughing at his jokes.

The team leads present next, describing their efforts and learnings over the past year, everything from legal's sale-leaseback trick (totally goes over all of our heads) to data security's latest protection protocols (shut down your computers at the end of the day, duh!) to the findings of the marketing team's recent focus group (we need to reach more rich people—no shit). Eric wraps up with what's coming next: a new office (probably in Manhattan, whomp whomp), expediting our expansion in the Midwest now that we've acquired a dedicated manufacturer (as if *that* were a flip of the switch), inking more deals with hotels and hospitals (hello! it took almost a year to ink the two we have), all to applause and whoop-whoops.

"But now it's top-shelf-bar time!" he shouts. The mixologist is already setting up in the lounge. He calls Starr up to connect her Canto account, then rejoins the Blue siblings as Drake's "Controlla" blares through the room. Jasmine grabs the mic, tells us that our mixologist's name is Meg, to make sure we tip her, and that Starr *is* taking requests, whatever she might say. She reminds us that there's a broken light in the single-stall bathroom so probably best not to use it (translation: great place for a hookup!).

The interns clamor to Meg the mixologist. Some of the OGs rush over to Starr to make sure that TLC and Dr. Dre make the playlist before it's overrun by Bieber Fever or requests from the Swifties. There's yet another dash to the cafeteria island when the taco order arrives. A beer pong game ensues between the kids only three or four years out of college and the thirty-somethings lucky or dumb enough—I can't decide—to have mortgages. Jon's already flushed from the alcohol when he hands me another beer.

A couple of hours later and I'm on my third Meg the mixologist special, something with mescal and maraschino, and then I get another with gin and maraschino and then mescal again. I'm digging the *M*'s, I tell her. I might have winked. I'm not drunk. Just feeling nice.

The cafeteria turns into a dance floor, but while most Bowlers still have their backs on the wall, I realize there are non-Bowlers here too.

Like Max's fiancée. I've seen Vicki only twice before. The first time, a year ago, at the last State of the Bowl after-party; the second at a marketing team happy hour back in March or something. Max was all about us meeting because Vicki was Peruana *Peruana* according to him—born there, like su madre, su padre, sus abuelas, sus bisabuelas, sus tatarabuelas, and so on and so forth back to the Incas or something. Like being born there gave her a bigger claim, and homegirl's mixed anyway. Light-skinned, so you know she's got that conquistador blood in there somewhere. We all do, I guess. *Does she speak Quechua?* I remember asking, as if I did. She didn't, but she spoke Spanish so fluidly it bugged me. If my parents hadn't pushed me to speak it more in the first place, maybe I would have. I could've sounded like her. Less clunky when I messed up shit like saying *sandiya* when it should be *sandía* or *caro* when I meant *carro*. She's younger too, late twenties or something, so she can get away with just wearing mascara because her skin is that fucking smooth. Very J.Crew, with that green sleeveless top she's got on and those pressed jeans and yellow flats. She smiles *a lot*, and the first time I saw her, I thought, *Why force your face to do that?*, but even when she's not meeting someone or looking at Max, the girl's grinning. I guess because she's the perky type, exactly what you'd expect from a kindergarten teacher and those super annoying pictures Max has of her on his desk, his screen saver, his phone, and GOD, we get it, you love your fucking fiancée, don't worry! No one wants to fuck you anyway.

She tiptoes and greets me with a kiss on the cheek and a gentle squeeze. Even her hellos are Peruvian. "¡Te ves divina!" she exclaims, always kicking things off in Spanish as if that's the language I should feel the most comfortable in. Like, hello! That's just another colonizer language, but anyway, she extends her arms as she holds my hands out to get a better look at what, I'm not sure. Truth is, I probably look like shit, but she gets a smile out of me anyway. I don't want to like her, but I think she's actually genuinely nice.

She'll start the first year of a PhD program next month, she tells me, licking the salt off the rim of her margarita. "Education policy," she says. "I thought my parents would kill me when I told them I enrolled."

"Never!" says Max, turning all kinds of pink. I look at him, look at her; the alcohol just slows down her eyes, no blotches like the ones he's got on his neck. This must be what they're like postcoital. "You're their only daughter. Imagine how proud they'll be to have a *doctor* in the family."

"Maybe if I were *that* kind of doctor." She runs her hand up and down his sweaty back. "My parents just want to see me married, with my own family, in a nice house on Long Island." She turns to me. Shit. I hope I didn't miss anything else she just said. "Same old song, right, Flores?"

"Oh yeah," I say. "Yeah! My parents wanted me to leave the house bien casada y ¡de blanco! Even now, when I'm like, 'Ma, I might freeze my eggs,' she's all '¿Pero de qué hablas? ¡Ya pronto encontrarás el amor de tu vida!' Like there's only one person in the entire world that your life and happiness depend on. Totally cursing me to her fate. What a joke." They say nothing to that, and by the looks on their faces, they definitely *won't* ask about my love life. I wish they would. I'd tell them all about Feast and how I swipe while I'm in bed, catching up on *Dancing with the Stars* or *90 Day Fiancé*, looking for an easy fuck, or maybe I'd tell them about the Magic Wand I hide from my mom and use only when I'm in the shower and she's not in the apartment or when she's too into the episode of *Caso Cerrado* to notice. I want to march into that living room with that wand up in the air and tell her, *This is the One, Ma! ¡El amor de mi vida!*

Instead, Max tells Vicki, "They just want you to be happy."

"Well, you make me happy," she whispers, and I think I may just barf on those yolky shoes when she says, "But you're a guy. You don't really get it," and I remember why I like her.

I laugh. "And he doesn't have parents, either! It's not like he has to worry about what they want or think," and I don't know why I say this, but her eyes harden and she tightens her grip on his hand, and I want to say that my father is dead too—I'm not some cold bitch—but I don't, and then Jasmine swings by, Starr so close behind she might as well sit on her shoulder, and they save me from Vicki's glare. They give her that weird "hello" they typically give new hires, Jasmine smiling her big-ass fake Joker smile, telling Vicki she looooves that top, jade is such a good color, and OMG, congrats, DOCTOR hottie, totally not hitting on you, just facts, *ha-ha-ha!* Are they still getting married in her brother's restaurant? What's it called again? La Imaculada? Meanwhile, Starr sways, totally off beat, to "Santeria" (WTF—Sublime?), twirls a fat curl in her hair, downs whatever mint-topped thing she's got in her glass. She's had too much, I can tell. Too quiet. She excuses herself and heads back to the podium when "What I Got" blasts through the speakers.

I follow Jasmine to the bar. She slaps my hand as I reach for another signature drink and hands me a glass of water instead. "I still can't believe they're together. I thought he'd hook up with a management consultant or a tax lawyer by now. Someone just as boring and slimy."

"He's not *that* bad."

She shrugs, hands me more water. "Anyhow, she's cool, but another party crasher, and party crashers were *not* in my budget." It's not just Vicki eating tacos and walking away from the bar double-fisted—there are at least a dozen faces I've never seen before up in here, plus the guys from the start-up next door, everyone playing Ping-Pong, drinks in hand, gyrating on the cafeteria floor.

"I didn't say people could bring a plus one. Did I?"

"No."

"Did you ever see it on ChitChat?"

"Nah."

"Did I ever, at any point when I was up on that podium, say, 'Hey, so text your homies and tell them to come through'? I didn't, right? Yet here they are, walking around like they own the place."

They *are*. People are so fucking entitled.

Fuck. Did I turn off my laptop? Or the monitors?

Fuck.

I put the glass down and make my way through the crowd toward the back of the office, trying not to panic. If anyone sees my work, it could be bad. Fucking data security has me paranoid now. Best to just put my laptop in my schoolbag and go home.

The hallway's weirdly empty as I make my way to the back. I hope I don't see a mouse.

What I do see is Starr rushing into the single bathroom, head down, wiping her nose. Slamming the door behind her. I'm guessing she ran in there to either puke or cry.

I stand outside the bathroom door. I hear her whimpering.

"Starr, are you okay?"

"Flores?" The door shifts. She must've been leaning against it. "I'm fine!" she exclaims in her usual upbeat tone.

"You sure?"

I hear the toilet flush, the water run. When she comes out, her hair is pulled back in a ponytail. She should've kept it down. At least then she could hide all that pink around her eyes and neck. This must be what *she* looks like postcoital.

"Hon, what's going on?" She just smiles, says one of the songs Jon played reminded her of an ex. I get that. Songs can hit hard sometimes. It's been over for a while now, but whenever I hear an Usher song, I think of Vasily. I wonder if it was those Sublime songs that did it for her.

But I don't even get a chance to tell her *Fuck that guy!* because she's already heading back to the cafeteria. By the time I put away my laptop and make it back there, she's dancing, cackling, no hint that she'd just been bawling in the bathroom.

And before I know it, I'm in on that dance floor too, right next to her, clinking our Solo cups, the entire episode forgotten for now. We dance in a group with a few engineers and a couple of guys I've never seen before. Some can actually move. One grabs my hand, gets so close I can smell the liquor on his breath. He spins me once, twice, over and over, until I feel like I'm disappearing into a kaleidoscope of flickering lights.

· · ·

THE SPINNING BROUGHT up the Meg specials, so I decide to head home. Outside, the clouds that brought the rain earlier have now parted and turned the night sky an inky blue. I wave to the smokers as

I head toward the subway station, and see Max, Vicki, and Nina huddled at the corner.

"Heading home?" he asks. "Or karaoke with the rest of them?"

"Definitely home. What about you guys?"

"Home, too," says Vicki as she fiddles with her phone. "And hopefully no more talk about the Bowl."

Nina snickers. "We were talking about Eric's speech. He's quite the motivational speaker."

"The guy's got cult leader vibes, for sure," I say.

"That's a very interesting way of putting it." She laughs, and after Max and Vicki get in their Uber, she asks if I could go for a *real* drink. This isn't someone I can say no to, so we end up at a bar a few blocks from the office, with a glass of Sancerre for her, a Sprite for me, and truffle popcorn.

We have small talk that doesn't feel small. She tells me that her parents tried for years to have a kid but ended up adopting her from Korea because her mother's mother was from Korea. And then Ethan came along when their mother was in her forties. "She thought it was menopause," she tells me. She found her biological mother twenty years ago, but spoke to her only once. Her bio-mother asked Nina not to contact her again. "She had her own family and wanted to forget about me, I think. I get it. She wanted to protect what she had. But that's still pretty fucked up."

She asks where my family's from (Peru), how long I've known Eric (fourteen years?), how we met (college).

"What do you think about his plans?" she asks. "The tank manufacturer, the hospital partnership. Do you think any of those have legs?"

I hesitate. I know what she's doing. She's an investor, gauging my allegiance to the guy who's running a company her firm has heavily invested in. But I've had several drinks, and no one that matters has ever asked for my opinion, even though it's always dancing on the tip of my tongue.

"That tank company is a mistake," I say. "We don't need it. We can have our shit made in China and ship it straight to the hospital or hotel or whatever. And you're right. The money's in the people hitting up our chat boards. The *afishionados*. They just feed us information. Where they live, what they do, how they spend their time, their money. You give access to some of that to the hotels, the hospitals, the designers, whatever—that's where we'll make our money."

"That's right! Your customers will tell you where you need to go. You listen. Pivot. You don't repeat the same mistakes. And you surround yourself with people that can do that if you can't. Tell me. Do you think Eric *knows* how to do that?"

"How to let people do their jobs?"

"When to recognize his shortcomings."

"That would mean admitting he's failed. He hasn't yet, and he's gotten us this far!"

"It might take a different type of leader to get you farther. You can't do the same things and expect different results. You have to change, get out of your comfort zone. Otherwise, how do you grow? And sometimes that means leaving the past behind. Goals that aren't tenable anymore. Strategies that don't work."

"People," I mumble.

"Sometimes," she acknowledges. "And not everyone. But you have to be willing to let go. Change your game plan."

Change your game plan. Max had said the same thing. These are Nina's words then, her plan already in motion. It's why Max has asked me twice now to put Eric on blast at next month's board meeting. It's why she's been to the office more times in the last couple of months than she has in the last couple of years. It's why she's here now, having drinks with me.

Her phone glows and buzzes with a flurry of messages. Her nanny, she tells me as she finishes her drink and asks the bartender to close out her tab. "I really enjoyed our conversation, Flores. It's good to know we have someone like you on the team." She pulls a business card from her wallet. "If you ever want to talk, about the Bowl or any other company in our portfolio or even Silver Blue itself . . ." The thick card she hands me is double-sided: the name of the firm emblazoned in silver on the navy side; the other side, white, with her name and contact information etched in metallic blue lettering. "We can always use good people."

13

PAULA

"SHE MENTIONED IT MONTHS AGO," VICENTE TELLS ME, KICKING THE PAVEMENT as we walk down the avenue with ChaCha. It had been several days since Renata left for her sister's house on Staten Island, telling Vicente that she intended to move to Puerto Rico permanently. Her trips had convinced her that that was where she needed to be. Even though Vicente and I had seen each other in the days after she left, he refused to go into any details until now. I don't ask many questions—I remember how it was when things ended between you and Vasily. You didn't want to talk about it. Mi niña. You always turn inward, never sharing with me your sorrows and fears or even your dreams, the way I imagine you did with your father. When you were hurting then, I wanted to tell you that everything would be okay, but would you have believed me? I wonder if you even gave yourself the grace to mourn the end of that relationship. I never did see you shed a tear for that man. Except for the memorial service, I can't recall seeing you shed a tear for Martín, either.

The sun is ahead of us now, compressed between the buildings sprouting on the edges of Long Island City. Monstrosities. Normally I'd suggest we walk the other way, toward Daniela's bench at the park, or sit in the backyard at Caramelo. But like you, Vicente is a private man. He almost never talks of his marriage, yet here he is, spilling it, so we keep walking, though I regret swapping my work sneakers for my sandals.

"I told her there's no way I'm moving," he exclaims when we finally turn onto our block, away from the crowds. And why would he move? They tried Puerto Rico once, and it didn't work, not for him. Besides, someone needs to manage the apartment building, he says, and he doesn't trust anyone to do it for him. Renata's childhood there wasn't a good one, there's a reason she left. Besides, that house will just get destroyed again when the next hurricane hits, and what's the point of constantly rebuilding? And their son is here, the only child they have left. He still has another year of school to finish in Boston; then he's off to graduate school, who knows where. "Where's the mother's love now?" he says. "The boy still needs us. Our children still need us, right?"

We make it to our building, the sun now gone, and sit close enough on the stoop that we don't have to shout over the slurred "soy peor, soy peor" blaring from a parked car. We don't even put ChaCha between us.

"Vicente, I hope you didn't say that to her," I tell him. "About the hurricanes."

I have never allowed myself to fantasize about how things might be between us if Renata were not in the picture. The possibility raises my pulse. In some ways, this is easier—this gray space. But how he dismisses what she wants, well. In the past, I wouldn't have reprimanded a man for this—not him, not your father. But I understand why going home may feel right for Renata.

"Your mother-in-law has Alzheimer's," I remind him. "Soon that home might be the only thing Renata has left of her past, until disease and another hurricane erase it again. Can you blame her for wanting to spend more time there? I'd want to, before it all becomes a memory."

He grunts. "That's not why, though you're right about erasing. The truth is, Renata has wanted to move back ever since we lost

Daniela. She wanted to get away from everyone's pity and seeing everyone else's kids grow up. She's always hated the winters here too. And with Facebook and whatever else she has on that tablet, all she does is keep up with her brothers, cousins, aunts, high school friends. They've all kept her there. That's easier than being here and constantly reminded. There, she might forget."

"I'm sure she knows that's not possible," I say. "But I can understand if she wants to be home, with her mother. Not all of us can do that. Or *want* that."

Not that I'm sentimental about my parents. How can I be? My mother left me with my father in Lima the moment I was old enough to "defenderme," as she liked to say—oh, the irony of that! She went to Piura with her new boyfriend. My father demanded I give him whatever I made from working as a housemaid. He spent that money in hotel casinos. Last I heard, my mother was still in Piura, my father somewhere in Chile, but that was eight or so years ago. I am fine knowing this much and nothing more.

"The years aren't going to stop for us," I say. "If Renata wants to be with her mother and family, then she should be. You'll find a way to make it work. Or not."

This is all we say about the matter or Renata. Soon there are others who pass by, happily filling the silence: Bienvenida, who washes and folds clothes for eighty-five cents a pound at the laundromat down the block; Amir, who runs the bodega and is still recovering from knee surgery; and Raúl, the ex–police officer who just got a job as a doorman in one of the high-rises a few blocks north. Maybe I should be uneasy at how many people see me and Vicente together on this stoop, but I'm not. Maybe I don't care anymore about what others might think.

Then you come home. The day's heat had stretched into the night. You don't kiss Vicente hello when you get out of the cab because you're too sweaty. At least that's what you say, and though you have always shown him respect, you never did show him affection. The resentment is palpable, and whether it is because you blame him for what happened to Dani or because you believed there was once something between us, I cannot tell.

He waves at you from afar, rising and tugging at ChaCha, letting her urinate on the rectangular patch of dry dirt with the metal sign specifically banning dogs. It feels like a standoff as you watch him, waiting for him to leave. He does me the courtesy of departing without looking back. You climb the stairs ahead of me without speaking to me, your usual form of punishment.

14

FLORES

"YOU SURVIVED," STARR SAYS AS SHE BITES INTO HER BACON, EGG, AND cheese sandwich—the breakfast of the hangovered—in the pantry the next morning. Her Bucknell mug and a few half-and-half minis sit on the counter. She's not wearing any makeup. Her hair is tied in a low ponytail, her lash extensions sag toward her cheeks, and she's started both coffeemakers for the others that manage to drag themselves into the office today.

Like me.

"I should've stayed in bed," I say. The Advil, Alka-Seltzer, and smell of coffee slowly set my foggy morning into focus. I pour Froot Loops into a bowl, hoping the cereal will settle my stomach. "Thanks for getting the coffee going."

"I'm doing this for Jasmine. She went to karaoke last night and is definitely *not* coming in today. Did you go?"

"I went straight to bed." I decide not to tell her about Nina, especially since Starr was so unnerved the last time that Nina was here. And what am I supposed to tell her anyway? That I suspect Nina and Max are plotting to get Eric out? That's not idle gossip; it's certainly not something someone so junior should know about.

"Me too," she says, and because she seems to be in a chatty mood, I decide to ask why she was so upset last night. "You mean the bathroom?" She laughs, in that pitchy way she usually does when she's nervous. "It's nothing. It's stupid. Just, you know, men!"

For all her smiles and penchant for gossip, Starr is tight-lipped about everything Starr. Every now and then, here in the pantry or at lunch, she shares glimpses of her private life: that she was "not an easy kid" in high school, that church and missionary trips had only made things worse, her worries about her sister—older and on the spectrum, she mentioned once—and how she needs to live at home. She's never cried in front of me, and to cry at a work party of all places seems out of character for someone who's always had a wall up, even with those of us who, I think, she considers friends. "They just lie and cheat, you know? I mean, of course you do with what happened with your ex. Oh my gosh, I'm sorry, Flores! I didn't mean to bring it up."

"No, you're fine," I say, and oddly, I really am. "He didn't cheat on me, for what it's worth. He just didn't want to live in New York anymore, and I did. Too bad it took him seven years to figure that out."

"Seven years! Stop."

I nod. "We were living together at the time. I thought we'd be together forever, but first loves are tricky like that, especially when you've got this tall, smart, Colin Firth type of guy with a great ass telling you it'll be forever. Plus my parents had practically been each other's first loves. I romanticized the idea, you know. Of my first love being the forever kind."

I'd fallen hard for Vasily. He wasn't beautiful in the way Romeo Santos or Keanu Reeves are. But he had confidence and wit. He spoke to our professors as if they were equals, challenging them to the point where they simply started to ignore him when he raised his hand in class. He wrote problems on the board as if they were poetry—long, fluid, indecipherable at times. At first his aloofness and disregard for authority bothered me. They underscored just how he could get away with that attitude because he was white and a man, and I wasn't. I envied and admired his assuredness and ease.

He was taken aback when I introduced myself after our third Regression Analysis class together. I thought perhaps what intimidated him was my height, my presence, how I made it a point not to melt into the crowd. He told me later it was simply the attention that seemed foreign to him. We spoke of that day's assignment, the mistake in the problem that our professor had highlighted, the other classes we were taking that semester. He was an immigrant, like my parents, and I appreciated how he didn't care about his accent or worry if something didn't come out right. He always spoke up. He lived with an aunt, in a four-floor house in Brighton Beach. He rented the basement apartment, not just a bedroom like I did at home, but still, we shared a disdain for our classmates who had a studio or one-bedroom apartment paid for by their parents, or even those who grew up in New York City and still had the money to live in a dorm. He had that thirst one needs to live in an unfamiliar country, in another language. This was not his home; he was from *there*, not here. I treaded that line closely too, but often felt decidedly from *here*. After all, I had a U.S. birth certificate and spoke more Spanglish than Spanish. That wasn't enough, though, to ever make me feel like I fully belonged.

Of course, he also *wasn't* like me or my parents. A straight white guy generally has an easier path to success laid out before him, even as an immigrant, though he may not see it. He had never seen a Black person in person until he landed in New York, never knew they existed in Peru or the many ways one can *be* Peruvian; never knew a Peruvian, period. Never met a Filipino American until he met Eric. Didn't know they could be brown-skinned, either. He was here on a scholarship—a full ride to my quarter—not just the precarious promise of a better life. He planned on going to graduate school in New York, certain he'd get some kind of funding. I was sure I couldn't afford it, but he urged me to consider it.

For years, he showed me the ways one can love. Tending to me
with a cup of coffee after I had pulled an all-nighter for an exam
or for work. Reading aloud obituaries of artists over breakfast and
Lucille Clifton poems before bed. In the winter, he'd warm towels
on the kitchen radiator and hand them to me after my baths. For
years, I thought we were good until we weren't.

"My parents would legit disown me," says Starr. "So what happened? Obviously, you didn't get married."

"Obviously," I repeat. "He applied to a doctoral program in
Sweden. On a whim, but he got in. He swore I told him I was up
for a move like that, but that's not what I remember. Anyway, he
decided the U.S. wasn't for him and we both knew Sweden wasn't
for me."

I had neither the desire nor the need to move to another country. I can't say, with certainty, that I told him I was completely
opposed to it. But when the time came, I had all kinds of excuses:
didn't speak the language, didn't have the paperwork to work there,
couldn't leave my parents, couldn't squander the opportunity they'd
given me to have a future here. Not for a future I didn't want, even
if that meant losing someone I loved.

I couldn't tell my parents when we broke up, not at first. We
continued to live together until he had to leave for Sweden, about
three months. The day I moved out of his aunt's building, I wept in
the passenger's side of my father's Astro van. Pa cried too. I couldn't
face my mother. When I was back home, I mostly watched television on their couch, ignoring her. Then, while they slept, I'd head
to the fire escape to cry some more, even though Vasily and I both
knew, had known for longer than I care to admit, that the end had
been a long time coming.

"So that was that," I tell Starr. "But then Eric offered me this
job. I didn't know how much I needed this place until I got here."

I leave out the parts that still taste bitter. How I was laid
off from my last job only weeks after I had moved out. Within a

year, my dad got his death-sentence diagnosis; even then, Vasily never bothered to call. How I had to take out loans to cover the medical bills, medicine, rent. The times I had to lock myself in a bathroom—in the hospital, at home, even here in this office—when it got to be too much. I don't tell her how that breakup and what came after forced me to question what love looked like. It's not marriage or kids or an overpriced dinner on Valentine's Day. It's not proven by the number of selfies you take as a couple or the public declarations of love you post on social media. It's not loud or necessarily visible to the world. It's not even the electricity that shoots through your body when your lover's lips are on your neck for the first or hundredth time or how their eyes become the only thing you need to make you feel seen, to give you comfort.

No, that's not what love looks like to me anymore. It is my mother's fingers interlacing my father's as he got chemo. The two of them walking to the park in the early mornings, absorbing the last bits of sun that would ever graze his skin. It is reading the lyrics of old vals criollo songs as my father fell asleep those last nights, hoping that my voice might give him comfort as it carried him quietly into the next life.

It is learning not when, but how to hold on and how to let go.

"I'm sorry, Flores," she says.

"It's okay." I head to the fridge for the milk, scour the drawers for some sugar, suddenly in need of some distance between us—a breath—before returning to Starr and the coffee. "So who is this guy? An ex? Someone new?"

"Not new. More like an old fling. He's in a serious relationship now. And I knew that, but I actually saw him recently with this person. I wasn't ready for it, that's all. But I'll be okay."

She picks up her mug, ready to return to her desk—a sign that this is as much as she'll say about the topic, even though I have so many questions. But she rushes off before I can tell her that bad romances happen and even *actual* love can sometimes feel like a terrible thing because it ends, just like everything must. And maybe because it *is* so beautiful and temporary, it can both fill you and break you, make you glow so brightly that you rival the sun or leave you whimpering alone on a fire escape under the moon. Or even have you weeping on an office bathroom floor under a broken light.

• • •

JASMINE BOOKED LUNCH for Friday, when the three of us had properly recovered from our respective hangovers and caught up on work. The new Italian spot is just far enough away that we can avoid other Bowlers and have a sit-down lunch, share some solid bochinche for a good forty-five minutes, and still make it back to the office by two P.M.

We kick off lunch with a bottle of rosé, our version of a summer Friday since the typical shortened workday that heralds the weekend in New York doesn't apply to start-ups. Jasmine is offended that the server cards Starr but not us. "At least as a courtesy," she tells him when he comes back with the wine and an overstuffed bread basket. I pop off my Invisalign, which makes Starr giggle and Jasmine cringe, before we clink our glasses to avoid seven years of bad sex.

Then we get into it:

Did you see Tanya and Roger making out at karaoke?
        No, I wasn't there!
What about Peter and Nate? They're still together, right? They're trying to keep it on the low, but everyone knows . . .
        Of course, who doesn't?
Did you see how drunk Nik got?

So that one, I do remember. Vaguely, perhaps, but enough that I can recall him slouching in the sofa behind the deejay table, right next to Starr, his cheek resting on his palm as if he were power napping. I may have even seen him put his head on her shoulder.

"Didn't he say something to Max about being white and Mexican?" I ask.

"Yes, and then he flirted with the guy's fiancée," says Jasmine.

"Well," Starr mumbles, "Max doesn't look Mexican."

"What exactly does a Mexican look like?" asks Jasmine.

"Excuse me, but you thought I was Chinese."

"Come on, you two," I say. "Please don't start."

"That was my bad," Jasmine acknowledges. "But now I know more about the beef between Taiwan and China. Anyway, I like a drunk Nik. He's way more real than the everyday Nik. Did you hear what he was telling Meg?" She grabs the edge of the table and starts swaying as she deepens her voice. "'We've spent millions, and no one knows who the hell we are. You probably didn't know about us until Jasmine emailed you, am I right?'" She cackles, picks up her glass. "You know that's gotta hurt his ego."

"For sure," I say. "He gets paid stupid money and for what? He's let marketing run loose with our cash and has nothing to show for it. Then gets pissed when we have to preapprove his spending. He should be embarrassed of the shitty job his team's doing," and I could go on, but Jasmine's eyes widen, and she clears her throat as she nods toward Starr. "For what it's worth, I *do* think it's getting better. We're making moves with the subway ads and the trade pubs. But that's all Max."

"That dinner after the last board meeting crushed him," Starr says. "Nik, I mean. We went out for drinks a couple of weeks ago, and oof! It was all he talked about."

"Who went out for drinks?" asks Jasmine.

"Me and Nik." Starr's shoulders cave just a little.

Jasmine sets down her glass. "Wait, you went out for drinks

with your greasy car salesman of a boss and didn't tell us? Did you know about this?" she asks me, but I'm just as surprised.

"Well, it was our first official one-on-one," says Starr. "And I've tried to go to the team outings, but every time, Max is all 'this is just senior staff' or 'just sales folks.' So yeah, if I have a chance to go out with the head of my team, I'm going to. No way is some guy going to sideline me."

They'd gone into Manhattan, to a speakeasy in the back of a cell phone store. They sat in a booth meant for two—the only one available, apparently. He sipped aged whiskey; Starr made do with a glass of the house red. They munched on a trio of cheeses, roasted nuts, and olives. She did most of the eating and most of the listening. "He said the brother asked some totally legitimate questions about our marketing plans and was very respectful. But the sister." Her lips turn into a rosebud as she flicks her hair back. "And now she's coming around the office. And even came to the party!"

"She's not fooled by the Nik show," I say. "All that buzz and pizzazz doesn't impress her. That's why he doesn't like her."

"He thinks she's trying to get him fired."

It occurs to me that perhaps Nina pointed out Nik's weak performance just to underscore Eric's. After all, Nik ultimately reports to him and executes plans only with Eric's go-ahead.

"I'm sorry," says Jasmine, "but can we go back to your boss taking you out for drinks? So it was just the two of you at a bar? Meanwhile, all of my one-on-ones with Eric are in conference rooms. Sometimes we do them at lunch, but drinks?"

"I've done my one-on-ones with Jon at a bar," I say.

"But you and Jon are friends," says Jasmine. "You're around the same age. You have a history together. It's a different power dynamic."

"Jasmine, you report to Eric," says Starr. "I mean, no offense, but why is the office manager reporting to the CEO?"

"Your point?"

"My point is, Nik is like a mentor. I'm not trying to be his friend or anything, but I do want him to be open and honest with me about my future here. Besides, it's not like I can say no to my new boss."

Starr had interned for us during her senior year of college, getting paid twenty dollars an hour to work just fifteen hours a week; this is partly why she's still at home with her parents and sister. Our chief marketing officer at the time promised to reevaluate her pay after three months, but just two weeks in, he left for Palm Springs and a job at a makeup subscription start-up that gave him money to buy out most of his options at the Bowl, if he wanted to. He bought one, just out of spite—that's how bad things had gotten between him and Eric. Starr made the Bowl keep the former CMO's promise anyway, adding calendar reminders so she wouldn't forget to check in with HR about her pay. They set KPIs that would get her to the "next level," amorphous goals that kept any pay increase or title change just out of reach.

This past spring, I urged her to hold out for a full-time offer, even as she contemplated those from two other start-ups that were more in line with her values—female-led companies that cater to women's needs. I discouraged her from both. After all, was anyone *actually* using vulva cream and butt masks (a fem care company)? Did she want to be worked to death expanding another company's footprint on the West Coast (a women's-only coworking space)? Were they *really* donating all those fem-hy products to underserved communities? Yes, I wanted her to stay because she was one of the few friends I had here, and because by then, she had told me, in fragments only but enough for me to understand, that she would eventually need to care for her sister and aging parents. She wanted to set the foundation for a career early on, hoping it would give her the means to care for them when the time comes. She also believes in the Bowl. Not with Max's cautious

optimism or Jon's cultlike devotion, but with the genuine belief
that something could be made with just a flicker of passion and
doggedness.

So even though Jasmine side-eyes her, I understand why Starr
couldn't say no. "It's weird that it was just the two of you," I say,
"but I get it. He's your boss. Anyway, truth is, you're probably not
gonna see a pay bump for a while, so get as many free meals out of
this place as you can."

Jasmine sputters. "Fuck the meals. Listen, don't get sucked
into this place like me and Flores. You don't have kids. You don't
have mounds of debt. Put in another year here, start that 'fuck you'
fund so you can leave whenever you want, and get out. Shit, I'm
not planning on being here longer than I need to be. Best case, I'm
done by next summer. Worst, next winter, but then . . ." Jasmine
makes the peace sign.

"Well, I want to get a promotion before I leave. What about
you, Flores?"

"She's never leaving," says Jasmine.

"I'd leave for the right opportunity," I say, "but with my student
loans and the one I took out when my dad got sick, I basically have
a small mortgage."

"A couple of hundred thousand dollars is not small," Jasmine
mutters. Starr's eyes widen.

"And look, I don't even know if I want kids . . ." I hesitate here,
unsure how or if I should put this into the universe by speaking
it because I can't say for sure whether it stems from a very real
yearning to be a mother or from simply wanting to check off one
more life milestone. Mostly, I think, it's from the innate ache of
knowing that without my intervention, my family's existence—our
memories, the life we shared—might end with me. "I'm thinking
of freezing my eggs." I say it quickly, finishing the rest of the wine
in my glass. There is a brief silence, the shock, I imagine, settling
in for them as it does for me.

"Good for you," says Jasmine. "Taking fertility into your own hands."

"That's really smart, Flores," says Starr.

"Look, I don't even know if I'll do it, but I had some tests done, and my eggs are healthy." Luckily our table is wood, and I tap my fist on it. "Apparently, you can be thirty-three and have eggs that are more like forty-three. Not very promising if you want biological children. And I don't have the money for it right now, but I might in a year or so. I need to be mentally prepared for it too, you know. I mean, I'd be a single mom. I always imagined myself *married* with kids. That obviously hasn't happened, but it doesn't mean I can't be a parent."

"Of course not," says Jasmine. "And your mom can help."

"My mom." I roll my eyes. "She's been a handful lately."

"Is she still seeing that married guy?" whispers Starr.

"They're 'just friends,' or so she says." Though it hadn't occurred to me to mention it before now, I tell them about the note. "It was under my dad's urn. I'm pretty sure she and this guy had a thing even when my dad was alive."

"You think she cheated on him?" asks Starr.

"I don't know. I once saw them holding hands under a picnic table while they were playing bingo." To this day, I'm shocked at how brazen that was, with his wife and Pa literally just feet away. "She's had feelings for this friend for a while, I think. And that's cheating too. There's definitely something between them now. She probably feels guilty. Why else would she ask for forgiveness?"

"She doesn't need to," says Jasmine. "Your mom's a grown-ass woman, Flores. And . . . this is going to sound harsh, but your dad's dead, may he rest in peace. She's allowed to rebuild her life. At the very least, she's allowed to have fun. If hanging out with this 'friend' makes her happy, who cares? If she fucks him, who cares?"

Starr nearly chokes on her bread, laughing.

"*I* care," I say. "You don't know my mom. She's not about casual sex. My dad was the only man she was ever with. Sexually."

"That you know of," Jasmine says.

"Okay, fine, that I know of. But it's more than that with Vicente. She has a history with him, and so do I! His daughter and I were friends growing up."

For a couple of summers, Dani and I were close. We only ever really saw each other in the warmer months, except for whenever an adult decided to host an apartment party in the cooler seasons. She was almost three years older than me, and I relished that this brash, loud soccer head who most of the boys didn't dare challenge took an interest in me. We rode our bikes around the park, chasing the lady that sold coconut and cherry coquito for a dollar, and the ice cream truck driver for rainbow-sprinkled vanilla ice cream cones. We were the only girls that dared to play handball with the older boys. We watched the soccer games with them too, on the opposite side of the field from where her dad sat. I had started making out with Hugo "Brace-face" Buenavides behind the handball court, which she was totally disgusted by. "You're gonna choke on his rubber bands," she'd warn, and I was too embarrassed to tell her that once they actually did pop in my face.

The summer that she died, we spent a lot of time at the pool, without our parents. My mother had seen too many babies in diapers at the public pools to care for it; my father wasn't going to get half-naked for nobody. I went only on Sundays, but Dani would sometimes go during the week with her friends.

When Pa told me she drowned, it didn't register. I was only twelve. Dani's quinceañera was happening that November. She told me once that she loved being a Scorpio because people were afraid of them, and that Capricorns made the best of friends because we were loyal. What I knew about life was that it was temporary, and so yes, at some point, Dani, like all of us, would die. But I knew nothing about death itself, definitely not that it could take someone like her, young and healthy, and in my ambit, and do it so suddenly. She was supposed to be at the park the next day. I was supposed to see her there.

Instead, the next time I saw her was inside the Ortiz Funeral Home. I made my way through a maze of teenagers, little kids, her abuela, her parents and little brother. She saved him, people whispered in the room, though my mother later told me it was a concussion that did her in. I made it to her coffin, and there was her body, adorned with a crown and the quinceañera dress she was supposed to wear later that year for her birthday. None of it felt like the Dani I knew, always in Tupac T-shirts and gym shorts— the dress much too poofy, and her face with a peach blush and hot pink lipstick. *This is not her,* I told myself, *that's not Dani.* I refused to cry for a stranger.

Her funeral was two days later, on a brisk summer morning. A storm had dropped inches of water the night before, its gray clouds moving quickly overhead. So when the hearse drove off with her casket, I pretended it was fall. It didn't matter if she was dead or alive—I never really saw Dani in the fall. I prepared myself for a long winter, another season without her.

"Anyhow, she died," I go on and hear Starr gasp. "She drowned or hit her head. Her dad and my mom—I don't know, the way they acted around each other made me uncomfortable. He never talks about my friend, either. And then after my dad died, he started coming around. It'd be one thing if my mom just needed to have her needs met, which, I get it. She's human."

"She's a mother, not a robot," Jasmine says.

"And I'm not, like, opposed to her having a boyfriend. But not someone who's married. He obviously doesn't care about his wife. He couldn't even take care of his own kid."

"Flores, that is harsh," says Starr.

"Let your mom live!" Jasmine shouts. "Focus on *you.* Plan for that family in case you decide you want to be a mom. And look, you don't need a partner to do that. You never know when or even if you'll meet the right person. There *is* no right person, actually, and you can't put your life on hold waiting for somebody that might never show up. If that person does, great. If not, I'll tell you this, as someone who's been a single mother since her baby was two: it's hard, but not impossible. Who knows? Maybe you'll meet someone tomorrow who loves Swayze as much as you do."

"You could always adopt too," says Starr. "Like, if the eggs don't work out or something. Maybe even a kid from Peru?"

"That feels like I'm taking advantage of a shitty situation," I say.

"But you could be helping the kid and his parent *out* of one," she replies as the server places our pasta on the table, and I think of Nina when my phone goes off. It's my mother. I let it go to voice mail.

"Well, I do want my mom's opinion on this too. I've mentioned it, but kind of jokingly. I haven't had a real conversation with her about it yet. You're the first people I'm actually telling."

My phone goes off again, and again, it's my mother. This time, I pick up. But the voice on the other side is not hers. It belongs to a man, one whose voice I don't immediately recognize because it's the first time I'm hearing it over the phone.

Vicente tells me she's fine, not to worry, but my mother fell. She hurt her head and arm. They're in an ambulance.

"Where're they taking her?" I ask as Jasmine mouths *What's happening?* I hang up, tuck my phone in my fanny pack. "It's my mom. Jaz, I'll Venmo you!" I shout back as I race out of the restaurant to Woodhull Hospital.

15

PAULA

A CONCUSSION. THAT'S WHAT THIS DOCTOR, WITH HIS TIRED SHOULDERS AND small voice, tells me after he closes the curtains around my bed in the emergency room. It's what the pain in my head and the blurred vision tell me too. Then he points to the X-ray they took of my left arm. No major breaks, just a hairline fracture that'll need time to heal. And the bruising—*Oh! Look at the green and purple!* I got lucky, he goes on, because osteopenia and injuries at my age can be bad, very bad, but good thing that the CT scan didn't show anything more serious. I imagine blood pooling in the crevices of my skull.

He gets closer, clicks on his penlight, and points it into my eye. Once again, the questions:

Are you dizzy?
   A little.
Any chest pain?
   Just an ache.
How did you fall?

I can't lie because Vicente came to the hospital with me, but I'm not going to tell everything that happened, either. I'm a terrible storyteller anyway. I repeat what I said earlier: that I tripped on a dog's leash as I was coming down the stairs and fell onto the sidewalk. My whole left side. My head just did a little bounce over the sidewalk. It was just a few steps.

I don't say that Vicente and I were going to his apartment for lunch when we saw Renata on the stoop in front of their building, loading boxes into the back of a small truck with her nephew. How she and Vicente began to argue right there, at the top of the stoop. That's when ChaCha began to bark, so I ran up there, grabbed her, tripped on her leash on my way down, landed on my side.

The reports will go to my general practitioner, but I should follow up with a neurologist too, is what I hear the doctor say. I might need physical therapy, depending on how the fracture heals.

I hear you sigh, and I'm embarrassed.

"Like I said, very lucky," the doctor repeats, taking another look into my eyes with his penlight, as if I need to be reminded—almost chiding me, like he would a child—of my good fortune. "At this age, it could've been a lot worse," he says, but looks at you when he says this.

• • •

A FEW YEARS before Martín left us, you got him a recliner for Father's Day. The heat from his body softened its cinnamon leather over the years as he sat there, reading *El Diario* or watching Mexican fútbol games on Univision. On Sunday nights, he'd fall asleep in it, and I'd wake him with an "Amorcito, vente a la cama," even though he looked so protected, cocooned in that skin, that I was sometimes tempted not to wake him.

After he died, you suggested I sell or donate it, but I'd given away so much of him already: most of his clothes, shoes, even the novelitas he bought at the bodega on Graham. There were pieces of him I couldn't let go of—his favorite maroon sweater that still held his scent; the burgundy leather church shoes he polished on Fridays in the hallway over old newspapers; the half-empty bottle of his cologne. And this recliner. This recliner that cradled him, warmed him, retains the imprint of his body.

It's where I choose to heal now, and where I am when Shanti comes to visit the day after my fall, with sunflowers and a box of pine tarts.

"Oh, Shanti! You didn't have to make these for me," I say.

"I didn't. I hate the kitchen as much as you do. These are from a very popular Guyanese bakery in my neighborhood." She places one sunflower beside Martín's urn and mentions how good he was; how he used to make her laugh. She is quiet for a moment, then runs her fingers across his urn, which makes me feel as if I am intruding on an intimate moment.

"Does your arm hurt?" she asks, sitting on the couch and fanning herself with last week's *People en Español*.

"Only if I don't take my medication," I say. "That first night— oh! I thought I might faint from the pain. It's not so bad now. The bruises are changing color." I pull down my collar and show her my shoulder. "I'm going back to work soon. I'd go back today if I could, but my daughter insists that I rest. And that's fine, but anything longer and I'll go crazy!" Shanti's eyes balloon. "Are you going to tell me to stay home too?"

"Those bruises look painful. You can't work like that! You should just sit here, watch movies, read books or these magazines. Give your body more time to heal."

"I don't like movies and I don't like books. I like people. Exercise. Besides, I need the money."

"You do *not* need the money. Your daughter has a good job. She takes care of you."

"We have to move, Shanti," I say, and explain how we need

to find a new apartment when our lease ends in September. "I'm not sure if we're going to live together or apart. At first I thought it might be better if we lived separately. Had our own space. I wouldn't worry so much about her because, well, I wouldn't see her. I know that sounds awful, but she could live her life and I wouldn't spend my nights waiting for her to come home. But my Yoli has no one. That job has become her life. What's the point if all you think about is work and money? And now look at me. You should have heard how they spoke about me in the hospital. *About* me, not to me. Like I'm a brittle old woman. I am a burden, and then I will die, and what will happen to my daughter? Who will care for her? If we were together, then we have each other to lean on, but she also needs to live her life."

"You need to live yours too, Miss Paula. Whether you live with her or not."

"Yes, but it would give me peace to know that she has someone to love her and keep her company. That'll be with her when she's old and back in diapers."

"There is no guarantee that any of us will have that, no matter how many partners or children we have!"

Martín had promised me that: to love and care for me, and never to cause me pain. He was wrong to promise me the impossible. Shanti was also promised eternal love and protection—until that night when it was her son who tried to protect her from her husband.

"It won't ever be true for my daughter if she puts that job before living her life." For a moment, I wonder whether it is appropriate for me to say this to Shanti, but she is a young woman too and would not pass judgment. "She doesn't come home some nights, you know. She'll just text me that she'll be back the next day like this is some hotel."

"Ah, so she *is* seeing someone, then?"

"I don't know, and I cannot ask her those things."

"Of course you can, you are her mother! And if she's just sampling the menu, that's okay too."

"That is *not* okay. You would never act like that. No woman with any dignity would." She giggles. "Is that why you came here? To get me flustered about my daughter's love life and then laugh about it?"

"Miss Paula, your daughter is an adult, not a child. And I can guarantee you, not a virgin! It's not realistic to expect a woman in her thirties to be one. It'd be very sad if she were. You should be more open to talking to her about her love life."

"She's only ever had one serious relationship, and I knew, from the beginning, that that boy was not right for her. They were too much alike. Life for him was school and work, not their relationship. He was Russian and wanted to go back to Europe eventually. For a little while, he said, but you know how those things go. A couple of years turns into forever. Like it did for me. And I was worried about how they'd treat her over there. I gave her my opinion once and she basically told me to mind my business. So, I did and never said anything to her again about that relationship."

"She might have appreciated your thoughts anyway. You obviously experienced something similar when you moved here."

"She had to make her own decisions, Shanti. And he did move to Europe, but imagine. If she had decided to go with him, I'd hate him for it. If he had treated her badly or cheated and she still stayed with him, I'd hate him too. It was better not to know. Certainly not about sex. Even when she was younger, I never felt comfortable talking to her about that. You know, when she got her period, it was my husband who took her to get maxi pads."

"Mr. Martin? What does a man know about such things?"

"A man should know, and the rest, she learned. One day we were at the Duane Reade, and she brings a box of tampons to the register. I was shocked, but all I could do was pay, and when we left, I asked, 'Since when?' because she was still in high school. She tells me that one day she didn't have a pad, and so her classmate gave her this long stick." I set my index fingers apart to show her just how long that thing was. "I don't think she was a virgin by that point, but if she was, that thing destroyed any proof. It was very unnatural."

"It is your reaction that is unnatural, Miss Paula." She laughs. "She is going to worry about you whether you live together or not, and no matter how many husbands, boyfriends, or children she has. Or doesn't. She is your daughter, and you are the only parent she has left."

For years now, this realization—that in this world now, it is just me and my daughter—has lived in the back of my mind, far from my skin, where it cannot threaten to rip through me. There are times I wish I could have had another child. For years, I tried, prayed to the Virgin Mary and my grandmother to please give me one more. I lost three. When Martín and I finally stopped trying, the relief was overwhelming. I could devote more time to my only child. I could give her a better education, dress her well, give her more of me. There would be less pressure on us to work an extra job or two just to pay the rent, or so I thought.

But when you have one child, there is the danger of putting everything into that only. All of your sadness and fears. Everything you hoped to be one day, and all the things you hoped to end—to not pass on—just to give that child the opportunity to be free of generations of burdens. Maybe this happens with every child, no matter how many children you may have, but with an only, it feels like you have just that one chance to get it right. And so you hope for the impossible—that with this singular opportunity to parent, you can somehow right all the wrongs.

Perhaps it is Shanti's words or her touch as she reaches for my hand, but that realization rises to the surface now. My lips begin to quiver.

"She is *my* only too," I say. "That is why I cannot be a burden to her. She is everything I hoped she would be. Smart. *So* smart. Hardworking. Beautiful, and I don't just say that because she is my daughter. She can make her own money. She'll never need anyone else for that. Not even me. But she is not happy. What does any of that matter if she is not happy? What does it matter if she doesn't have love?"

Shanti sighs and grips my hand tighter. "Maybe what she needs is not the kind of love you think she needs."

16

FLORES

WE MEET IN THE HALLWAY A LITTLE PAST TEN A.M., AFTER JASMINE SENT US A ChitChat that Ethan had arrived and would be waiting for us in the conference room. The siblings had requested this meeting to give us feedback on what we planned to present at the next board meeting. Eric and Jon think of it as a "practice run," a way to assure our major investors that all we need is an infusion of a few million dollars for Eric's vision to succeed without seeming desperate. Or maybe, they joke, the meeting is to ensure Nik comes out intact, given how Nina got under his skin at the last dinner. The two laugh, but neither Nik nor Max seems amused.

As if this last-minute meeting isn't stress-inducing on its own, my mother has decided to talk to her boss about going back to work today. I texted her an hour ago, told her to keep me posted, but she hasn't replied. Why can't she just tell me she's fine or at least send me a thumbs-up? Better yet, why can't she just stay home? She makes light of that fall, even though at the time, I could think only of the worst: that she is dead, bleeding from her brain, that it was caused by some underlying and undiagnosed condition. A heart attack, Alzheimer's, a brain tumor. Why else would she fall? She insisted it was nothing but a "stupid fall," and when we argued about her going back to work, I reminded her that even stupid falls can be lethal.

I never bothered asking what stupidity brought her to Vicente's house in the first place, but I can guess. Maybe she thinks Pa's already forgiven her. In any case, why the rush to go back to work now? What's her paycheck gonna do for us anyway? All of it makes me wonder about us living apart.

Just thinking of her gives me heart palpitations. Or maybe it's this meeting.

Ethan greets the men with pats on the back; me, with a firm handshake. Nina dials into the Zoom meeting from her home in Palo Alto, her company website picture popping up on the screen. Too early for a mom to turn her camera on, she says.

I barely start detangling the cables to connect my laptop to the screen when Eric asks if I'm ready with the deck. I give him a look, mutter a *yeah*, plug in my laptop, and quickly search for the file.

The deck is a shell of what we plan to present at the board meeting, composed of bullet points and summaries, along with several charts that both Eric and Jon had me work on these past few nights and over the weekend, after they'd agreed to let me expense however many coffees and Seamless orders I needed in order to finish by today.

Nina's questions come quickly:

How much will it cost, and how long will it take to upgrade the Fisk & Tanks' facilities?

How much revenue do we expect to generate from it in the first six months? Twelve months?

Which hospitals are we targeting? Why not the ones in Philly, D.C., or those out west?

Why influencers, and why would they agree to work with us anyway?

They tackle the soft questions first. "Well, we pay the influencers," says Nik, searching the room to see if anyone else finds the question as simplistic as he does.

Instead, Eric gives him a hard look. "I get it, Nina. You're wondering about fit, but Nik has vetted these guys. Or gals, right? And they're all about lifestyle and self-care, and that's what we see the community talking about on our platform. You see, for them, having an aquarium is a way to make their home more beautiful, more serene. A place where they can decompress. And that's exactly what these YouTubers and podcasters are about. Beautifying your home, your life. Plus, they're married to guys with huge followings, so hopefully we can piggyback on that."

But Nik can't help himself. "I mean, we know that women need stress relievers at home and at work. They're also the ones making purchasing decisions. Look at office managers. Most are women, and they have a ton of buying power. If we can sell them on the aesthetics and the stress relief that comes with having an aquarium, it'd be like striking gold."

Everyone in the room exchanges glances as we wait for Nina to respond, but when she says nothing, Ethan turns to me and asks, "What do you think? Would you sit on your couch after a long day at work, look at an aquarium tank, and think, *Ah! This is just what I needed!*? Or would you hit the spa or the gym or, I don't know, the club?"

"None," I mumble. "I watch reality TV." My phone vibrates. My mother, finally. *Todo está bien*, she writes, with a thumbs-up, and this gets my heart racing once again. She will *never* not tell me everything is fine. Right now, I choose to believe her.

"*The Bachelor* and those *Housewives* shows, right?" Ethan says. "See, that's these women, the influencers. They've been on these shows or are married to someone who's like a pseudo celebrity. Am I right, Flora?"

I can't even look at him; otherwise, he'd see the knives in my eyes. *Years* now, and this fucker still can't learn my name. Of course, no one dares to tell him what it is, and why would they?

He's given us $30 million. No one in this room is going to correct him, not even me.

But then the only person not in the room does. "For fuck's sake, Ethan, her name is Flores," says Nina. "And if she's like any breathing human being, she probably gets her stress relief from sex or wine or exercise. Maybe even a good therapist." The room goes silent. My face and neck start to burn. "Snooping around other people's online conversations isn't going to cut it, guys. You're all going to need more than these stereotypical sexist assumptions to make this work. You hear me?"

Eric glances at Ethan, who shifts his gaze to the fingers he's tapping on the table. Clearly, don't expect a rescue from him today. "We hear you," Eric replies, which means he'll want numbers to back up the marketing strategy and justify the cost, or to simply shift the focus to the questions left unanswered. Numbers I'll need to finagle at my desk in that corner, well into the night, trying my absolute best to make them work.

I know what'll happen then. At the meeting, I will be in an-other corner near the screen, much like I am here, clicking slides, watching Eric, Nik, and Jon do their dance. I'll jot down the questions they can't answer, figure them out, then serve them up for Eric to deliver in a sunny email to the board that feels more like an invitation to a five-year-old's pizza party than an actual response. Then it'll happen again. I—"Michelle," "Maria," "Flora," that woman in the corner, whatever her name is—will be back at it with the numbers, weaving their tale, as my mother's voice repeats, firing me up because she's right. *Te lo dije—tóxico.* She's *been* right.

This is how they finally get to me. I admit, at first I didn't care how I got my money—I just wanted my options to be worth something, and if that meant a little fudging here or storytelling there, then I'd do it for the peace of mind that'd come with the payout and all it promised. Not just as a way to tackle my debt, but as a way for me and Ma to start over—in a new place, with my father's memory, but without his ghost. Without ours.

I text Max as soon as the meeting is over.

Let's go

17

PAULA

SANDEEP'S CHAIR NEARLY TIPS OVER WHEN I WALK INTO HIS OFFICE. "I AM going to call an Uber to take you home right now, Miss Paula," he says, picking up his phone. "Do not take another step."

"I am fine, Sandeep!"

"How can you say that when you are limping in here? Clearly you are still in pain."

"I'll take another Tylenol if I need to, but I'm ready to get back to work."

He clicks his tongue. Doesn't he understand that I need to work? I can't be home, waiting for my daughter to give me money so I can buy coffee at the bodega. I want my own money. And I need to get out of those four walls. It gets too quiet, and when it does, the floors creak or the walls shift, and I swear I hear Martín.

"Sandeep, please. Just give me a few hours. If I don't feel good, I promise I will go home. You won't even have to ask me."

He exhales, still holding his cell phone. He is only a few years older than me, but that gap can sometimes feel like a few decades. He considers every decision, every situation presented to him with skepticism, from which brand of toilet paper to put in the employee bathroom to the cost of the Thanksgiving place mats he wants in stock by Labor Day. Not even his own children can escape it. Both are in medical school, unmarried but living with their girlfriends.

One son is with a lawyer, he told me once, a good girl from a good family. He gets along splendidly with her parents. The other boy is with a Catholic woman from Boston, which has given him and his wife much consternation. This face he makes now—I imagine this is how he looks when he and his wife speak about this son.

"Okay, okay. But if you feel unwell, you will come and tell me, Miss Paula, and I will call an Uber. I'll make sure Shanti keeps an eye on you too."

"Don't insult me, Sandeep. I don't need a babysitter."

I head to the register, where a line of customers has formed. Shanti is already rushing to ring them up, and she mouths a *thank-you* when she sees me. It takes me a bit longer to put on my Dolla-Bills smock, but I manage to do it alone.

. . .

A WEEK AFTER my fall, my bruises have mostly faded. My arm still aches, but the pain has subsided, and the headaches are gone too. I am grateful to work, to be doing *something*. I am not yet ready to sit in front of a television while I wait to die.

"That's unfair, Ma," you tell me as you reheat the fried fish and quinoa you made last night. You do all the cooking now, which I hope might turn into something permanent. I'd much rather do all the other chores around the house than massage kale. "Just because you stop working doesn't mean your life has no value. There's more to someone than just their work."

"This coming from you, when all you ever do is work?" I've come to expect these rebuffs. Since Martín died, you challenge me more, treat me like we are equals instead of mother and child, even if you contradict yourself. Of course, you pay the bulk of the rent here, and this has, I admit, forced me to tolerate the ways you push against my boundaries. How many times have I wanted to remind you that you should at least, out of respect, listen and not argue with me? Or not roll those eyes at me? I confess, there were times I wish I could smack them into place, and I am ashamed of what that says about me. I've come to accept, however, that this is what happens as one ages: children feel entitled, compelled even, to tell their parents what they think without asking if anyone wants their opinion in the first place. Without even looking in the mirror first. And why should you? The older I get, the more I avoid the mirror too.

"Tell me, Yoli, what would you be without your job, eh? What are you besides those numbers you fuss over and whatever title and salary they decide to give you? You breathe, sleep, and eat that job. You know why? Because it makes you feel useful, valued."

"I do it for the paycheck. Besides, Pa couldn't work in the end. That didn't make him any less valuable."

"He was sick. At least he didn't suffer in that state for long or die of old age."

"Yeah, let's look at the bright side. He withered away from cancer instead. Only took a year for him to die." You snicker. I can never say the right things. "Anyway, it's not like you didn't do this to yourself. You broke your arm walking your boyfriend's dog. It could've been worse, you know."

"Eh eh! Remember who you are speaking to, Mónica Yolanda! The dog was getting agitated. I went to hold her so that Vicente could speak to Renata. His wife. Okay?"

"Oh, I know who she is. You seem to forget."

"What is the matter with you? I would never disrespect another woman like that. Understand?"

"You went to his house! Just be careful, Ma. Renata may be small, but those bruises may end up on your face next time."

"No soy ninguna cualquiera," I say, and I stop myself from saying anything about the nights you don't come home. "I'm not a child, Yoli."

"No, you're more like a teenager."

"Enough! You may be the one paying the bills around here, but I gave birth to you."

"What, you want some sort of pass for that? Look, I just want you to take it easy with work and avoid any more drama. We have more important things to worry about, like where we're going to live. I'm seeing an apartment this weekend. I know you want to do your own thing, but it's a two-bedroom. If you're interested, that is. Obviously living in Vicente's building isn't an option."

I walk out of the room, slam my bedroom door. For my own child to speak to me this way, like I'm some silly girl with no restraint or self-respect—it's intolerable. I know my place in Vicente's life, and in that moment, I saw the place my own daughter had put me in hers. A teenager, you said. As if I needed to be mothered. When had I come under your care in this way? I wonder if it was after your father died or if you always saw me as fallible, juvenile even, utterly incapable of being my own woman.

18

FLORES

MAX AND I SIT AT A CANDLELIT TABLE AT LES VICTOIRES, A WINE BAR IN THE
West Village that once upon a time served hot dogs and beer. The
velvet chairs, the wood, the candles and tea lights, and especially
the empty piano in the far-off corner make me wish I was on a date
with the promise of a nightcap and the thrill of a first kiss looming.
Instead, I'm here with a soon-to-be-married coworker.

I flip open the menu to make sure the food offerings haven't
changed, though there's never a need to look at a menu when I'm
out with Max. He orders a bottle of Cabernet Sauvignon to start
us off, along with a cheese and meat board. As the server leaves,
I jump in to request their truffle fries, though he argues, unironi-
cally, that we could have gone to the McDonald's down the block
if I wanted quality fries.

With our food and wine orders placed, he goes on to tell me
exactly how we'll show the precarious state the Bowl is in. Not too
dire, but enough to warrant a change in leadership. Show everyone
who's given us money how we need a different leader—or at the
very least, a different strategy—to get us back on track. Max and I
never actually say that the goal is to get Eric out, even though that's
the hope. We can't say it aloud; at least I can't. It feels treacherous.

For all these meetings, I work closely with the heads of each
team to present their slides and ultimately control the master

document. Once the presentation for the board meeting is complete, I'll circulate it to senior staff. But when it comes time to present, I'll swap the original marketing team slides with the ones that emphasize the historical downward trend of our sales numbers, not just year-to-date; the exorbitant cost to acquire new customers based on the proposed marketing strategy; and the projected losses for the next twelve months. Basically, a rapid decline if we are going to shift resources to expanding Fisk & Tanks and cranking up our overall marketing spend rather than investing in the only avenue that matters—community building and engagement. This, Max believes, is where our strength lies. This is what will get us acquired.

"And this is the out we need," he says, nibbling on a cube of Alpha Tolman cheese. "That is realistically the only way we're going to make any money here. Not partnering with some hospital or hotel or buying a manufacturing plant. Those take too long to see the actual upswing, and we have neither the time nor the capital. And these investors—they're not going to give us more money. I wouldn't. Not with Eric in charge."

"We've established that," I say, hoping to end any more discussion about Eric himself. There's no need to keep beating up on the guy. "So, you'll give me your slides on a thumb drive?"

"Definitely. After you send around the final deck, I'll give you this." He pulls a thumb drive out of his back pocket, the word CANTO scribbled in orange against a navy blue background. "It'll have the slides you need to swap in. This way, no one can trace them before the meeting."

I scoff. "You really think they're looking at us, don't you?" It's why he suggested we pick a place in Manhattan to talk.

"Of course! We spy on everyone. That's the business we're in. And now we're not even subtle about it. There are cameras in the pantry, for crying out loud."

"Someone's stealing the Emergen-Cs, or so Jasmine tells me.

But don't worry. Those cameras will come down soon. Legal hates them."

"That's because they don't like records of anything." He leans in and whispers, "They know we're sketchy."

"They're paranoid control freaks."

"Anyway, point is, they're looking, so we have to be careful. I'll give you the thumb drive. You swap out the slides and that's it. You're done. Easy."

"You think that's easy? Everyone will know that I switched the slides."

"By the time it's over, it won't matter. Besides, I'm the one presenting, so all the heat will be on me. No one's going to be looking at you, trust me."

They don't as it is, but he's right. All eyes will be on him, and he has no intention of glossing over questions or seeing any silver lining. He'll say what he believes is the truth: that nothing we're doing is actually making a difference, and unless we change course, we're screwed.

"He'll fire us," I say.

Max wags his finger. "Eric won't fire me. Nik needs me. The *company* needs me. Plus, there are investors that would absolutely lose it if he did. And he'll never fire you. But if for some reason, this goes to shit, just say you don't know what happened ¡y ya!"

"Easy." I swirl the wine in my glass. The hints of cherry and pepper, the soft light, the gleam of the wood, the familiarity of the place—it's comforting. It doesn't quite soothe my *unease*, but it helps another feeling come in: resignation. Max has no reservations about the plan, which makes me wonder if I've been blinded by friendship all these years. "You know why I wanted to come here?" I ask.

"The fries," he jokes.

"Yes, the fries. And because this is where Eric and I used to come for drinks after class. This place was called the Greasy Pig back then."

"Very classy."

"It smelled like an old rug. Anyway, we were too young to even be here, but here we were, every Thursday with the other nerds in our Regression Analysis class."

"Did you think you were cool, Flores?"

"Fuck yeah, we were! We drank whatever was on the happy hour menu. Beer, mostly. It was all we could afford back then, and way before we got all fancy with our wines and whiskey."

"No Lagavulin neat back then? Let me guess," he says, shutting one eye and squinting at me with the other. "Corona."

"Yes, but I'm not *that* predictable. I'd have it with a shot of tequila."

"That is *very* predictable." He laughs. "And Eric?"

"He drank Stellas."

So did Vasily. The first time he came out with us was because Eric insisted that Vasily join us. Prices were mad cheap, Eric told him, and we had just turned in our midterm assignment. Vasily could be back in Brooklyn by dinnertime if he really wanted to (he already had a reputation of being an early riser). *Just one drink*, Eric coaxed him, and he was effervescent even then; it was hard not to be persuaded. But Vasily agreed only after I said I'd go for a beer too. Just one, because that's all I drink when I'm out with people I don't really know. But I wanted to get to know *him*.

So I nursed a Corona by the bar for a solid hour, Vasily sipping a Stella beside me, in the same place where Les Victoires makes the walk-ins gather now as they wait for a table to open up. We talked mostly to each other, occasionally with other classmates, but always as a pair, as if we were already a couple. He asked if I liked chess, and I admitted that I had never played the game. Vasily, it turned out, had won tournaments back home, and in the years that followed that particular evening, I learned to play, and did so, badly. While we talked, he'd tug on the collar of his sweater, sometimes nibbling on his nails. Meanwhile, Eric pounded pint after pint, his cheeks already burning from the Jell-O shots being passed around. I thought he'd stop after two. He was slimmer then, almost gangly, and I worried that his body could not handle the amount of alcohol he dared to drink. So Vasily and I closed out his tab and put him in a cab bound for Flushing.

Then we walked over to Chess Forum. The back was filled with tables of older men and college students. Chess pieces lined wooden shelves like saints observing their play. He visited the shop often, usually after class, to watch games, play five-minute ones, and chat with the owner if he happened to be there. To this day, I avoid even walking by the place.

We then went in search of something *I* love: Belgian fries. He ordered his with a side of wasabi mayo; I got the ketchup mash-up.

"This is just ketchup and mayonnaise," he told me as we walked toward Washington Square Park. A chill had settled on that October evening. The air was steady, the full moon illuminating our walk. "It's . . . basic," he said, even as he leaned in to double dip. "And you are not."

"I'm pretty basic," I said. "Maybe that's not the right word, but you know, regular."

"With your background, your brain, and that face," he said, "you are definitely not." It was the first time someone made me feel beautiful without saying I was. "And you go to one of the best schools in the world. Hardly basic."

"I hope not, especially for what it's costing me. But I see my education as an investment. It's how I'll be able to travel, own property, support my parents. I'll never have to depend on anyone for money. At least that's what I tell myself. If I'm wrong—well, then the joke's on me!"

"You can't go wrong with finance."

"Maybe, but it's not my passion. I can't imagine it being any-one's. But it's safe. Basic. If I were bolder, I'd do something I'm actually passionate about instead of going down the standard route of the good immigrant daughter, chasing money and security."

"And what is your passion?"

"I don't know. Sometimes I'm afraid I'll never find it. Or worse—that I don't have one. But that might not be a bad thing. Most people who do what they love need family money or a rich spouse to support them."

"I plan to be rich."

The next morning, I got a text from Eric: *Ur welcome! :D*

I count that night as our first date, even though Vasily never asked me out on one, nor did we formally couple up. Some things don't need to be said to be understood.

I don't realize I'm smiling until Max raises a glass. "Here's to fond memories."

I bring the wineglass to my lips. I haven't thought about that night in years. Funny how the feelings linger—the excitement that brewed in the pit of my stomach, how Vasily and I got closer and closer until our forearms rubbed against each other at the bar, the laughter between bites of hot crunchy fries on a cool night. Then the salt on his lips.

I'd like to think Vasily and I would've gotten together even without Eric as matchmaker. He always gave himself credit for getting us together, and felt it was on him to set things right when our relationship ended.

"You know, Eric's not all bad," I say. "Not as a person and defi-nitely not as a leader."

"I never said he was. And I understand why you hesitated in the first place. You're closer to him than most. Your loyalty says a lot about your character, Flores. It's admirable." He leans in. "But sometimes we have to pick between ourselves and our friends. This is one of those times."

"It's about money, Max. Let's not pretend it's about anything else."

"And is there something wrong with that? You want to pay off those loans. Take care of your mom. All these years, you've been crunching numbers in that corner with no real salary increase or promotion. If you want *something* to show for all the work you've put into this place, then this is what we need to do. Believe me, Eric getting out of his own way is actually the best thing that could happen for everyone, including Eric."

"I'm gonna lose him as a friend," I say.

"There are no friends in this, Flores." For a moment, my mother flashes before me, and I wonder if it's at all possible for a person to be in two places at once. Her lesson quickens my heart. He pours more of the Cab into my glass, then into his. Suddenly he reaches for the fries on my plate. I slap his hand out of the way before he snatches what is mine.

19

PAULA

"GOOD MORNING!" VICENTE SAYS, SMILING AS HE PLACES A PLASTIC SHOWER curtain by my register. He is tan, darker than usual, probably from his days at the beach or his walks with ChaCha. It suits him, this sun kiss. So do the crisp yellow polo shirt and dark blue shorts he's wearing. He looks well enough to loathe, but I simply try not to stare at him for too long, which is harder than it should be.

I haven't seen him since I fell. Not that he didn't check in on me—he did. I couldn't avoid his text messages, but I didn't always respond to them, and when I did, it was with one-word answers—*bien, no, okay*. He went to the beach at Robert Moses one morning and sent me a picture of the ocean. I replied with a thumbs-up. I watched all the funny videos he forwarded on Messenger and responded to each prayer he forwarded with an *Amen*, saying it aloud as I typed, so the Lord could hear me. He even called me twice. The first time, I picked up. He asked how I was doing, was my arm better, did I go out at all. I didn't pick up the second time he called. Still, I fear I must've called him with my thoughts.

I ring up the rest of his items—a tin of butter cookies, foam scrubbers, a bottle of Fabuloso. My chest tightens and thumps, all the way to the inside of my ears.

"How is that arm?" he asks.

"Better," I say, and my arm throbs in response. I shove his items into a bag, making as much noise as possible to avoid yelling at him. Shanti's eyes are already on us.

"I didn't know you were back," he says. "I would've come sooner. But you know the prices at Bottom Dollar are just a little better."

"Those thieves and their knockoffs. Just so you know, nothing in there is worth a nickel."

"Their bottled water is cheaper."

"I forgot you're too good for tap." I hand him his shopping bag. "We have reusable bottles in aisle six. Much cheaper than buying plastic water bottles every day and ruining the oceans."

He smiles. "What time are you done?"

The pounding in my chest gets louder and I can feel my cheeks turning the bright pink of that Fabuloso.

"Five o'clock," I hear Shanti say, and throw her a look as if that will somehow shut her up. He's halfway down the center aisle, heading toward the exit, when I smack her arm with my good hand. She giggles. "Miss Paula, you didn't tell me you had an admirer."

"I do not, and you should know better than to think such stupid things."

"It's not stupid! You are single and attractive. And he's quite handsome."

"He's an old friend and he's married."

"Well, we don't all live forever."

"Shanti!"

"I don't mean his wife!" She laughs. "Although she won't. And neither will the two of you!"

· · ·

WHEN MY SHIFT is over, he is standing by a parking meter outside the store, without ChaCha. "I didn't think it was a good idea to bring her," he explains. "She's part of the reason you got hurt in the first place."

"In that case, you should've stayed home too." I make my way through the crowds on the avenue, the day bloated with heat. He catches up quickly. Sweat coats his skin, just enough that his face glistens. His shirt floats over his chest; meanwhile I'm soaking in this long-sleeved shirt I feel forced to wear just to cover my injured arm. A pool of sweat has started to collect in the dip in my bra, right between my breasts.

It's not until we turn a corner, onto the quiet street with the cherry trees, that I clear my throat. What exactly do I want to say to him? That day I fell, he asked me to go to his apartment for lunch, and that's all that it was. An invitation to share a meal on a day I was off from work. It was hot. We were walking down this very block. We didn't want to spend money or be outside in this heat. He had leftover arroz verde and papa a la huancaína, which he made the night before and claimed to have perfected over the years. He'd made chicha morada too. I was curious to see how good he was in the kitchen. Really, I was.

He had almost whispered when he asked, "¿Te invito a comer?" And then he reached out his hand, and his fingers took ahold of mine. It was just a few seconds, but my body jolted. My blood rushed through it. I did not realize until that moment how long I had gone without someone else's touch, without the warmth of another's skin pressed against mine, or how much I longed for it.

I knew Renata wasn't there; she was at her sister's, after all. And everyone on his block would be at work—maybe one or two chismosas would be sitting on their stoops or at their windows, nothing more. In his apartment, it'd just be the two of us, with ChaCha as our only witness. If I must confess, I did not know what would happen, but I knew I wanted *something* to happen.

So I said yes. Who in their right mind says *yes* to a married man who asks you back to his apartment? What did I expect to happen there? It wasn't just lunch; he and I both knew that.

Renata knew it too. It's why she crossed her arms and her head fell to the side when she saw us approach their building, laughing, our fingers touching. She didn't even acknowledge me.

"¿Esta viuda?" she had asked him. "¿Traes a esta viuda a mi cama?"

I was insulted. We were going to have lunch, I told her, nothing more. How dare she assume anything else?

But she ignored me and spoke only to him in a murmur that I found more threatening than if she had raised a hand to strike me. That might have been less painful to bear than her words. *This widow*, she kept repeating, *you bring this widow to my bed?* Was she shocked? Disgusted? Did she expect to find him with a younger woman?

Then her tone changed. *A esta pobre viuda.*

In the days that followed, I kept hearing those words and the pity and disdain they were laced with. *This poor widow.* And I heard a version of this contempt from you too—the acting "like a teenager." *Como una chibola.* That's what you said. Her words already made me feel small, and when you reprimanded me, I wondered if whatever desires I had, carnal or otherwise, were somehow supposed to have died on that bed, with Martín.

My mistake, I think, was finding comfort in an old friendship. Too much, perhaps, and now here is the old friend's wife. Where was my pride? Where were my boundaries?

"I don't think we should see each other anymore," I tell him, despite the massive stone lodged in my throat. "I don't want any trouble with Renata. Or to give my daughter any more headaches. All I want is to work and live in peace, Vicente."

He rubs the back of his neck. "Paula, I'm sorry. I didn't know she'd be there. She'd left! She wanted space, time apart. I didn't think she'd show up with her nephew and a truck and move her stuff out. She didn't even call or text me."

"She doesn't need to! It's her home. She has every right to come and go whenever she wants. I'm the one who shouldn't have been there." My chest is heavy; my body feels bound, and I want to shake off the restraints. "You are married, Vicente. You shouldn't have invited me over, and I shouldn't have said yes. Even this"—my good arm going back and forth between us—"this shouldn't happen. This walk, our talks. It's wrong."

"Don't tell me you're still worried about appearances?" he scoffs. "At our age? Renata and I may still be married, but you know the truth. You and I . . ." He hesitates, then finishes the sentence with the one thing we've been telling ourselves all along. "We're friends, Paula. Are you telling me that after all these years, after everything we've been through, the good and the bad—are you saying that we can't be friends?"

We can't, I want to say, because the truth is that I don't want us to be friends anymore. I don't want to be made a fool of, either. I want to see him. I want our walks, our talks. But I cannot be that desolate soul, so unmoored without her anchor that she can find solace only in someone else's. That she can find it only in another.

"I can't disrespect Renata or myself, Vicente."

"There's no disrespect! She and I are . . ." He pauses, shrugs his shoulders. His hands land on the sides of his thighs. "I don't know what we are."

"Then tell me what *we* are?" I cannot stop myself from asking this, and immediately regret it, because the truth is, I don't want to know. If he's unsure, then I can still pretend that this thing between us is okay. We can keep pretending, and I won't feel like a silly teenager.

His silence is just long enough that I mutter, "Please don't tell me." My voice is brittle, and I regret saying anything to him at all. Even letting him in in the first place. I pick up my pace. This time, he does not follow. "Don't come to me with tonterías!" I manage to yell back, my hands shaking. He better never dare reach for my fingers again.

20

FLORES

IT'S JUST AFTER NINE A.M. WHEN I SEE JON THROUGH PULSO'S WINDOW, RACING to the door. He texted me late last night, as I tried to decompress with a glass of wine and the latest episode of *90 Day Fiancé*, asking if we could meet before work. He has a disdain for what he considers overpriced coffee—the K-Cups in the pantry suit him just fine—and he's usually scrambling to get his kids to day care in the morning. So the text alarmed me, though he assured me that everything was fine; he just wanted to talk.

He sidesteps his way up the line toward me, panting, waving his shirt to cool himself off. "I need some iced coffee stat," he declares, rubbing his eyes. "I don't even know how the fuck I drove in." He gives his head a shake, then takes a good look at me and laughs. "Man, you look like shit."

I give him the finger. "Maybe don't work me to death," I say. What I really want is to point out that the coffee shop's warm light doesn't soften the lines on his forehead; that I have only a pinch of gray compared to the fistful on his head. If anything, he looks more like forty-eight than thirty-eight. But I don't bother, because if there's one thing Jon enjoys, it's getting a rise out of me, like an older brother pestering his little sister. Still, I can't help but inspect my own reflection when we reach the glass covering the pastries.

We find a table in the back corner of the shop. He tells me

about his weekend plans to barbecue in the backyard; set off the leftover fireworks he bought at Walmart; skid down a slip and slide without crashing into his daughter. I tell him about the Peruvian Independence Day celebration and how I hope to make a trip to Rockaway Beach. I leave out the hours I'll spend watching *Say Yes to the Dress*, *Dateline*, and *Reba* reruns.

"No dates?" he asks. "Too bad I don't got any single friends, but you know some are gonna be getting divorced soon."

"Great," I say. "So what's up? We both know you don't like to spend money on coffee, so why are we here?"

He sips his latte, looks around the room. His leg shakes under the table. "You know how life's a helluva lot easier if you know someone's got your back?"

"Are we talking about dating? I'm fine being single, Jon."

"No, I mean, you know how big we are on trust, right? You gotta have your ride or dies. People you can depend on, and that's hard sometimes because with some people, you just can't be sure." He pauses, leans in. "Like your boy." He cocks his head, but I don't react. "Has Max said anything . . . *off* to you? Anything about other people at the Bowl or investors? Like Nina Blue?" He blinks repeatedly, clearly expecting me to dish.

"Why would he say anything to me about her?"

"Oh, come on. You saw him at the party. He was chatting her up like they were homies. Getting her drinks, walking her out. With his fiancée there." His eyes bulge. "The guy has no shame."

"Because he was sucking up to an investor?" I chuckle. "All of you do that. Seriously, though, did it ever occur to you that the guy might actually be a gentleman?"

"*That* guy?" he snorts. "A gentleman? Look, I know Max thinks he can save the company or whatever, but he needs to stay in his lane and away from investors."

"Because he talked to one?"

"Because he flirts with one. Because he whispers in corners

with them like they got secrets. And I'm sure it's not just Nina. All year long, he's been out there meeting with potential partners, doing Nik's job for him."

"Wasn't that the point?"

"It's one thing to make your boss look good. It's another to get too comfortable with the people funding your business. Makes you question his motives. His loyalty."

"People are only loyal to themselves, Jon."

"Wow! If that's what you're saying now, after one year of being all buddy-buddy with that guy—"

"I'm saying in general, people are only loyal to themselves."

"Not us. We've been loyal to each other and the company. But you gotta be careful with people like him. We don't know what his agenda is, and let me tell you, people got eyes on him. You know what I'm saying?"

So Max has gotten Eric's attention, and not in a good way. Eric has always had the eyes and ears of his employees who are closer to the ground—the interns, the first-jobbers, the nonmanagerial new hires. He takes them out for coffee so as to inspire confidence and trust in their leader, when really, he's just fishing for intel on his employees. His real questions are embedded in the idle prattle, the kind that causes you to let down your guard because he makes you feel like he's just one of us. What did you think of the holiday party? Have the Friday lunches gotten better? How's that new designer (the actual question he wants answered)? If he asks about anyone in particular, then there are doubts about that person's performance, their intentions, and ultimately, their place in the company. Whether someone is loyal and trustworthy is, perhaps to our detriment, the most valued of traits. It's why the head of HR puts grads from the executive team's alma maters at the top of any candidate pile; why we always give preference to a candidate that another Bowler can personally vouch for.

I earned Eric's one night back in college, when he was short on cash and I paid for the pizzas we were having for dinner. And that's how it was between us for years. We got each other, whether it was paying for food, sharing class notes, studying for exams. Or hooking me up with the first real relationship I ever had. He was always looking out. It's probably why he offered me a job here in the first place.

But when someone's loyalty is questioned, they better tread lightly. We try to make it easy for them to leave. Shuffle them within their department; give them a new boss; take away their responsibilities until they are essentially forced to leave because there's nothing for them to do. They get bored and frustrated, and exit the company of their own accord. If a person happens to lead a team—well, that's a bit more complicated. Part of the team is spun off and given to another leader, or the person gets a new boss— typically an outside hire—and that new boss makes the not-so-hard decision to say it's just not working out, so the person is given a month to find a new job, and if they can't, well hey! They can still say they work for the Bowl for a little while after if it'll help them land their next gig. No hard feelings.

I wonder if this will ultimately be Max's fate.

"Are you saying Eric wants to get rid of Max?"

"No, and that's obviously not my call, but . . ." He shrugs, and I know it's *exactly* what he's saying. "Look, it's one thing to suck up to people at work or our partners or whatever. It's another to be all up on investors. Just be careful with the guy, that's all I'm saying. Maybe some distance would be a good thing. Have fewer coffee breaks."

My skin bristles, my body confirming what I already know. Eric doubts me too. It's why Jon's here. Eric sent someone he trusts, and in doing so, he's creating that distance Jon speaks of now. They are watching me too, who knows for how long, just as Max suspected. And it pisses me off that he was right.

"Are you guys gonna tell me who I can and can't be friends with now?"

"Who you roll with is on you. Just watch what you say around him. And I can tell you that because you're on my team. Max knows more than he should as it is. And we both know that was a bad idea in the first place. But if he says or does something off, tell me. You'll tell me, right?"

I nod.

"Good." He looks straight at me, unblinking, as if we're playing chicken. I don't hold the gaze for very long. I wish I could be a better liar.

21

FLORES

"MA, YOUR LIPS CAN'T GET ANY REDDER," I WHISPER AS SHE FISHES IN HER bag for her lipstick when Shea Stadium comes into view. That might not be its name anymore, but if you've lived here long enough, you still call it that.

She wraps her arm around the pole on the 7 train and frantically reapplies. "This heat is already melting my makeup," she says, then offers me the lipstick. I hesitate at first, then pull up the camera on my phone to touch up my own lips and the red stripes I drew on my cheek, an homage to the Peruvian flag. Once a year, we dress up in red and white—the colors of the flag—and head to a Peruvian Independence Day celebration, usually the one at Flushing Meadows Park. Aside from her ruby-red lips, my mother is in a T-shirt bearing the Peruvian coat of arms, white mid-calf jeans, and a pair of rhinestoned silver sandals. Her shoulder bag, emblazoned with Shipibo geometric patterns, is packed with a bedsheet, bananas, and Band-Aids in case those sandals give her blisters later. I opted for a Paolo Guerrero jersey, white shorts, my new cherry Jordans, and a red Mets cap I got off eBay. My camera dangles on my shoulder, ready to capture the colors and outfits that grow only more vibrant the deeper we get into Queens.

It is the only holiday that I will never *not* spend with her. For my mother, it is bigger than Christmas (a money dump, as she puts it) or Thanksgiving (an excuse for gluttony), even though she never objected to the presents or to my father cooking both pernil and turkey on those holidays. Fiestas Patrias commemorates the day General San Martín declared Peru's independence from Spain after more than a decade of war. Not that it liberated every Peruvian, as my father always reminded us when this day came around, but my mother loved it because it was a day she could almost feel as if she had returned to Peru.

A steady stream of blood and bone pours into the park. The air is already saturated with the smell of burning charcoal. My mother doesn't complain when I make her wait as I snap pictures of other red-lipped smiles, women in polleras, or the backs of a young family, dressed in traditional Shipibo clothing, making their way through the crowd.

The gatherings we had when I was a kid pale in comparison to this. The food vendors aren't confined to a small fenced-off nook; instead, there are rows of tables and stands filled with dishes I only ever had on weekends or special occasions, when my father was still alive: papa a la huancaína, arroz verde, tamales de plátano and yuca, bags of canchita, cups of mazamorra morada and arroz con leche. Our lungs fill with the smell of seared hearts, once beating inside cows, now burning on wooden skewers over charcoaled grills, seven dollars each.

"Ladrones," my mother mumbles as we walk by. She texts Norma, who is selling her juanes somewhere in the middle of the park, but I know Norma will charge the same price for her anticuchos and my mother will simply have to swallow her grumble. Coolers filled with cans of Inca Kola, water bottles, Doña Pepas, and Sublime chocolates are hauled through the crowds, a dollar apiece. Then there's the chicha morada and cremolada, chicha de jora, and freshly pressed juices made right at the stand. There's even ponche, whipped on the spot, with dark rum, beer, or pisco, your choice. My camera snaps and snaps, and I lament that it cannot capture the rumble, the burning, the sharp air that fills my mouth and sears my eyes.

I know Norma won't have salchipapas, so I buy some from a woman and teenager cranking them out under a massive beach umbrella. It'll be the first of many I eat today.

"¿Y la dieta?" my mother asks.

"What diet?" I say, savoring the smoky cuts of meat.

We order two ponches with algarrobina and pisco from a trio of men churning them out from blenders. When one hands over the drinks, my mother asks for la yapa, that additional dollop any self-respecting Peruvian knows to expect from a street or market vendor back home. "Is this a Peruvian celebration or not?" she demands. The man's laughter is like a whistle, and I realize my mother is flirting, which makes me tip my cap just a little lower to hide my smile. I'm both embarrassed and amused. He obliges, pouring an extra bit of pisco in each of our drinks.

I twirl the liquor into the froth as we walk over to Norma's table, her teenage son doling out heads of her juanes: rice, chicken, olives, and slices of hard-boiled egg wrapped and then cooked in banana leaves, twelve dollars apiece. "I should've sold that too," she shouts, gesturing to the ponche. "But I only have two hands, and can you believe I have to pay my own child to help me?"

"Your ponche is the best, Normita. These guys used a blender," my mother says, wide-eyed, disgusted that they took a shortcut to make the drink. The truth is, my mother wouldn't have bought all her meals or drinks from Norma anyway. She's always complained about Norma being una carera. Ma would've at least opted to buy a cheaper drink from someone else. She orders a plate of food nonetheless, and gestures to me when Norma totals up what we owe.

It's also the price one pays for good gossip. A bargain, if you ask me.

"Have you seen anyone from the neighborhood?" my mother

asks, though she is really interested in hearing about only *one* person. If anyone would've seen Vicente, it's Norma.

She lists the folks she's seen so far, my mother muttering *aha* at each name, until Norma finally leans in and says, "I saw Vicente with Renata."

So the scandal's made its way around. Of course I sneak a peek at my mom. Her body tips back; her eyebrows suspend above her sunglasses as she holds her ponche to her chest. She says *ah sí* to every bit of info Norma divulges: they got here early, she tells us, with all the other vendors; walking around, waving hello to people like they were Obama and Michelle. And who told Renata she could just put up any old picture on the Peruanos Unidos Facebook page without asking? Anyway, they didn't look happy, para nada, and everyone knows she's left him, but they were very cordial. All business. Vicente just kept jotting down stuff in his little notebook, probably to make sure they get their cut in the end because they're one of the organizers, and they're *always* sure to get their money. *Orgullo Peruano*, they say, but no—dólares americanos, that's the source of their pride.

Of course, it's no surprise that Vicente is here. That day in the ER, I found him sitting in a chair in my mother's exam room, holding her gym bag. She was nowhere in sight. My blood congealed. He held me. She had just gone up for a CT scan, completely routine, he reassured me. She had also asked him to leave, but he refused. And though I promised to update him on her condition, I had no intention of doing so. That was up to my mother. As we chat with Norma, though, I begin to wonder how much *she* knows about that fall. Were there rumors swirling about my mother and Vicente? Did Renata say anything?

My mother pulls out her phone and navigates to the Peruanos Unidos Facebook page for today's schedule and map. Renata had pinned the post, but my mother scrolls farther down and stops on a close-up of Norma and her juanes, a picture taken in the park several summers ago, when Norma's face was rounder and her roots whiter—a picture clearly taken between touch-ups.

The dance performances start in less than an hour, so we leave Norma and make our way to the stage, stopping to greet one acquaintance after another, people I barely remember, but who, according to my mother, I've interacted with in the past. *You used to jump rope with her when we lived on Dupont*, or *We went to a pool party at her house when you were six or seven*—all failed attempts to jog my memory. I nod and smile out of politeness, say hello to so-and-so's cousin and this person's daughter, and all the while my mother asks about their parents. Some, we're told, are too tired to sit out in the sun for hours; others can no longer eat the deep-fried picarones they love so much, let alone dip them into puddles of miel de chancaca or indulge in a cold Cusqueña to ward off the heat, so why bother coming at all? My mother grows less enthusiastic with each update, whispering to me how all those years of drinking must have brought on this person's stroke, and how that other person was never good about taking care of himself anyway, even before the diabetes, all in an effort to explain their fates and perhaps rationalize how those fates would never befall her.

Soon we see Vicente make his way toward us, grinning, wearing a navy blue-and-white striped Alianza Lima jersey, emblazoned with the Cristal beer logo at its center, and carrying a notebook tucked under his arm. My mother slurps her ponche, turning away from him. He greets us both with pecks on the cheek, careful to avoid my mother's arm while she barely mutters a hello.

I compliment him on the crowd and how well organized the event seems, just to kill the awkward silence. "I've been doing this for years, and this has been the best group I've worked with," he says. "And yes, a great turnout too. Don't you think so, Paula?" My mother shrugs and continues to mash her straw into what's left of her drink.

"How long *have* you been doing this?" I ask.

"A long time, except for when I lived in Puerto Rico. This helped keep me going after . . . well . . ."

He doesn't need to finish the sentence; I know enough about his *after*. I manage a grin and nod, the only acknowledgment I can offer at the moment. Anything else—a hug, a word—might force me to look at my own wound, one I'd rather leave alone.

"Back then, the park was the last place I wanted to be," he goes on, "but I had to throw myself into something for our community. This was perfect." He scans the crowd, beaming; his exhalation hits me with a bit of envy. His breath doesn't grow shallow when he talks about Dani, like mine does when I talk about Pa.

His attention turns to my camera—its heft, broad eye, and thick strap—and he leads us toward the front of the stage, where, he tells me, I'm sure to make the best use of it. Along the way, he shakes hands and pats backs, the crowd filled with folks eager to greet him. A celebrity, like Norma said.

"Right in front, just like when you were a little girl," he says, stopping just left of center stage. "Maybe we can put some of your pictures on our page."

My mother pulls the bedsheet from her bag and sets it down on the dry grass. To my surprise, he sits down with us, and I suddenly find myself sandwiched between him and my mother, who has yet to utter a word. She unwraps Norma's juane and begins to eat it, her back turned slightly toward us.

"You know, when you were a kid and we did these celebrations in the park," Vicente tells me, "it felt like every Peruvian from every corner of New York showed up. This feels bigger, but the circle's getting smaller. Every year, you find out someone else has died or is sick or has moved back to Peru." He pauses, as if acknowledging a moment of silence before moving on to a happier memory. "Anyhow, even though ours were smaller, we always had dancers. The music, the movement. It transported everyone home. I remember how your father used to carry you on his shoulders. At some point, you'd jump off and shove your way to the front of the stage."

"You remember that?" I ask, suddenly back in the skin of the child me, the mesmerized-by-the-world me. When I didn't just want to *see* the dancers but catch the wind from their whirling skirts and the flicks of fire they spun from their handkerchiefs. Absorb the sound of their feet pounding the floor.

"Don't you remember?" my mother cuts in. "You were so captivated by them, I thought you might jump onstage and join them. It's because they had that fire. That duende." She gestures to my camera. "It's what you're trying to capture with that thing. Only duende is something you conjure."

"And I can't make magic, Ma?"

She rises. "It's more than that. And you can't conjure it when you've become a spectator in life."

She leaves to dispose of her banana leaf and ponche, finding an excuse, as always, to walk away from an uncomfortable conversation. It's a tactic she used on my father too. Better that she goes. I have no desire to argue with her in front of an audience, but what right does she have to reproach me about spectating? Has she not done that herself all these years? The only ambition I've ever known my mother to have was to be a wife, and she accomplished that—if you can even call that an accomplishment—early in her life. She had no other ambitions that I know of, no fire that burned.

¿Yo apagada?

So what if my flame seemed like it had dimmed to her? If I find comfort and beauty through a camera lens—as a witness and for my own pleasure, with no desire to share it—does that make it any less alive? Does that make *me* so?

Strangely enough, her walking away gives Vicente the opportunity to have an uncomfortable conversation with me.

"Yoli, I wanted to apologize for what happened that day your mother fell. I never should have let her hold ChaCha. I'm sorry she got hurt and for scaring you. I know she's all you have left—"

"It's fine," I cut him off, in no mood to listen to his deep dives into my psyche. "She's doing much better now. Thank God it wasn't anything more serious. But that's life, right? Parents eventually become like children."

"Your mother is an adult," he says sternly, "and yes, at some point, if you're lucky to have her that long, you will have to take care of her. That's what your father would've wanted, and I think that's what you want too. It's why you're still with her. But don't feel like she's alone because she's not. Neither are you."

"I don't mean to be rude, Vicente, but if you're going to tell me we have you, well . . ."

"You do. Your mother is a great friend."

"Then treat her like one," I say. "Look, I'm her daughter. No matter how much we argue, I will always be here. To care for her, to protect her. Even from so-called friends. Especially married ones. Understand?" I sit a little straighter. It's the first time I've ever told a man not to fuck with my mom. I couldn't even do it when I should have with Pa. I wonder if she ever told him about that time I saw her and Vicente at the park. I wonder if she's ever told Vicente.

She returns as the musicians take the stage, dressed head to toe in white. Red handkerchiefs are tucked in their shirt pockets. They are all men. They exchange nods and smiles, a camaraderie I instantly envy, as they settle behind their instruments.

Then La Cantante appears. The lips of her red dress kiss the floor. Her hair, the color of algarrobina, curls and settles on her shoulders. Her tumi earrings reflect the sun. She calls out—*mi gente peruana*—and her voice sends a tremor through me. We stand as the Peruvian national anthem reverberates through her throat, clear and unaccompanied, with no instrument to guide or embellish it. The crowd responds, a rumble that serves only to drill

La Cantante's voice into the earth. I close my eyes for a moment, and because I do not know the words, I pick up my camera. First, my eyes catch my mother and Vicente, in profile and mid-song, their faces almost pained as their open mouths cry out; then, a few feet away, a man, his mouth shut tight, holding the flag above him; a child in a marinera dance outfit gripping her mother's hand; an old woman seated in a folding chair with a framed image of El Señor de los Milagros resting on her lap.

La Cantante finishes to chants of *Peru* and introduces herself as Carolina, our MC, then the musicians and their instruments. She encourages us to eat the many, many delicious foods and beverages available from our compatriots, and, by example, reminds us to drink water in this heat. She calls out to the cajón player, and when the crowd is just the right kind of silent, he pounds one set of fingers across the sandalwood box, then the other, palm after palm, smacking the center, then the top, moving so quickly that my eyes, my camera's shutter, can't keep up. The dancing swells in the belly of the crowd. First the children, then the women. My camera turns to them now, clicks its black tongue until my mother's hand lands on my arm and I look in the direction of the stage. The beats of the cajón close in, and as the player speeds up, there's an *eh!* and an *epa!* I close my eyes, and suddenly, the music is inside me. In my jaw, my throat, the sound so loud it explodes from my rib cage and races through every limb and capillary. The sun-baked grass gallops beneath my feet. My face tilts skyward. The sun blazes against me, and I find my body swaying, my arms electrified as they call on the ceaseless sky, simultaneously imbibing the sunlight and beckoning the rain.

· · ·

WHEN THE PERFORMANCES are over, Vicente takes us behind the stage to meet La Cantante. She doesn't just have a beautiful voice, he tells us, but is also an accomplished dancer, having studied many forms of Peruvian dance and run a school in Lima for years before coming to New York with her musician husband, the cajón player.

When Vicente introduces us, we kiss each other on the cheek. The kiss feels like a blessing. I quietly pray that some of her seeps through my skin; her smell of cinnamon, her vibrating words giving me a yapa of that magic she conjured on the stage.

"Your voice," I manage to say, unsure how to speak to this woman who didn't seem real. "The dancers were incredible! And the music!"

"There were a few bad notes and some missteps," she says, eyeing her husband. "But there's beauty in imperfection."

"Vicente mentioned that you have a school," my mother says. "Are these your students or your troupe?"

"I had a school in Lima, but I just started giving lessons in Paterson. This troupe is from Long Island. The musicians are from Corona."

"We really need you here in New York," says Vicente. "Our kids, like Yoli's age, they only know about our dances and music from these celebrations and whatever videos they find on the internet. I'm not sure her generation even cares about keeping this going when we're gone."

"I do!" I say, jolted by the fear that this too might somehow come to pass. I show La Cantante the pictures I took of her and the performances and offer to help however I can. She hands me her card, an image of her singing into a silver microphone, her lips a blood orange, the light capturing the golden sheen of her obsidian dress. My fingers trace the card's edge, a gold that glimmers like the foil on a prayer card.

22

PAULA

I DON'T ASK ABOUT YOUR CONVERSATION WITH VICENTE UNTIL WE GET HOME, when we're away from the crowds and anyone who knows us.

"I told him he needed to act right," you say, "that's all. He's married. Sometimes people need to be reminded of the promises they make."

For a moment, I consider telling you about what happened with Martín, but I can't speak ill of the dead. Or at least, not about your father, even though we've turned him into a kind of saint now that he's no longer with us. Don't we all do that? Turn our very human loved ones into near-perfect angels when they can no longer hurt us. I don't ask any more questions. Still, I wonder if you would have reminded your father of *his* promises.

• • •

I NEVER KNEW her name. Never cared to know. But I had my suspicions. Back when it happened, Martín had been working at the elementary school for years. He did it all—cleaned classrooms, watered plants, set traps in the schoolyard for any rats that tried to get inside. He befriended most of the teachers and staff, talking up his daughter on the honor roll at the middle school—I'm sure of it—and complaining about the Mets and Bill Clinton, like he did

with everyone. Back then, when his workday was over, he drove to
Middle Village and picked me up from Elsie's. Do you remember
her? She was the only Peruvian patient I ever had. She owned a
hair salon in Corona once, and oh! Now that was the one thing
she never forgot. Her hair. Every morning, first thing I did was
wipe her down with the agua Florida and some water, then brush
that hair of hers in front of her gold-framed mirror. Her only son
had Down syndrome. He had a job handing out mail in an office
building in Manhattan and lived in a group home some blocks
away. Poor Elsie had gotten Alzheimer's in her fifties. So young,
and when I think about it, younger now than what I imagine being
in your fifties felt like then. It took just over a decade for the illness
to take her. By the end, she didn't remember me, barely remembered her son. Maybe that's why I can sympathize with Renata and
the situation with her mother.

During those car rides home with your father, I listened to
Martín's stories about work. There wasn't much I could tell him
about my days with Elsie, except maybe when her son stopped
by to drop off groceries or what topics came up that day on *El
Show de Cristina*. But Martín always had something interesting to
say about the people who worked at the school. Javi, the security
guard, was a Dominican in his early thirties with plans to move
to Florida. Mrs. Annie, the principal, had twin grandchildren in
the fifth grade. Mrs. Baptiste, their teacher, couldn't wait for the
twins to graduate.

And then there was Miss Laura. I wasn't exactly sure what she
did, but she was some kind of administrator, not a teacher. She
was the person the mothers went to when they had questions about
after-school programs, middle schools, signing up for lunch duty. It
was always the mothers, of course.

And it was always Miss Laura whom I suspected. He knew too
much about her. She shared more than what a coworker should
share in a casual conversation, and because Martín liked to talk, I

ended up knowing more about her too. She had grown up in Ohio, a place I vowed to never go, but came to New York because she loved a movie about ghost hunters that took place here. She played the guitar well enough to sing at a bar in Manhattan on Friday nights. Her boyfriend, a pianist, traveled so much that poor Miss Laura was often lonely. She was saving money to go to India one day and learn from a real yogi. Once, Martín suggested we see her play at that bar. She was the very reason why so many vegetables at the store are organic now, too pricy for us, and why we have to go to Western Beef in Queens for reasonably priced tomatoes, I told him. I wasn't going to support *that*, but go ahead if you want, I said.

The signs came on suddenly, or maybe I didn't notice them until it was too late. On those car rides home, he began to turn up the music on the radio instead of talking to me. At first I didn't mind the salsa and merengue and the usual radio jockey antics, but his silence was unusual, and even when I asked him about his day, he said it was fine. Lo mismo de siempre. He started to leave for work earlier than usual. Then, in bed, he started to turn his back to me. You're a woman now, so you'll understand what this means. There were weeks he wouldn't touch me.

That year, as the summer approached, he shared little about his coworkers, and what he did share could double as an epitaph. Javi moved to Orlando. The twins graduated. Mrs. Annie retired.

And Miss Laura had gone to India. Not that he told me this. She had sent a postcard, an image of a river and mountain on one side, and a handwritten note on the back that said she'd made it, was studying with true masters for two months, and hoped he was having a good summer. I tore it up and tossed it in the trash.

It was the summer that Dani died. I didn't want you at her wake. I wanted you to remember her alive, not in a casket, made up to look like something that bore only a passing resemblance to the living Dani. But Martín insisted. You needed closure, he said. So he took you to the wake and the funeral, held you as you said your goodbyes, I imagine, and in the moments when you sat quietly in your bedroom, weeping. That, I know.

When I mumbled that maybe he also needed to say goodbye, not just to Dani, but to the rest of them, especially that Miss Laura, the man burned like a devil. Called me callous and childish, and accused me of protecting only myself for not wanting to go with you to the wake or funeral. There was no point in arguing that. You would get through this, I thought, because children are resilient. But adults? Mothers? I could not face Renata. I could not face Vicente. I could not think about their child without thinking of mine. What good would it do to cry with you? I couldn't let you see me do that, either. For months after Dani died, I'd walk to the river, sit on its edge at sunset, and let her loss and that fear of losing you slip into the current, hoping the water would carry it all away just as the sun plunged behind the Twin Towers, the Empire State Building, the land across. Who knew I'd sit there again for many nights, years later, when the Towers fell, crying again over how unfair and inexplicable it all seemed.

It was then, shortly after Dani died, that Martín told me he'd fallen in love with someone else. Of course, a part of me already knew. First, I asked if he was bringing any diseases home. Not that we were being intimate anyway, but I needed to know. He hadn't acted on his feelings, he said, didn't even know if this other person felt the same way. I made an appointment with my doctor the next day anyway.

Then I asked what he wanted to do about it. I didn't believe he was in love. Infatuated, maybe. He might even have cared for this person. But love? What about me? What about the promises he made to me? He wanted to forget, he said. It was a good thing, then, that I tore up that postcard.

When school started that fall, there was no talk of Miss Laura. He didn't talk much about work at all, now that I think about it. There were no weekend fútbol matches in the park to distract us, either. Vicente had stopped organizing them after Dani died. So you and your father spent the weekends grocery shopping, making dinners together, watching movies, playing card games. I was on the outside, and I have to say, it was where I wanted to be then. It pained me to know that he had feelings for someone else, and that his focus was on you and comforting you rather than our marriage. I resented him for being the better parent instead of trying to be the better partner. Because while he was good to you, and in your eyes, the best father, the way he took your side on everything made me feel like a failure. He told me that if I couldn't love you the way a mother should, it wasn't *your* fault. What does that even *mean*? Doesn't everyone love differently? You needed me to love you in a way I didn't understand. I'm not sure I'll ever know how, but who was he to point the finger? In some ways, Martín didn't know how to love me, either. He never helped me work through my shortcomings, even when he saw the rift between you and me. Maybe he thought I was inadequate to deal with the hard stuff. Maybe it wasn't his responsibility to mend the rifts between us, but I would've welcomed the help.

Our marriage did get better. Time took care of some of my resentment, and so did Miss Laura's absence. But I never could overcome that distance between you and me. A distance he created, and one that only grew as you got older, with the swells and slumps that come with being a teenager and growing into your own person. There were times I did not recognize you. When you made yourself sick over an exam or a big meeting. How you found fault in our food, that it was so unhealthy, and made exceptions only when your father prepared you a meal. How you spent hundreds on sneakers, jeans, trips to the Caribbean and Europe with your boyfriend. Each time I hoped you'd bring us back a souvenir. A token from the places you'd seen and which Martín and I never would because we could never afford them. What I wanted was a sign that no matter how far you were, you hadn't forgotten us. Hadn't forgotten me.

Martín couldn't possibly know this worry. You loved your father. I could never resent you for that. What hurt is that you loved him first, and eventually I needed him to get to you. That's how I'd come to know about the boyfriend you had in high school, the choir you didn't make, the colleges you didn't get scholarships to, jobs you didn't get, and later, your relationship with Vasily. Martín became a bridge. For me, a bridge to you. For you, I think, a bridge across whatever waters troubled you.

I'm trying to move across the river now without that bridge. Sometimes the current feels too strong. I don't despair. I can move with it, I think, if I am patient. If I can accept his absence and my own limitations, and that there are simply some things I cannot control. If I can move with all of that, then maybe I can get to you. Maybe I can make it across my own river too.

23

FLORES

THE MOON ARRIVES EARLY TONIGHT, ENTERING IN THE WANING DAYLIGHT. THE sun drapes its thinning skin over the river, turning its water into a mirror of the sky. Its rose, lavender, and golden hues are visible from the windows by my desk. My teammates have left, eager to take advantage of every bit of August as autumn looms. I stay in the office, scrolling through the photos I uploaded to my drive. Normally I'd drag every blurred image or a composition that doesn't resonate with me immediately into the trash bin. These images are different. No matter how unfocused the subject or how incongruent the components of the photograph, if there is a glimpse of that *something*—what, I guess, my mother would describe as duende— then it never goes into photographic purgatory. It is something I could identify as a child but which for years has eluded me, and that has slowly begun to reveal itself after my father's death.

It's probably why I still have most of the first images I took soon after he passed. Images of the view above me as I stood under a canopy of trees in Inwood Hill Park; the one beneath me, as I tiptoed over the moonlit rocks on the banks of the East River; the sun before me as it skimmed the water in Rockaway Beach. Imperfect photographs, except for the memories each one brings back now. Leaves crunching under my feet as my father and I walked through the park after Dani died. The river's water lapping at the stones where he and I witnessed the death and rebirth of the skyline, and where we sat in silence in the months before he passed. The light contemplating the ocean's depth on a beach we visited every summer when I was a kid. Places where I hoped to still find my father. I wonder if I'm still searching, or if these images will always capture something I know is there but can't quite see, not even with the aid of another eye.

It is better than sitting in my room, surrounded by cotton-candy-colored walls, the white trim peeling, my mother whispering, "No todo es trabajo, hija," and of course she is right. But what if that is all there is for me? There is clarity and safety in this routine, in what is expected of me, which is both comforting and terrifying. This resignation and repulsion weigh on me as I finally respond to Max's message, taunting me from the edge of my screen for several minutes that seem like an eternity.

Estas?

• • •

MY STATUS IS set to busy, and the last few times he has messaged me this past week, I haven't responded immediately. I haven't told him about my conversation with Jon, but since then I've avoided his requests to grab lunch, coffee, make a quick stop at the bookstore; any and all banter by the pantry too. I realized that perhaps I wasn't the only Bowler with whom Jon had had a conversation. Jasmine seems particularly irritated by Max, more so than usual. He had asked if she could drop something off for him at the post office, she told me, and she promptly reminded him that she managed the office and wasn't his damn secretary. Starr doesn't even entertain a conversation about him. We catch him rushing to a conference room one morning, and when I wonder aloud where he's going, she tells me she avoids him. Odd since he's second only to Nik on her team, and that is when I realize Max has suddenly become That Guy. Then again, maybe he always was.

What's up? I reply.

• • •

THE NEXT DAY, we decide to grab salads at Leaf in Brooklyn Heights. We stroll along the Esplanade to catch both the cool of the river and the bite of the sun. He elbows me awkwardly as he blurts a *Finally!* and I stumble a little at the nudge. He jabbers on about a sci-fi show he and Vicki are bingeing before picking up on my vibe and finally asking what's wrong. I tell him about my conversation with Jon.

"That guy has a problem with me talking to Nina?"

"Not just Nina. The other investors too. No one likes an ass-kisser, Max."

"Being polite is not ass-kissing. Her investment is what pays our salaries."

"There's more to it than that, but neither you nor Jon are telling me the whole story, so it doesn't matter."

"There's nothing I haven't told you."

"Bullshit. You didn't tell me about that coffee you had with Ethan a few weeks back."

"We talked about my career. His other investments. Places I can go to after this. Maybe even Silver Blue." So he's already thinking of a move. Not that this comes as a surprise, though it gnaws at me that he never mentioned it. "Look, I'm not going to say no to someone that wants to be a mentor. It's not like anyone here is taking my future seriously."

"Jon wants me to rat you out if you say or do anything disloyal. They know something's up. I'm just telling you so you can keep your head down."

"So that's why you've been avoiding me."

"I can't be on their radar. I need this job." We're supposed to move out of the apartment next month. The last thing I need is to be unemployed. "What if there's another way?"

"What other way, Flores?" he shouts. "He'll never leave on his own, and there aren't enough board members willing to get him out. But if we can show how bad his plans are and offer alternatives, then maybe we can at least get them to shift his focus."

"I get it! I just don't know how I can do it and then look at myself in the mirror."

The prospect of betrayal eats at me. I have always considered myself a straight shooter, even if I don't always say what I feel, what I think, or the truth. And there are certainly benefits to silence. I never told anyone how, the summer that Dani drowned, she and I had first filled our lungs with smoke from Newports behind the handball court, or about the time Eric and I got a look at the Regression Analysis midterm days before the exam, or about that guy I messed around with in Miami during Angela's bachelorette weekend. Except I had to tell Vasily after that guy's girlfriend found me on Facebook and told him I'd fucked her boyfriend, I hadn't, even though I wanted to. Does a kiss even count? It might have been more than a kiss, but whatever, it didn't matter, Vasily left me anyway—I should've just fucked the guy.

I never did tell anyone about the time Pa shoved my mother. For those few seconds, it was as if I had hit the floor, not Ma. How her eyes pierced him—I felt them on me. Then Pa dropped to his knees, held her legs, apologized, kissed her hands as if she were the Pope, even though blackmail was probably a good enough reason for her to whoop me the way she had.

Days later, when he dropped me off at school, he apologized to me for raising his hand to her, how I never should've seen that because it never should've happened and no one—much less someone who says they love me—should ever do that to me. I confessed to him then that Ma didn't hit me because Ms. Sosa accused me of cheating. No. She hit me because I threatened to tell him about how I'd seen Ma and Dani's pa holding hands. Something that I thought I'd gotten over, even after Vicente started coming around—until I found that note. The messed-up part, I told Pa, was that it had occurred to me to threaten my own mother.

He tucked my hair behind my ear, and I winced, even though I didn't mean to. He exhaled and teared up. Sometimes a friend needs you to hold their hand, he whispered. I wanted to tell him he was wrong—it wasn't that kind of a hold—but instead I cried and let him hold me because I knew nothing had changed. He had still shoved my mother and it was because of me, and she had still held another man's hand, a man who wasn't my father, and my friend had died on a lush and radiant summer afternoon, as bright as lemonade and minty green. And although I got caught that one time, I'd still cheat—on tests, on my ex—because even at the risk of self-sabotage, it is easier to try and fail, or to blame others for my failures, than it is to simply accept my shortcomings.

"So what do you propose we do?" Max asks. "Take him out for coffee and try to reason with him? A lot of us have tried that, and it hasn't made a difference."

"But have any of you actually told him to step down?"

"Not directly, no," he admits, "but he doesn't need anyone to tell him that. He knows."

"This company is his entire life. It's how it is with everything the guy's ever done. And he thinks he's doing right by it."

"Then imagine telling someone like that that they're doing it all wrong. You can't."

"I owe it to him not to screw him over."

"Believe me, he wouldn't pay you the same courtesy. He is not the person you met freshman year in college, Flores." His body tenses next to mine, his steady smile and placid facade collapse. He places his hand on my shoulder and gives me a gentle shake as if waking me, and my heart drops to the pit of my stomach. "He is a narcissist. He doesn't care about you or anyone else at the Bowl. The only thing he cares about is his name and reputation. That's what matters to him. But that's not you, Flores, and it's not me. We care. About Jon, Jasmine, Nik, everyone who's put in so much of themselves here. And we have careers to think about too. Not Eric. He'll sell the company for pennies if he needs to, just to save face, and then he'll go on to start his next company because that's what he is—a serial entrepreneur. But we can do something now to change the narrative. We just need the cojones—and forgive me for using this metaphor, but that's what it is—the cojones to actually do what no one on C-staff or the board is willing to do. And that's not even to call him out, but to call *them* out. Make them do something." He steps back toward the edge of the pavement before it drops to the cobblestone street. His hand drops too. "Or we just wait. We wait until he makes a shitty deal and see what happens then."

He stands on that edge waiting for an answer, some reassurance that I'm still in it. After years of being played—by Eric, Jon, even Max—I feel stupid for feeling a modicum of guilt, but as much as I want to play the game better than they can, just considering the deception gnaws at my insides.

So when I'm back at my desk, I shoot Eric a text.

Hey! Wanna grab a drink tomorrow?

• • •

THE NEXT DAY, Eric and I head to Roni for the twelve-dollar pizza slice and house wine happy hour special. He never asks why I want to talk, and I assume it's because he knows the reason. And although I had proposed drinks, I thought he might counter with grabbing a cup of coffee instead, just as a way of keeping things more formal between us.

The problem also with waiting until happy hour to have this conversation is that it's on my mind *all* day, and even though we've known each other for years, it doesn't change the fact that Eric is the reason I have a paycheck. My anxiety builds, and by the time we meet at the back entrance and head over to Jay Street, I start to think that maybe Max is right. Maybe it's just not worth it.

Eric seems distracted. He's on his phone, apologizing as he replies to messages, sucking his teeth at whatever he's typing up, tsk-tsking when he shares the latest news alert. Did I hear about the drama at Simply-City? That interior design shop with the CEO who ChitChatted his COO, a woman, and asked if she had a brain? The guy just stepped down, he tells me.

"He should know better than to put that shit in writing," I say. "It's why legal's always on us about 'the record.'"

He shrugs, slipping the phone into his pocket. "It's why I only ask people if they have brains in person, and I only ask dudes."

Our walk is mostly filled with his banter: how this heat makes him miss the December cool but not the February freeze, and how he's dying to try the new oat strawberry matcha bubble tea at Boba Queen. On the surface, he hasn't changed much from the person I met in college. He's all ease, disarming, vibrant, the same tools he brought to class when he didn't know the answer to a professor's question or had yet to find a summer job even as the academic year was winding down. Except now he tells people that he meditates twice a day to stay focused; goes to a Kentucky monastery every year for a silent retreat; and has his life coach on speed dial. I cannot make out which parts of him belong to the person he needs to be rather than who he really is. Maybe I want to see the cracks just to feel less broken.

We grab a couple of glasses of the house red and pay an extra two dollars each for the pepperoni squares. Several bites and a few healthy gulps in and he's already looking at his watch.

"You're a busy guy," I say, "so I'll just cut to it. I know things are . . . different between us, but if you need to say something to me, you can. You don't need to send Jon." His jaw drops, and although he may have mastered the performance of his public persona for a screen, when he is one-on-one and in person, he is a terrible actor. "Don't pretend. Jon would never talk to me about Max unless you asked him to."

"I didn't send him to talk to you about anyone," he says. "Jon's not my muscle. And it wouldn't be weird if I did ask him to speak to you. He's your boss." That may be, but it's not as if anyone else needs their manager as a buffer. Not when Eric grabs coffee with almost every Bowler, no matter their title. No—that's not it. Truth is, there has been distance between us for some time—ever since that one night in K-Town.

Eric had booked the largest room at his favorite karaoke spot, with three screens that covered an entire wall, plush red velvet couches, bottles of champagne chilling on side tables, and the occasional callout to meet in the adjacent room if you wanted drugs. Eric was married, no kids yet (although one was on the way), and like he does even now, he partied without his wife. It was soon after I started at the Bowl and not long after my breakup with Vasily, a period in which I first became familiar with my own capacity for grief.

After a couple of early Madonna songs and too many folks disappearing into the adjacent room for the promised drugs, I decided to leave. Eric offered to walk me to a cab, it was so late, I remember him saying. And I did fumble a bit on my feet, but he was just as drunk, so much so that he leaned against a store's metal grate as we walked to the corner, just to avoid tipping over.

As we waited for my cab, we found ourselves on each other, making out messily across the street from the Manhattan Mall. We never did talk about it. Maybe he'd forgotten about the kiss or simply pretended it never happened, like I did.

"What did Jon say to you exactly?" he asks.

"To watch myself with Max. That he's too *friendly* with Nina." I shrug. "Look, Jon already runs my work life, but he wouldn't tell me who I can and can't talk to."

"I can't, either," he says. "No offense, but why would I care if you and Max are friends? I mean, I can't be friends with him. Don't get me wrong, the guy's one of my best hires. He's mastered the art of schmoozing. He's done some creative and cool shit in his career. Plus, he's got all these degrees and speaks a million languages, so he's legit. But I'm not gonna grab a beer with the guy. That's just me, though. I'd never tell anyone *not* to talk to him. If he was a real problem, for whatever reason, he'd be gone, no question. And no matter how much Nik loves him."

"Then what's the deal?"

"Ask Jon. There's probably more to it than just the ass-kissing." He takes a gulp of his wine. "Or you could just take his advice."

He doesn't take his eyes off me, and I know better than to look away. He's playing me. "Why should I do that?"

"Like you said, he's your boss, but he's also your friend, right? Maybe he's just looking out for you. Maybe he knows something that neither of us knows about."

"You know everything," I say, to which he shrugs. "Tell me, why is it you can't get a drink with Max? You just said he's one of your best hires. Don't you want a good relationship with him?"

"A good working relationship, but not a friendship. He's pushy. He tells everyone what he thinks even when no one cares. Especially investors. He thinks he's always right, and sometimes he is, I'll give him that. But he's also condescending. It'd be one thing if he was confident. That's something people can respect. But condescension? That shit will turn everyone off, including Jon."

"And you, it seems?"

"I can handle his ego. We have our disagreements. He thinks Fisk & Tanks was a bad idea. He doesn't believe in our physical expansion. He thinks the hotel partnership is a waste of time, but that's the beauty of being a CEO. It doesn't matter what anyone else has to say about whatever it is they think they know about. In the end, it's not a fucking democracy, and only one of us has the title that matters."

And there it is, the king gripping his crown. The funny thing is, I don't disagree with what he's saying. There has to be one ultimate decision-maker, someone that gives that final yea or nay that determines which path to take no matter who's advising them, how qualified those advisers might be, or how viable their ideas actually are.

"I need to surround myself with good people," he goes on. "People who are smart and are gonna get it done. Max is one of those people. You are too! But in the end, all that talk is just noise. I take it in, for sure, but I trust my gut. Always have and always will. It's gotten me this far. You should follow yours too, Flores." He finishes the rest of his wine, leaves the pizza crust on the paper plate. "Are we good?"

We're not. We haven't been good for a while. Up until this point, it was never clear to me when or if I should let the place go, even though I can taste its toxicity, feel it thinning out my veins. Eating at that gut that he now so assuredly advises I follow. I followed him. Our friendship is what brought me here, kept me here all these years, even though I've known, for quite some time, that he and I are not good, no. Not good at all.

But I nod anyway, assuring him that we indeed are, and when he asks if we should get another round, I say yes, without thinking, not flinching when our knees knock under the counter or rest against each other, or when he eats the last of my crust. We're good, I say when we embrace, my chest pressed against his. We're good.

What's one more lie at this point anyway?

24

PAULA

IT IS ALMOST NINE P.M. WHEN YOU GET HOME, CARRYING A ROSE. YOUR HAIR IS tied in a knot atop your head. Your face is flushed.

"Ma," you say by way of greeting, and hand me the flower.

"Is this for me?" I ask.

You nod. "I bought it from a woman on the subway. I figured you'd be mad." You pull your bra out through your sleeve and hang it on a chair by the table as you head to the bathroom. This time, you close the door behind you.

"Why didn't you call?" I ask. "I wouldn't have made dinner."

"I texted," you shout, and when you return to the kitchen, you fill a mug with tap water, take a large gulp, then refill. "Besides, it's not that late. And I had dinner. A delicious salty, spicy pepperoni pizza."

"With anyone special?" I dare ask, remembering what Shanti said. How I had to get comfortable with you having a sex life, and even if you were not open to sharing, I should at least pretend I was willing to hear about it. The truth is, I craved physical contact too, and didn't want you to be deprived of it only because you did not have a partner.

But instead of telling me about a date, you say something more worrisome.

"My boss."

"Your Chinese friend?"

"He's from Flushing, Ma. His parents are from the Philippines."

"The one that's in love with you?"

"You know men and women can be friends, right?"

"Maybe if one of them is gay."

"Vicente's not gay."

"Vicente and I are old. You, on the other hand . . ."

"I'm what? Single? Lonely?"

"You have a lot of . . ." You are an adult, but I still cannot find the right word. Regardless of your age and that *thing* you're hiding under all those towels when you announce you're taking a bath, you are still my child. So I pick the word that seems the most accurate and the least troubling for me to mutter. "Energy."

"Energy?"

"Yes, energy. A lot of it."

"Ma, I really don't want to talk about my sex life with you."

"It's not just about . . . that." I was never one to have difficult conversations, and certainly not with you. For all your hardness, hija, you are a thin sheet of ice. I never doted on you as a child, the way your father did, and not because I didn't want to. I didn't know *how* to. I tried to copy Martín, but the hugging, the spontaneous kissing, the hand-holding—it never felt natural to me. Making sure the apartment was always clean, organizing your desk and shelves, setting your clothes out the night before, and doing your hair in the mornings—that *did*. But the rest, well. I don't know how to quite explain it, except that I did not understand exactly what would be expected of me as a mother. Affection—the thing you wanted and probably needed—wasn't something I had been given. That is not to say I couldn't have tried then or can't try now. I should. But you are grown and all the things I wish I had been at your age: self-sufficient, independent. You're also uncertain and adrift. All the things I was, and still am, perhaps even more so now.

"I saw your face at the festival," I say. "The way you moved when the music played. You came alive. You were happy. Completely awestruck. You took in everything with those eyes. It reminded me so much of your father. The way he looked whenever he set his eyes out on that river or the ocean."

"You mean with fear?"

"With reverence. But yes, even with some fear."

"What did you expect after that spiked ponche?" You laugh. "Estaba entre pisco y nazca. Anyway, I don't want to talk about Pa."

I sit at the table and point to the chair across from me. You hesitate for a moment, then sit. "Your job, hija," I say as you groan. "It has possessed you. Maybe it's not even the place, but the work itself. Maybe it's your friend. But the other day, when you were in that park, you let go. You were this other person. Like a child again."

"When was I ever a child, Ma? If I wasn't helping you clean apartments, I was helping Pa dodge bill collectors. The reality is, I need the job, especially now that we have to move. You want me to give it up so I can do what? Take pictures at dance festivals?"

"You were happy, that's all I wanted to point out."

"I'm happy with a steady paycheck."

"Yoli, what makes someone happy changes with time. I was the happiest when I was in love. That sounds silly when I say it. But even love changes. Circumstances change. You know this. Maybe this job made you happy once. Just like Vasily did. You have to be willing to see when something doesn't anymore and let it go."

"Do you love what you do, Ma? I can't tell if you do or if you're just there to pass the time because you can't let go of Pa."

You do not mean to hurt me, but my voice quivers. "I don't know. But I know that I loved your father, and loving him made me happy." In saying this, I realize that in my sixty-three years, my source of happiness has been defined by relationships: marriage, motherhood, friendships. In other words, my joy depended on others. That, I confess, is a fear of mine: that I won't be able to find my own joy and purpose.

"Then what should I do?" you ask. "I can't just quit my job. We need to be out of here and in a new place by October. And I don't want people chasing me for their money. That's what being a kid was like for me, Ma. Picking up the phone because you and Pa didn't want to talk to any collectors, telling them you weren't here when you were right there washing dishes."

"That won't be you! You can find other work. Have faith, Yoli. If not in God, then in yourself."

Your lips pucker and I wonder if it's possible that you are actually listening to me. My chest swells. Is this bit of advice making a difference? I may not have been the mother you wanted me to be or even the one you needed, because we had Martín. Martín, who always covered the gaps and patched up whatever wounds I had inflicted, whether I meant to inflict them or not. Martín, who loved you, loved me, not always in the ways either of us needed, but who tried, and when he left us, I realized the extent of the void he had once filled. I'm trying, not just because he's no longer here or because you are all the family I have left, but because *I* am here; I matter too.

"What about you, Ma? Are you ready to have a little more faith in yourself? Let go a bit?"

"Of your father?" I reply. "How can one let go? I have the memories, but what haunts me are the things we didn't get to do. Go back to Peru. See the Pacific again. Make another trip to Pucallpa with you. But of course he was so terrified of flying, who knows if we ever would have gone back."

You lean over and whisper, as if he might hear you, "He was worried that if you went, you'd want to stay."

"I might have," I confess. "But I couldn't imagine being apart from you two. It was so hard being separated from him in those early years." I pause, that sense of abandonment I had kept deep down resurfacing. "Sometimes, Yoli, I wish it had been me first."

I can see your eyes begin to fill, and I turn away. "Pa wouldn't have been able to go on without you," you say.

"Of course he could have. You find a way. But when he was alive—" I clear my throat. "I'll always wonder if I did enough. Not just if I should have made him go to the doctor sooner or given him more uña de gato. But if we could have done more together. If I could have done more while he was alive, on my own."

"You still can."

"No, Yoli. I always thought we'd have that store to go back to. That was supposed to be our future. We had so many good memories there. But that's all it was. A memory. Maybe I wouldn't have so much regret if we had done things differently. Who knows? But he deserved to live. He had his flaws, but he was a good man. He didn't deserve to suffer the way he did. Not him."

"But why *not* him?" you say. "It wasn't a punishment, Ma. Being 'good' never spared anyone from illness or accidents or death. Why would it spare him?"

"Because he and I still had so much left to live. And I know that sounds ridiculous because Death knows no age. Doesn't care if you're good or bad. None of that matters. And our marriage wasn't perfect. No marriage is. But I miss what we were as much as I miss what we still could've been. And here I am, trying to figure out who I am, if not a wife and mother."

"That's funny, isn't it? I'm still trying to be the person he wanted me to be."

"All your father ever wanted—all *I* ever wanted—is for you to be happy."

"What does that even mean, Ma?" you say, exasperated. "Do you know? Because I don't. Sometimes I think I'll be happy if I just had this job or that promotion or even got this picture right. But the happiness goalposts keep moving. Nothing seems like it's ever enough. I sometimes think that even if Pa were still here, it wouldn't be enough to make me happy."

"That might be true," I whisper. "But I can't tell you what happiness is for you. I'm still learning what it looks like now, for me." And this is the truth, hija: without Martín, without you, I'm not sure I know who or what it is that I am. Without knowing myself, how can I possibly know what it is to be happy?

"Maybe that's the problem. We're holding on to who we were. Me, trying to be his daughter. You, his wife. Maybe those versions of us are gone too."

Those words weigh on me. Perhaps I cannot let go of my former self. She lingers around me, reminding me of what could have been, of my regrets and remorse. I hear some of that in you too, a fear that we can't quite move forward without unloading our past. But maybe we need to hold on to *some* pieces of our former selves to reimagine who we are. Maybe that's why we move the rest of the night throughout the apartment without saying another word to each other, disappearing into bright rooms and dark corners, negotiating in silence with our ghosts.

The next morning, I wake to the red rose you gave me blooming on my nightstand. The sun's light filters through my bedroom window, as if I am still in a dream. A lightness comes over my body, as a voice with intense clarity makes itself known to me. One that reminds me that I am still here, not in pieces or as a shadow, but in flesh and bone, and entirely whole.

. . .

I SPEAK TO Sandeep a few days later. A storm had wrestled the night, turning the morning into an autumn afternoon. A white sky blocks the sun, and the trees rattle with the touch of a menacing breeze. I stop by Dunkin' Donuts for a hot coffee for me and a latte for Sandeep, a small offering. When I walk into his office with the coffee cup in hand, he sets down his newspaper and his eyes balloon over the frames of his glasses.

"A fancy drink," he says, opening the cup's lid and taking a gulp. "You must want something important, Miss Paula."

"I do," I admit, taking a seat across from him.

"Then you should have brought me bourbon." He laughs, but when I don't, his face grows worried. "Now you've made me nervous. What is it? You're not leaving, are you?"

"No," I say, which doesn't seem to soften the concerned look on his face. "But I do want to discuss my future here."

My future. It is much harder to say than I thought it'd be. I don't think I've ever thought about my future in the sense that it is only mine, not tied to another person. I do not recognize my voice. It's as if another person is speaking, someone who I am only now coming to know. It feels foreign to speak this way, and even more so to say it in English, a language I doubt I will ever master—one foreign language on top of another.

"I want to be a manager."

"A store manager?" he asks. "Here?"

"Wherever you may need one," I say. "Now, I know I may not have as much experience as some of the others—"

"You don't."

"And I'm older than most of the kids that work here—"

"They are all over eighteen."

"But I work hard. I've been a good employee these past few years, *and* I want to learn. This is not some job I'm doing to pass the time or because I'm bored. It may have started out that way, I admit. But I've come to love the store and I love what I do. I think—I *know*—I have what it takes to manage one."

"And you want more money."

"Well, of course I do. Why shouldn't I want more money? It's more responsibility, more time. But I can do it, and I can do a good job."

"There is more to running a store than hard work, Miss Paula. You need to know how to actually *manage* it. That means hitting sales targets, hiring the right people, managing inventory, negotiating with our partners."

"I do a lot of that," I say. "Every summer and holiday season, I help hire the right number of workers. Never too many, never too few, and I keep an eye on their schedules. I make sure we change our merchandise and that the aisles are always full and well organized, whether it is my job that day or not. Everything else, I can learn. I'm also very good with Facebook. I can update that page of yours you barely touch. We can offer discounts on there to the schools, day cares, the YMCA! Some of these people don't even know about our products unless they pass by the store. We can do more if we make actual connections with the organizations." He begins to shift in his seat, so I try another tactic. "And this would be good for you too, Sandeep! You have been talking about taking a step back from this place for as long as I've been here."

"That is mostly talk. Just like you, I have no plans to retire."

"And you shouldn't. But with my help, it'll be easier for you. You won't need to rush between this store and the one in Queens. You can take more time to do the things *you* want to do. Your wife goes to London every year to visit her sister, no? Imagine being able to travel with her to Europe. You can even spend more time at that beach house in North Carolina—"

"*South* Carolina."

"Yes, there, at the beach. Golfing. If you give me a chance to manage this store or even the other one, I know I can do it."

"But why do you want to do this?" he asks. "At our age, after working our whole lives? Do you need the money?"

"More money would be good," I say, "but I *want* to do this. I am capable. I am smart. I like what I do here, and I can do more."

I hesitate for a moment, but if I am going to be more open, more transparent and clear about what it is I want, I must put it into words. "For years, I thought my husband and I would go back to Peru when we retired. His family had a store there. It was where we first met. He may not be here anymore, but I think I would like to have that at some point. My own store, that is. But I need to learn how to run one first."

My chest opens. A longing I had held, in my breath and in my body, pours out. How I had nurtured this, harbored it like one might a secret or a newborn. Except this dream had been just that, one that I believed could be only for me and Martín, the two of us, and back there, in Peru, in *his* store, the place where it all began. Never did I imagine it only for myself; never did I imagine starting here, where it actually ended.

"You will tire of the work," Sandeep tells me. "It's not easy, not at our age."

"At our age?" I laugh. "I can understand you being tired of this. You've been doing this for decades now. It's still new to me. I'm still learning."

He tightens his mouth. His eyes slit as he nods. I sit very still, my head high. Let him size me up. The worst he can say is no, and I will simply go back to being a sales associate, no different from what I am now, though I know it is not what I will always be. Whether it is here or elsewhere, I have made my intention clear. I've decided to move forward.

"I will not pay you more while you train," he says. My heart leaps, but still, I shift forward, ready to protest, when he raises his hand. "But if in three months I see that you can actually help me run this place, then we can talk about your title and pay."

I fold my hands on my lap and swallow the lump in my throat. This is actually happening! "And what would that title and pay be?"

"Assistant manager." My heart races. "We can talk about pay in three months."

I nod, and though I don't want it to, my whole body trembles. I smile as tears start to form. Quickly, I blink them away as he clears his throat to avoid what I'm sure would be an awkward scene for both of us.

"I expect you here at this hour every morning," he says, "and you may have to close the store on more nights than you'd like. Once these kids go back to school, we'll need to find others to replace them."

"All over eighteen," I say. "I'll see who can stay part-time."

"Yes, but you'll also have to fill in the gaps."

"Like I do for every holiday and summer." He sucks his teeth, and maybe I shouldn't continue to make the point that I'm more than capable, but I've earned this. "I can do this, Sandeep."

"I believe you can," he says. "Frankly, Paula, I didn't think you wanted to. I don't know if *settled* is the right word, but that's what comes to mind when I think of most people our age. Maybe a little bored. Waiting for the end." His eyes grow large. "I'm sorry I never asked. I, of all people, should've known better." He leans on his desk, half smiles, and as if Death itself is listening, whispers, "There's still so much life yet in us, isn't there?"

• • •

THE FOLLOWING WEEK, I close the store with Shanti. She has been distant ever since Sandeep announced to the staff that I would be taking on more responsibilities at the store and that they should come to me before going to him with any questions. Most didn't seem to care. A few of the women joked that they'd now call me jefa, but not Shanti. She tells me nothing is wrong, even though she prefers to play with her phone instead of chatting when things are slow during our shift. She doesn't ask if I need help sorting or folding the products. Even now she rushes to her car and doesn't offer me a ride home. She only points behind me and says, "There's your friend," as she locks the gate.

Vicente is by the lamppost, holding ChaCha. He walks toward me the instant Shanti turns toward her car. He wears his mischievous grin, along with a white cotton shirt, khaki shorts, and those black socks from aisle 2. Even under the rose evening sky, or maybe because of it, there are glimpses of the man I knew years ago. I wish I didn't crave his presence. I wish I didn't miss it.

"How is your arm?" he asks.

"Good."

"You look good. Working late, I see."

"Remember how you asked if I was happy with the bonus?" I say. "I wasn't. So I told Sandeep I wanted to be a manager."

His eyes widen. "And he said yes?"

"We're going to try it out for three months to see how it goes, but he seems happy so far."

"That's wonderful!" He steps forward, but I stiffen as he leans in for a hug. "I thought you might want to stop working after that fall. I should have known you were more ambitious than that. And of course he said yes! You're one of the best workers he has."

"So is Shanti," I say. "I don't think she's too happy about the change."

"I'm sure she wants to manage a store too. She'll get over it and you can be friends again."

"Do you think it's that easy? That people just get over things like they never happened?"

"Well, I'm here now and you haven't told me to fuck off."

"I already did. But then you hang around me and my daughter at the festival like nothing happened, and now you're here. Do you think I got over it?"

"I was hoping you did."

"I haven't. And you and Renata were at the festival together. I thought it'd be inappropriate to ask with my daughter there. She was having such a good time. But I assume you two are back together?"

"What do you want me to say?" he nearly shouts. "I've spent almost forty years with this woman. We're in our sixties. We have a child together. We lost a daughter. I can't leave her."

"And I can't be someone's mistress. Whether that's in their bed or in their head."

"I'm not asking you to do that."

"No, you're asking me to be your friend, and right now I can't do that, either." I walk faster, but he takes ahold of my good arm and calls out my name. Hearing it from his lips makes me tremble, and I find myself wanting to say all the things I promised myself I'd never say to a man. That I can't recall ever saying to Martín. I was not in the habit of talking of love; I think you know this. Not with you, not with my own husband. And certainly not in the end. What was the point then? He did not need to know how much pain his absence would cause or the regret I had for not telling him all these years, despite our mistakes, of all the ways I loved him. Or how much I hated that our time together was ending.

Now here is Vicente, who fills a void. Vicente, who makes me feel like it is possible to love again. Differently, but still love, and who I know I cannot be with.

"Stop!" I shout, jerking my arm free and finally, mercifully, letting go of so much that I had held in. "Yoli and I are leaving. We are moving. I don't know where yet, but we're leaving the neighborhood, and I don't want to talk about it. And as much as it hurts to leave, we have to. We need to. *I* need to because what I feel for you . . ." It takes me a moment to regain my composure. "What I feel for you is something I have not felt for anyone in a very long time. To you, this is just a friendship. Or at least that's how you want it to be. And I value our friendship. It's one of the most important ones of my life. But if you care for me in any way, I need you to let me go."

This may be the first time I've ever been clear with anyone about anything, except perhaps that conversation with Sandeep, because Vicente steps back and nods, and suddenly I feel like I can breathe. I will miss him. Maybe he is right—maybe with time, I can get past the void I want him to fill and instead accept him for what he *can* offer. Maybe I'd rather have his friendship than not have him in my life at all. It is a question I don't feel the need or desire to answer now, and that alone is liberating. I walk home, leaving him on the corner with ChaCha. I don't turn back, not even as her cries dwindle to a whimper.

• • •

WHEN YOU WERE eleven, I had an affair. Not a physical one, no. That was impossible with a child who watched my every move and a husband who was with me nearly every moment I wasn't at work. Martín would pick me up from work during the week; on Saturdays, we ran errands as a family—laundry, shopping at Western Beef, separating clothes to send to his nieces in Peru. On Sundays, we headed to the park.

One particularly hot Sunday afternoon, as Martín played a soccer match, I brought Vicente a bottle of water, as I often did, but this time, we talked about more than just the players and the match and bingo. He was distracted and kept fidgeting with his pencil. When we heard a cheer, he asked me who scored the last goal. I didn't know. We could tell who did when we saw the players huddle around Cabezón.

At that point, he noted the score, threw the pencil on the table, and sat back defeated. It wasn't the match, he told me. He had to sell his house, the very first one he bought with his brother in Elmhurst. His brother needed money. It didn't seem like a huge loss to me; after all, he had all those other properties he bought with that settlement money from the bus accident. I didn't say this, of course.

Later that summer, after I had spent years caring for Elsie, she died. It was expected, but like everything you know is coming, no matter how ready you think you are, you never truly are. Her absence made me realize just how much I need to feel needed. What a terrible thing that is—to feel validated only if someone else needs you.

While I waited for a new assignment, Martín lost his weekend job cleaning the Citibank in Ridgewood. We tried to never spend more than we could, but that year, we had sent more money to Peru than we usually did: money to your aunt for the store; some to a cousin who needed knee surgery; some for an investment in a plot of land in Pucallpa that turned out to be nothing but a scam. The lack of money squeezed our necks. You were on the phone with the gas company and debt collectors. They were unmoved by the voice of a child. It was easier to have you pick up the phone than it was for us to deal with the shame and the pressure, and for that, I am sorry. For the most part, we *did* watch our money, but whenever we lost a job, the anxiety dried up my mouth. I took to cleaning, sorting—anything I could do around the apartment to keep my mind occupied. Praying to La Virgen when no one was looking. Martín didn't want to speak of it. My pessimism, he'd say, didn't help the situation. Just have faith, he insisted.

And I can pray all I want, but was it so surprising then that I needed to get those worries, that anxiety, out of me? That I wanted someone to listen. I had no intention of sharing our financial troubles with Vicente. It made me look weak. It would've shamed Martín; he'd see it as a betrayal.

I told Vicente anyway. He listened. In the background we heard the referee's whistle, the players yelling on the field, the laughter of the women in the distance. To that noise, I added my anxiety about paying rent and finding another job. He put his hand over mine for the very first time. It wouldn't be the last. He was sure I'd been in this situation before, he told me. We all had, and we came out of them. We could do it again.

You see, he said just what Martín had said: to have faith. But unlike Martín, Vicente added the practicalities. Did I consider cutting back on groceries, cable TV, driving the car? Did I stop sending money to Peru? See! That has to stop, he told me. And even when he stopped talking, his hand continued to stay on mine. I didn't want him to let go.

His words and touch stayed with me during the week. I recalled them in the mornings, before I called the agency to check on a new work assignment and whenever Martín left for walks that seemed more and more like a retreat from me, from us. My mind kept going to Vicente, and I had to remind myself that we were just friends. He saw me as nothing more. That was clear from how he touched his wife, if ever lightly, whenever she was near, and from their kisses even when people were watching. But at the end of those Sunday nights, after a full day with him, I grieved. The length of an entire week loomed; a week that turned into months in the winter, when there were no soccer matches, and I'd see him only at the occasional party he'd host in his apartment.

All of that ended the following summer, on a Saturday in June, when Daniela drowned in the pool across the park.

Years later, when Vicente heard that Martín came home from the hospital, he called.

"He wanted to see how you were doing," I told your father as I sat on the edge of our bed, checking his drains. By then the windows of wakefulness had shortened, and he was able to stay alert for only an hour before falling asleep again. I spoke as much as I could, never wanting the silence to linger for too long in the room. When I mentioned Vicente, I did so the way I spoke of everything and everyone else that had come to pass that day, a more local version of the local news—the weather, updates from former coworkers and high school classmates who had called to check in on him, what new information had come out about that man with the Peruvian mother who had killed that boy, su tocayo, down in Florida. He grunted at any updates of the latter, sometimes wondered why so-and-so even bothered calling, then asked me to thank them.

But when I mentioned Vicente, Martín lifted his head off the pillow. "Did he ask for me or for you?" he managed to say. He had never been rude to Vicente, even though he had always suspected a crush, which he sometimes teased me about. He probably thought I could joke about *his* crush too. Maybe I should have. But Vicente had all the things Martín had imagined for us and more. Not just one house, but several, even though he owed them to an accident. Two children, even though he had lost one. Respect from the community. And he was alive and healthy. He still had possibilities. Maybe he resented Vicente. A part of me did.

But it wasn't this that made me regret mentioning Vicente to Martín then. To think that there was a time when the days ahead of me seemed vaster than an ocean because of Vicente's absence. A man who did not love me, but who I was infatuated with. Whenever our phone rang with calls from "unknown" callers or envelopes inked in red piled up on the kitchen table or Martín and you retreated into your own silence, I'd tell myself it was okay. I had Sundays, with its music, the matches, the moments of stillness that often came whenever I sat in that chair beside Vicente. I had Vicente. I could tolerate those rough days because Sunday would always come.

But as I sat beside Martín, I feared the days that *were* to come. I could not imagine an hour without him, let alone what was left of my life. To think that once I could not fathom a week between me and a man I did not love; how I longed for that one day of rest. After he got sick, I'd tell Martín to rest, and he'd ask why. He had an eternity to rest. Was I, then, condemned to a lifetime of grief? Those last days, I feared the hours and all the days that were to come, and what I would be without him.

25

FLORES

THE BOARD MEETING TAKES PLACE IN THE MIDDLE OF ONE OF THOSE WEATHER disturbances that crawls its way through the South, then descends almost without warning on our frail city. At least that's how everyone is acting this morning. Physical and parental infrastructures have collapsed, like they do with every storm. Jon's stuck in traffic at the entrance to the tunnel; Nik is still waiting for the nanny who's traveling all the way from Woodside to the Upper West Side; and everyone else is stuck on either an A or a C train as the storm floods the tunnels and platforms along the 8th Avenue line.

Jasmine relays these excuses to me at the offsite space she booked weeks ago in Lower Manhattan just for this meeting. We needed the larger space to accommodate all the attendees and for privacy, both of which we lacked in our office. She circles the conference room table, straightening the notepads and pens she's laid out (mostly for decoration). She's been here since eight A.M. setting up the food and coffee, checking the dongles and tech, making sure that none of the pens have run dry. The meeting's scheduled for ten, and we've got the room only until one, which is when we have lunch reservations at La Piccola a few blocks west. She fans herself with one of the notepads, looks at her watch. "We were supposed to start fifteen minutes ago."

Her anxiety is contagious. Not that I wasn't already on edge when I walked in. "Look, at least most of the board is here," I whisper, "even the ones who don't give a shit anymore."

"We need the fucking leadership," she grits.

She has a point. Most of the board—made up of the founders and other investors (including Ethan)—are here, except for Eric. The leadership's backup crew, including Max and me, is here too, in case someone has a question a department head can't talk their way out of. Better that we look unprepared rather than an executive of the company. But how important is this meeting if the CEO and other leaders aren't here on time? If it's not a priority to them, why should it be a priority to anyone else?

"At least we can count on Max to kiss ass until they get here," says Jasmine as Max regales the others with details about his family home in the Berkshires. "Must be nice to have a granddaddy with all that money. One day, though. J.Lo."

"J.Lo," I mumble.

Her eyebrows crinkle. "With energy, please. Otherwise, you'll jinx it."

She opens a bottle of the alkaline water specifically requested by one of the board members and takes a massive gulp just as Nina makes her way toward us. She kisses my cheek, a gesture that catches me off guard and makes Jasmine choke on her water. Ethan catches up behind her with a plate of fruit. "Hello, Jasmine," he says, then turns to me. "Good morning, Flores," which is more shocking than Nina's greeting.

Just then, Eric enters the room. "Hello, hello!" he shouts. He's more formally dressed than usual, sporting a fitted white button-down shirt, gray embossed denim, and a pair of gold-star-patched sneakers. Ethan takes ahold of Eric's hand, pulls him in for a quick hug—the equivalent of the kiss on the cheek his sister gave me. Eric quickly makes himself a plate of bagels and fruit while Jasmine connects my computer to the conference room screen. The center one mirrors what's on my laptop, while the other two show a blow-up version of the Bowl's logo: an outline of a fishbowl reminiscent of a horseshoe, with an oval and a triangle flushed to the right to represent a fish, and two bubbles floating just above it.

Eric joins Max's circle, and Max in turn pats him on the back. A part of me wants to shout, *Careful! The guy's about to stab you there*. Max is going to take those numbers and plunge them into Eric as though they were knives. And I'm handing them to Max.

Sweat crawls down my hairline and onto my cheek. Within minutes, the rest of the Bowlers arrive in quick succession, as if someone had pulled the stopper from the drain, and the water that had backed up and arrested most of the city now had a clear unobstructed path. Two investors confirm they are dialing in, so the meeting begins.

We start as we always do, with a brief welcome from Eric that is essentially your standard feedback sandwich: first he expresses pride for what the company has accomplished since our last meeting; then he acknowledges (briefly) the challenges we face when it comes to growth; and finally he ends with an upbeat view of the future the company can have with everyone's support.

He turns to me with a clear directive.

"Hit it, Flores!"

• • •

ERIC RACES THROUGH the first few slides, explaining that our focus is on expansion through the acquisition of Fisk & Tanks and our hospital partners, before turning it over to Jon, who gives the financial review. No one wants to hear a long-winded explanation about the numbers, so he looks back at the first half of the year, highlighting our accelerated growth for new customers in the first quarter, but glosses over the hard stuff: how that growth didn't meet our target and then decelerated in the second quarter. The only person who wants to know why the numbers flattened is Nina.

"It's historically a slow quarter for us," says Jon, without further explanation, then immediately goes into afishionado membership fees and promotional money from manufacturers, all with the enthusiasm and optimism of a game show host. So much so that you don't notice how he whisks through our markdowns and the hefty salaries we pay our engineers and C-staff (even the ones we had to pay to go away). Before Nina could ask another question, Eric reminds us that every graph that dips south is an opportunity—a chance, for example, to beef up our membership benefits or fine-tune our assortment with more exotic fish and livelier accessories.

More important than that, he goes on, there are still many hearts to lift and untapped customers, including the kid who wants to put together his very first aquarium, the tachycardic banker who needs something soothing to look at when he gets home from work, the restaurant manager who wants to create the right ambiance for his diners. Growth opportunities abound, and Nik and Max are going to get into that next.

And that's when Max's face flushes. The original slides for the marketing team highlighted their plans for a national television commercial, the December subway takeover, and the sponsorship of one of the largest restaurant expos in the country, with no mention of cost. And that's when Eric would ask for more money.

But the slides that I replaced in this deck include those exorbitant costs. Factor in the expense of building out Fisk & Tanks' operation in the Midwest, the additional hiring we need on the operations side, and we'd run out of cash by the end of the year. Max is ready to call out the flaws in Eric's plan because the real issue isn't that we need money, but that we don't know how to manage it.

All I have to do is click, and it'll all be there for everyone to see.

Maybe it's Eric's speech that gives me pause. Maybe it's the skepticism already visible on Nina's face or the indifference on everyone else's. Or even Max's blotchy neck. I wonder if he's lost his conviction. Or maybe I'm just tired of doing everyone else's bidding.

"My computer's acting up," I say, pounding the keyboard. I unplug from the monitor so that only I can see my laptop's screen. "Just give me a second." I close the presentation and find the file I had originally circulated. I scroll to the slide where I had cut Max off, making sure the ones that follow are the originals.

"You ready?" he asks. I tell myself that I'm doing him a favor, even as his eyes plead with mine. He looks up at the screen, and his face and neck become a coral reef. "Are you sure you have the right document up, Flores?"

Jon's eyes dart between us. "I think you're good, Max," he says.

. . .

IT'S BEEN MORE than a week since the meeting, and Max still won't talk to me. He ignores my ChitChats about lunch and coffee, even though I apologize and offer to explain what happened. I sneak a peek at his calendar and see that he's traveling, first to a conference in Los Angeles, then to another in San Francisco, and finally to Chicago for a meeting with our ad agency. He won't be back in the office for another week. I stalk the other channels on Chit-Chat for signs of him, but there are none, not even a comment or an emoji on the debate over whether a song he loathes should be crowned the song of the summer. His Instagram posts are stale. The last post is a picture of a slice of buffalo chicken pizza that was taken on the Fourth of July—well over a month ago now—where he tagged Vicki and Jacob Riis beach. I even check her page for more recent signs of him, but her last post is a throwback Thursday beach selfie taken that same weekend.

When Friday night hits, Jasmine and I head out for a happy hour drink, which turns into several happy hours, so I text him.

I couldn't do it

OK so maybe Eric could be better, but he had my back
when no one else did

And yeah, Jon can be a dick sometimes, but he looks out for
me too

Plus I don't have much faith in Nik

And if you just looked at Nina's face! She's not buying any
of Eric's bs anyway. She's gonna make sure things change
no matter what

Let her fix this mess

I'm drunk when I send these, each sentence in a separate bubble, close to midnight, after a guy I'd made out with at the second bar follows us to Madame X. It's not until the next morning that my texts are read. He never did reply.

. . .

IT'S MONDAY AND I'm at my desk eating a salad from the deli down the block when Jasmine texts me.

Something's up . . .

I haven't seen her yet today. She hasn't moved from her post at the front desk, and her status on ChitChat has been set to busy. She usually doesn't care if anyone sees our ChitChats, but if she's texting me, it's because she doesn't want legal's or data security's nose in our business.

The head of HR, she tells me, asked her to free up Bio for the rest of the afternoon. Not an unusual request—folks on the top of the totem pole often ask her to move meetings around just to have that room. But she hates having to shuffle people around and explain they have to move their twenty-person meeting to a room that holds only a dozen and that the rest would have to move to dial-in or sit on the floor because a lone C-staff member needs privacy.

This isn't one of those meetings.

He's in there . . . she goes on . . . *and legal just walked in*

So someone's getting tossed. A thrill travels up my spine. She must be salivating at this bit of gossip too, unfolding as we speak. The last time this happened, an engineer was let go for drinking on the job and shutting down the website for several hours. Another Bowler was fired for having manufacturers send free aquarium samples to her home, which she bedazzled then resold on her Etsy store.

We speculate on who it could be. Did the coke-snorting accountant finally mess up? Did that QA analyst share one too many bar cart videos? Did the romance between the head of operations and a customer service manager go sour?

Nah can't be that, Jasmine asserts. They're both in Mexico, on separate vacations, or so they say. And whatever's going down is going down today, in that room.

I look up from my desk to see who's missing, but it's lunchtime. Most Bowlers have stepped out to grab food or are eating in the cafeteria. Except that Max and Nik walk in. I knew he'd be back from his trip today, but figured he'd spend the rest of the afternoon working from home. I'm glad he came in; we can nip this in the bud today. He can ignore my texts all he wants, but we work together. He can't pretend I don't exist. I want things to go back to the way they were. He'd love this bit of gossip, and though it squarely falls within mine and Jasmine's FrieNDA, I have to make some sort of peace offering. This news will be public soon anyway. She won't mind if I share.

I wait until he settles into his desk before I ChitChat.

Hey, I write.

My cell phone buzzes.

Hi, he replies.

I turn to my phone. Jasmine's one-line message is a string of exclamation points. I go back to my computer screen and my Chit-Chat with Max.

Can you talk? I ask. My heart pounds.

My cell phone screen is still lit. I can see the typing bubbles appear, disappear, then reappear. I wish Jasmine would just spill it already.

Sure. Coffee? 3pm?

I give his message a thumbs-up. My body relaxes back into my chair. This'll be good. We can clear the air. I can apologize properly for what happened, make him understand that I think we'll get our way anyway, without either of us having to burn any bridges.

My phone buzzes again. I read Jasmine's message twice to make sure my eyes aren't playing tricks on me.

Starr's in there now!

I stand and look back toward the designers' workspace. Starr's desk is in fact empty. I wonder if anyone else has noticed her absence. I catch Max's eyes, pretend to stretch, and sit back down.

I bombard Jasmine with questions.

Anyone else in there?
    Just HR + Legal
Did she look upset?
    No
Did she have her stuff with her?
    Laptop

Half an hour later, Starr's back at her desk, all smiles and chatting with another designer, as if she didn't just have a meeting with two of the most nerve-racking teams at the company.

Then another text.

Nik just went in!

My eyes pop, though it wouldn't surprise me if Nik had actually crossed the line with Starr. What was he doing taking her out for drinks at swanky bars in Manhattan anyway? And taking shots with her at the summer party? It took her a year to get the job here, so if there's one thing that's true about Starr, it's that she's always advocating for herself. If he tried something, she'd speak up.

I'm too distracted to concentrate on work. I head to the bathroom and take a good look around the floor to see if anyone else realizes there's something amiss, but everyone's in their own bubble. There's the regular banter in the pantry and the conference rooms, overstuffed with people at the tables and on the floor, balancing their laptops on their knees. I come across one conference room where there are only two people, looking intensely at each other, but when I walk back to my desk, I realize they're on speakerphone, likely having a difficult conversation with whoever is on the other end. In the main work area, people are chatting on their cell phones. Others gather around one desk or another. The TV displays the latest congressional hearing. A typical day at the Bowl.

Maybe Nik got a warning. Maybe it wasn't Nik at all—maybe Starr was put on a performance improvement plan. Or she's unhappy about her comp and asking for more. But then why would legal be involved?

I spot Max talking with one of the data scientists. At least this is good gossip, something that'll break the tension between us when we talk later. I can explain why I backed out during the board meeting and then we can speculate on what the whole Starr, Nik, legal, and HR meetings this afternoon were about until we find out what really happened, which we will. There are no secrets at the Bowl.

I get back to my desk and wonder if I should message Starr about what's going on. She might get mad at Jasmine, though, for telling me. Carl asks about a formula on his screen, but I can't make sense of the numbers. I check my cell phone, but Jasmine hasn't texted. I'm about to put my headphones on when I hear Nik's voice. He's back at his desk and, like Starr, seems completely unfazed by whatever conversation he had with HR and legal.

If he's not getting booted, then who is?

Minutes later, my cell goes off.

O M G

The all-caps and spacing send a tingle down my spine. My body stiffens as I brace myself for Jasmine's next text.

Max

I shoot up. His desk is empty, his laptop gone. His seat is spun out toward the hallway that leads to the front of the office and that conference room.

"You good, Flores?" asks Jon.

I take off Pa's jacket and fan myself with my hand. I can't recall ever feeling this warm in the office. "Yeah, I'm fine."

I don't bother messaging him when three P.M. rolls around. By four P.M., I open our ChitChat thread and see the words that mark the end of one's journey here at the Bowl.

THIS ACCOUNT HAS BEEN DEACTIVATED.

26

FLORES

"JON TOLD ME ABOUT STARR," ERIC SAYS AS I TAKE A SEAT IN BIO, WHERE Max had also been summoned to earlier this afternoon. After his account was deactivated, I walked past his desk to see if he was really gone. His desk was still marked by his presence: his Moleskine notebook, the bottle of champagne his team had given him for his birthday months ago, the framed pictures of him and Vicki. I assumed that by then everyone who mattered knew he'd been cut, including Jon, but he said nothing when I stepped away from my desk and was completely stoneface when I returned, even though I couldn't hide my worry. I had to press cold water onto my face just to get my blood circulating and to stop myself from vomiting.

When I got back to my seat, there was a ChitChat from Jasmine. An ominous sign, since she had been texting me all day. Could I meet Eric in Bio in fifteen minutes?

So here we are. He's alone; no one from HR or legal is in the room, which momentarily settles my stomach.

"You okay?" he asks, and I hate how terrible I am at hiding any sort of emotion.

"No," I say. I clear my throat and straighten. "My friend just got fired."

"So you don't know anything about Starr?" he asks. "In that case, I'll tell you what I can. You understand it's an HR matter, so . . ." He taps his fingers on the table, interlacing his fingers as he decides what—and how much, I assume—he wants to share. My heart races. "Starr told Jon that something happened between her and Max. Jon came to me. I told him to go to HR. He did. Legal got involved, did their thing." He pauses, and his face softens. "Remember how I said that if I felt someone had to go, I wouldn't hesitate. Believe me when I tell you that he had to go."

My mouth dries out. I cannot move. What could've happened between them? Max, who seems so devoted to Vicki, it's almost nauseating. And *Starr*? She never once said anything to me or Jasmine about him, that I can recall, or even hinted that she had any real issues with Max other than she thought he was a suck-up, but didn't everyone? And she confided in Jon? None of it makes sense.

"Anyway, that's not really the reason I want to talk to you." He leans back in his chair. I'm struck by just how much he's aged. The streaks of gray, the delicate skin under his eyes, the laugh lines carved around his mouth. Had I completely missed just how much this place had worn him out too?

"I knew about his plans," he says grimly, and I'm no longer searching his face for a glimpse of the familiar because at this moment, I see the wall between us. He is not my college study buddy who ate my dad's empanadas or who rode the E train with me after class. He's not the guy I made out with sloppily after a bad breakup. He is a source of neither inspiration nor doubt. Instead, there is a distance that, up until this moment, I realize I chose to overlook for the sake of an old friendship. Don't we all do this?

"I know you were in on it. Swapping out the slides." He waits for me to react, but I don't move. I barely breathe. "What was the point, Monica? To make me look bad?"

For a moment, I sense his disappointment, and though my instinct is to apologize for hurting someone, it isn't this time. He knows me well enough, I think, to know that my intent was never to cause him pain or embarrassment. I simply wanted to make sure I'd be okay, or at least try. "Not exactly," I admit. "The point was to get the board to do something."

He scoffs, and that hint of disappointment turns to anger on the very next breath. "A few slides about how shitty you think my plans are and what? You thought they'd replace me? These people invested in me just as much as they invested their money in this company. Did you honestly think it'd be that easy?"

"No," I say. "We thought it could at least plant the seed."

"Because you think I need to go?"

"You're burning through cash," I say. Then, as if those on the other side of the floor could hear us, I whisper, "We don't have much runway left. We'll have to lay off people soon if things don't change, or worse. And I can't keep spinning stories for you, Eric. I want the time I spent here to count for something. I know you do too! What you've done is remarkable, but at some point you need to recognize when it's time to step aside. And I'm not just saying this as someone who has a real financial interest in this place. Who's invested time and energy, just like you, just like a lot of people here. I'm saying this as your friend."

"My *friend*? Let me tell you something as a friend. You may think you know when it's time for me to call it quits, but you have no idea. You have no idea what it's like to run a business or to be responsible for dozens of people and their livelihoods. You don't know what it's like to have everyone tell you that you can't do it because you don't have the experience, the talent, the training, the funding, the pedigree. And I guess I don't even have the support of my own team. Or my so-called friends. You have no clue because you've never been in my position. You can't possibly understand this kind of pressure. You never even bothered to ask me how I'm doing, *friend*. But you think it's time for me to go. You think you can decide when I need to move on when the truth is, Flores, you should be asking yourself that."

"I didn't go through with it," I say.

"But you were going to. Nik said you had the slides, and then in the middle of your presentation, your laptop freezes? You suddenly changed your mind?"

My eyes widen.

"Yeah, Nik," he says. "This whole idea to try to get me out? Max told Nik that an investor had approached him about making changes to the leadership. Nik went along to see which investor was behind it, and which employees, besides Max. I never thought you'd be one of them." I so badly want to vomit on Jasmine's ocean floor. "We've known each other for a long time, Flores. We've been through some really rough times. When things were hard, we did what we could to be there for each other. And I'm still here for you, no matter what. I want you to know that." He lifts his head, his eyes bulging. "But as a friend, I gotta tell you. You gotta go."

• • •

"I WAS PLAYED," Max whispers over the phone. It's been two days since we were both given the option to resign from the Bowl or be fired for cause. With the former, I still had a few months to exercise my options; with the latter, I'd lose all right to any that had vested. It wasn't much of a choice.

That evening, after my talk with Eric, I was allowed to return to my desk to collect the few items I had there. Max wasn't. His items, he was told, would be collected and delivered to him in the next day or so. His picture frames, seat cushion, personal humidifier, and the diffuser with the bottles of his essential oils had all been collected, tossed in a cardboard box, and delivered to his apartment just this afternoon. The champagne bottle he got for his birthday wasn't in there, he told me.

At first he didn't want to talk, not even after I texted that I had been booted too. Not that I had much to say, either, if I'm honest. I just liked knowing I wasn't alone. All those years and this is where I end up. Even when I thought I did the right thing, here I am, unemployed, embarrassed, still listening to the person I let into my head. Truth is, I can't blame Max for what happened. I wanted Eric to go. Maybe Jon too. I just didn't want to lose my job. Then again, I didn't want to pretend anymore.

I have enough in my savings to cover three months of living expenses, if I put my student loans on forbearance and negotiate a little with the bank on my personal loans, which is the first thing I do. In a few days, I'll update my résumé, upgrade my LinkedIn account, and send a mass email to friends and former colleagues letting them know that I'm looking for work. I can't file for unemployment benefits just yet. I don't even want to think about whether I can afford to exercise my options when the time comes.

I don't reach out to anyone at the Bowl and ignore the texts from Jasmine, Jon, and the rest of my team, even Starr. I want nothing to do with the company. I hate the place. I hate my landlord. I hate Navient, Chase, Discover, my jacked-up teeth, and fucking CareCredit.

I hate that I cry about it.

I want to hate Max too, but I can't, not even as he tells me what it is that got him fired.

"It was this thing with Starr," he says. A *thing*, not a real relationship; something that happened years back, when they both worked at Canto.

"You knew each other?" I say. Neither of them had ever mentioned it. It was one of those places that churned out employees like any other global platform. Besides, Starr had interned there one summer years ago. Max rarely spoke of the place.

He claims it had been casual, a summer fling that was over by Labor Day, when he left for another job. "It was ancient history. It never affected how I treated her at the Bowl. Never. But she thought I was the reason we didn't give her a job offer sooner and that I was bullying her. You know we didn't have the money to hire her full-time."

"Yes, but, Max, you were definitely harsh on her work, and you totally excluded her from your team happy hours," I say, recalling what she'd told me months ago. It's why she was so dead set on drinks with Nik, even if it was just the two of them. The memories pile on: Starr crying at the summer party, the way she made herself scarce whenever Max was around—in the pantry, in the reception area, at our weekly company meetings.

Why hadn't I seen it? Why hadn't she confided in me?

"Her work isn't great, Flores," he scoffs. "And I never meant to keep her out of team outings. She just . . ." He hesitates, then whispers into the phone. "Vicki would come sometimes, and it'd get awkward with Starr there."

"Then maybe don't bring your fiancée to a work outing," I shout, "and don't mess around with your coworker!"

• • •

"I HEARD THEY were still hooking up," Jasmine tells me that night over the phone. "They definitely did at Canto, and even after. Whenever he came to New York. Right up until he got engaged. ¡Vete, lava los platos!" she yells to her son. I hear a fork clank against a dish, then she whispers, "They were fucking."

"How do you know?"

"You're not the only one I have a FrieNDA with," she says.

"But you could've told me *something*."

"Come on, Flores. We all thought you might have a thing with the guy."

• • •

"WE HOOKED UP a few times," Starr tells me, after first expressing total shock at my being cut. I told her Eric didn't trust me anymore because of my friendship with Max, and that I can understand why. She does too. I don't expect her to tell me anything, but now that it's over, she spills. "But we never hooked up at the Bowl, just to be clear. It was at Canto. Summer after freshman year. I was an intern, he was an account manager. I remember thinking I was so lucky that he even knew who I was! I mean, he was cute and smart and so nice. Everyone had a crush on him. I was young. Like, really young. But obviously it wasn't love or anything. Anyway, I got another internship, and he moved to Chicago and that was it."

Except I know that wasn't it. Jasmine said they hooked up even after he moved back to New York, but I don't pry.

"I honestly never expected to see him again," she goes on, "but then Jasmine's like, 'Let me tell you about this new guy,' and seriously, I was shocked when I found out he was hired. Shocked! He seemed way too buttoned up for the place. I was nervous, obviously. We hadn't seen each other in a while. But I messaged him on LinkedIn because I didn't want things to be weird, you know, and we went back and forth and everything was fine! And I was honestly really looking forward to having him at the Bowl. Like, *really.* I mean, he'd done so many cool and clever things since he left Canto. He's very smart, professional, and I thought, *Finally, a real leader!* you know?"

But then a couple of months into his role at the Bowl, he began critiquing her designs. First at her desk and then, mockingly, at their weekly team happy hours. He had invited his fiancée to one such happy hour and then another. By then, the criticism and jokes were starting to grate. So during one of these team outings, Starr mentioned to Vicki that she also used to work at Canto, and asked if Max had ever mentioned it because they knew each other well.

"I was a little tipsy," she explains, and after that, Max's critiques were no longer confined to her desk or poorly timed jokes at happy hour. He made them in team meetings, even cross-functional ones. "We're supposed to be on the same team, but he was belittling my work in front of other leaders," she said. The happy hours got smaller, more selective, until she was invited only to the larger, cross-functional outings.

And then came the summer party, where Max charmed everyone, from the folks setting up the food trays to the investors, showing off his fiancée like that somehow put him a cut above the rest of the single, unattached messes drinking on the floor. Vicki wouldn't even look at her until they both ended up at the bar.

"She started interrogating me," Starr goes on. "When did I work at Canto, if I ever worked with Max since the place is so big. Basically, she wanted to know how well I knew him." She pauses, takes a long, exasperated breath. "He was being a jerk to me, Flores. So I just told her."

"Told her what?"

She pauses. "That her fiancé tastes like cinnamon gum."

Tastes. "Is that why you were crying in the bathroom?"

"No," she says. "He came looking for me. I tried to walk away, but he grabbed my wrist really hard and told me to never speak to his fiancée again. I told Jon the next day, and I wanted to tell you too. There, in the pantry. But, I don't know, you seemed sad about your ex, and you and Max are close. I wasn't sure if you'd believe me."

Even though Jon told her to go to HR, she thought it was pointless. Max seemed too valuable to lose and no one would take her word against his. So she took Jon's advice and got Max to admit what he did to her in writing.

"I got it on ChitChat," she says, but doesn't offer to show me the messages, and I don't ask to see them, even though I want to, badly. But there was enough in the messages to report it to HR. "They told me they'd investigate. That day he was fired, HR called me into Bio, just to let me know it was happening. He'd been traveling, but they asked him to come into the office. Apparently, there was other stuff going on too. Honestly, the whole thing happened faster than I thought it would."

"They waited until after the board meeting," I mutter. I'm too embarrassed to tell her that I was involved with the "other stuff," though I'm sure she already knows.

"I really didn't think I could tell you, Flores. But Jon said he was going to talk to you. Believe me, I never meant to get you wrapped up into this."

"This isn't your fault," I say. "I'm out for another reason entirely. I'm honestly just pissed I didn't see any of it."

Maybe I didn't want to.

27

PAULA

FOR DAYS, YOU SAY NOTHING ABOUT LOSING YOUR JOB. YOU ISOLATE IN YOUR room, watching television, eating, drinking, or with your phone in your palm, your headphones on, listening to whoever is on the other end of the line. This morning, you went to yoga with Manuelito. A free class, you say.

I reheat the leftover sopa de gallina, boil some rice. You sit at the table, but don't touch or even bother to look at the food. You always seem so strong to me, hija, that I never ask what hurts. I always believed that you'd come to me if you really needed me. Which is why I struggle even when I ask now, "What happened, Yoli?"

I expect a "Nothing, Ma," but instead, you sit back in that chair and whisper, "You were right. I trusted someone I shouldn't have."

My impulse is to say, "Te lo dije," because so-called friends don't exist in the kinds of places you've worked, and you should know this because how many times did people try to make you look bad or take credit for your work, all the lies and hypocrisy and behind-the-scenes scheming. You got too comfortable and made the mistake of trusting. What did you expect?

But I hold my tongue. I wouldn't want to hear those things, either, no matter who said them or their intentions, not even if they came from someone who loves me.

Instead, I find myself reaching for your hand. You wipe your eyes. "I trusted people," you whisper, "like some trusted me before. And I messed up."

I pull my chair in closer. "If you mean Vasily, you didn't love him," I say, and your eyes become moons. I was once a woman in love, Yoli. I wanted a life with your father, no matter what that looked like. Here or in Peru—Mars, for all I cared!—it didn't matter. I did not see that certainty with Vasily, but how could I tell you this then? What I saw was a young woman swept in the current, riding it without questioning if this is what she really wanted. But when the time came to make the decision of whether to follow him or your instinct, you were right to trust yourself. "If you mean this job, well. You deserve better."

As you catch your breath, I dare to ask the one question that I, for the first time in my life, have only just begun to ask myself. One that, I hope, we never stop asking because if we did, we would be resigning ourselves to our circumstances instead of making use of them. "Tell me, hija. What now?"

28

FLORES

I FALL INTO A FAMILIAR PATTERN IN THE DAYS AFTER I LEAVE THE BOWL. I shower, twice daily. I lie in bed in a tank top and shorts watching a string of movies inspired by Jane Austen books, simultaneously loving and loathing Jennifer Ehle, Keira Knightley, and Gwyneth Paltrow, but of course adoring Colin Firth, Alan Rickman, and Greg Wise, then cursing that inclination to ignore the faults of men, even fictional ones—except Colonel Brandon, who can do no wrong—all while I sip on Sancerre that's been in my fridge for who knows how long, until I finally turn to the bottle of champagne I took from Max's desk.

Jon has the audacity to call, saying he tried to warn me and that he's sorry things ended the way they did. Eric will get over it, he tells me. I don't care if he does.

Fuck him. Fuck all of them.

I linger in this state for a week. My mother soothes me with fresh smoothies, pollo a la brasa, and endless ají verde sauce from Pio Pio. She even leaves powdered donuts from Dunkin' on the kitchen table and gets the coffeemaker going before heading to work. She doesn't coax me to eat or leave the bedroom. Only once did she suggest I join her at the gym, after I left for a yoga class with Manny. But she didn't insist when I declined, nor did she ask about that yoga class, and I am grateful that she somehow understands that I need this. I need time to let go—of the job, the people, the habits I picked up along the way. Release all that I am feeling, so I can think clearly.

This morning, a late summer rain lingers outside my window. My thoughts go to my father. I wonder how he contemplated letting go. Did he think of the people he loved or the moments when he felt most alive? Did he wonder about the life he might have had or what lay ahead? If there was anything there at all? Or did he cling to a memory, one that gave him hope, that hinted at the possibilities? Like that photograph with his mother and mine.

Maybe this is why I turn to the camera now. It is a way for me to seek, to hold on. To remember, to let go.

The rain drips outside my window. The clouds stay steady and low, heralding the wind, but inching apart for the sun.

I grab my camera, kneel by the windowsill, close my eyes for a moment, and snap as the wind stretches the arms of the old willow toward the river. The sky reddens as the thunder grows louder, closer. My walls creak. The television blinks and freezes. A car alarm wails in the distance. The room darkens, then rumbles.

Years ago, when I lived with Vasily in Brighton Beach, a tremor woke me in the middle of the night. A quiet roar that had traveled north, and even though my bed shook for several seconds, it did not wake Vasily. The only sign that I wasn't dreaming was the clinking of my bedside lamp. In the dim room, without the aid of my contacts or glasses, I couldn't see clearly, but I could hear the lamp's jewels collide against one another, like they're doing now, the sound echoing in the darkness.

And now it takes only seconds, measured by a few jeweled collisions, for the wind to knock the dead willow off its base, exposing its roots, the rocks, and the cement that had held it in place for as long as I can remember. Its slow fall feels deliberate as it cuts the street in half, crushing two cars in its descent.

I snap several pictures on my camera before sending one from my phone to my mother.

Dios mío ten cuidado, she texts back.

The air gushes through the window, carrying with it the salt of the river, the smell of the exposed earth, the last sweet breath of summer. The thunder is still close; the sky lights up, and the rain patters on what remains of the willow and the broken concrete.

I dress quickly and head outside, where others have already gathered to make sure the cars are empty. The willow's trunk has crushed the top of the SUV parked just under it. Its branches have destroyed the windshield of the silver Altima parked across it, on my side of the street. There's speculation as to who owns the SUV; there are three of the same brand and color on the block. But everyone knows who owns the silver Altima. I text Manny.

I make my way across the street and around the crushed car to the tree's bare roots. A slab of concrete is attached to them. My camera lens homes in on the loosened soil at the base of the trunk and into the gaping hole left on the sidewalk. Incredible, how deep those roots dove; how powerful the wind that finally had its way. The exhalation of the wet earth, thick and almost alien, penetrates the air. I take in heaps of it like a ravenous animal. The other spectators wrap their arms around their torsos, bracing themselves against another sudden show of the wind's strength. If only I could follow her, see what other creatures she uproots with her breath.

I rush back upstairs to swap out my wide-angle lens for my macro one. From my bedroom window, I hear the commotion outside as more neighbors gather around the uprooted tree and damaged cars, shielding their faces from a sun that only now has begun to eye its way through the storm. As I search for the lens in my top dresser drawer, I catch my reflection in the mirror. My cheekbones are flushed. My curls, now loose on my crown, slip over my brows.

My collarbone glistens in sweat. I *see* my own body—proof of its effort and vitality, its own inner workings. I could not remember when I had last seen myself like this. Not just moving for the sake of it, but doing so with purpose, with intention.

The images I had slid into the edge of my mirror come into focus. My parents and me on the steps of St. Thérèse's after I received my first communion. My father and me dancing at my modest quinceañera party here, at home. My arms wrapped around his waist on the night of his last Thanksgiving. Then the framed picture of my parents and grandmother on that boat in Yarinacocha. He wasn't one to smile for the camera, but he did in these. He smiled even as he learned to let go.

At the very bottom edge is La Cantante's business card. She is not looking at the camera. Her saffron lips lean into a silver microphone. Her skin gleams beneath her matte black dress and against the smoky backdrop. Her fingers open, ready to give, to receive. Beside her card is another, slightly bent from how I shoved its dense blue body between the wood and the mirror.

I pick up the cards and text one woman, then the other, before heading back into the dissipating storm.

29

PAULA

IT DOESN'T TAKE THREE MONTHS. IT TAKES JUST THIRTY DAYS. THIRTY DAYS of clearing out the beach towels and pails, the goggles and flip-flops, and whatever remained of the summer wares by moving them to the endcaps near the entrance with a big SALE sign. I arrange everything Halloween and pumpkin-scented at the front too. Even small shifts, like moving certain candies up the shelf and closer to the registers (gum and mints for the adults) and others down (M&M's and Sour Patches for the children), seem to make a mark. I join Sandeep on calls with distributors. He introduces me as his right hand (he doesn't use the word *man*, which is very modern of him), so no one is surprised when I bring up renegotiating costs or, at the very least, payment terms, since we've been customers for a very long time and always pay our bills.

At the YMCA, I recruit the boot camp and yoga instructors to spread the word in class that DollaBills, right on the avenue, is looking for help, and if anyone's interested, they can talk to Paula, a cue for me to wave my hand. Starting pay is fifteen dollars an hour, I tell whoever is interested, with room to grow. I hire two friends of acquaintances this way. Weeks later, even those in class who never approached me about DollaBills greet me by name.

Sandeep comes into the store less often than he used to. What was once every day for a few hours is now five days for even fewer hours. He still sits in the back office with his feet propped up on his desk, constantly on his cell phone negotiating with the landlord about the air conditioning or with his wife about their son's wedding, but he watches me more and corrects me quietly, patiently— not the way he usually sounds on the phone or when he's wandering the floor. He might find it awkward, I think, to yell at a woman his age. Then again, maybe this is who he is when he is teaching. Assertive but guiding in his tone. Maybe it's both. All I know is that the teacher seems satisfied with his student.

And while all things progressed better than I expected with Sandeep, there is still that rift between me and Shanti. When I first tell her to move the flip-flops to the sale endcap, she asks, "So you're the boss now? No one told me." But Sandeep did, I remind her, and she tosses aside whatever is in her hand to do as I asked.

At first her behavior strikes me as that of a child throwing a tantrum. Except you point out that Shanti is no child. "She may seem like one to you, Ma, but she's an adult. Look at it from her perspective. She's worked there longer than you and has two kids to support. You'd be mad too."

When the Halloween candy and decorations arrive, I ask Shanti where we should put them. Even though she gives me a sideways look, she suggests putting the pumpkin and ghost decals on the windows and placing a couple of electronic witches and scarecrows right by the door.

"Won't that scare the little ones?" I ask.

"Not if we can put a few pumpkin pails with stickers next to them," she says. "They can trade in the stickers for candy at the registers. Nothing expensive, so Sandeep won't get angry." She suggests peppermints, which is very clever because they are, after all, his favorite, and, apparently, also the favorite of many adults that come in. Their kids, well, not so much, but that's fine because sometimes, not always, their adults end up buying them actual good Halloween candy. Shanti beams each time these last-minute additions make it to the pile of items already on the register.

She helps me sort and arrange the shipments that come in of Thanksgiving decorations, Christmas lights and wreaths, Santa figurines, dreidels, menorahs, red and green candles—all the holiday items we need to plan for as soon as October hits. She interviews every job applicant that I do, jotting down her observations in her notebook, or at least pretending to, and making everyone a little bit nervous in the process. It's a good strategy. The ones that are flustered by it simply get up and leave or are offended that she's taking notes for a job that's "not that serious." We get rid of the lazy ones quite easily this way.

She hasn't asked for a raise yet, but I've told Sandeep that she is trustworthy, creative, very organized. Someone we need to help run a store. She can certainly manage one too.

"I don't need two managers for this place," he tells me.

"No, but you need one good manager for each of your stores."

"Let Shanti worry about her own future," he says, and this is when his tone simmers. "You need to worry about *your* store, Miss Paula." It takes me a moment to process what he's saying. My skin reacts first, tingling in that pause. "The Jackson Heights one. I need you to start splitting your time there."

My heart picks up. "When?"

"Starting next week."

• • •

THE JACKSON HEIGHTS store is two trains and forty minutes away in Queens. It's not as large as the Brooklyn store, but still a good size and quite busy. About ten employees work there at any given time, with Sandeep popping in for half of the day, then heading home straight after. Now I will replace Sandeep.

The neighborhood itself has more music and street food options, as if it is simply an extension of everyone's home life. Several Colombian restaurants and bakeries, and even a few Peruvian ones, scatter the neighborhood. I can get coffee and a buñuelo for three dollars. The low buildings mean there is more sunlight. The 7 train calls out from Roosevelt Avenue every few minutes. The store is only half a block from the train station, but of course I still worry about commuting from there in the winter evenings when I have to close it.

"It'll be fine, Ma," you reassure me over dinner. "I can meet you at the train station if you want. With all this change, we're both gonna have to get out of our comfort zones, you know."

"I was hoping to stay here," I say, "in this store. Now I have to worry about the trains. You know how unreliable they are late at night."

"They're always unreliable," you say. "And we have to move out anyway. You'll still need to deal with a commute. Maybe we should learn how to drive. We can get our licenses and buy a car! Or we can just move closer to that store."

For the first time, the idea of moving doesn't sound like a betrayal. My body doesn't brace itself at the thought of leaving. The impulse to resist the notion isn't there. It doesn't even feel like I need to whisper when I say, "Maybe." The prospect doesn't scare me anymore. Instead, the idea of change feels promising. As if anything is possible.

30

FLORES

MY MOTHER AND I SIT IN THE LIVING ROOM NOW. SHE HAS NEVER CONSIDERED leaving this apartment or the neighborhood, despite how pregnant with grief our lives here have become. I thought those last few days of Pa's life would release our attachment to this place. During that time, Ma was seldom in their bedroom. She mostly stayed in the kitchen, making the only soup she knew how to make just to fill the air for him with its aroma, or cleaned the rest of the apartment, determined to wipe away any hint of Death. She dusted every baptism, communion, and quinceañera favor she collected over the years, wiped down her crystals and santos, decided the stored bedsheets and towels smelled like mothballs and hauled them to the laundromat. She scrubbed the refrigerator shelves clean of the sticky stains left behind by syrup bottles and Tetra Paks, and left the television in the living room on at full volume so she could listen to reruns of *O Clone* no matter where she was in the apartment. She checked on my father's bags, picked up the cup of tea I'd leave on the nightstand. That was how my mother spent most of her days then. At night, she lay beside him, but only after I had succumbed to sleep, or when I was out. Whenever I did catch her there, she'd dart up, her face cast down so I couldn't catch a glimpse of it.

That last night he was with us, she slept beside him. I took to the fire escape, with wine in a mug and a gummy Eric had slipped into my pocket before I took leave from the Bowl. A poor attempt to ease the sorrow. It was only magnified whenever I heard laughter coming from the neighbors next door. New folks from the Midwest. I found myself quieting down whenever they were around, even though I wished I could tell them to shut the fuck up, close their damn window—a man is dying over here. My father is dying.

In that moment, I couldn't recall when it was that I had last heard my father laugh. Before he got sick, he often clutched his belly when he laughed; that, I did remember. But he held his belly the same way when he was in pain too. Joy and pain, I realized, had the same point of origin. Perhaps the heart is where we carried both, but where I felt it—at least where I could pinpoint their genesis—was my gut. From there, the sensation exploded. From there, it could consume me.

I didn't think then of what my grief would consume. Hope, in some ways, and the relationship I had with my mother. With myself. What I did not expect is how grief would devour the excess— the expectations I had about myself, and not just the ones that originated in me, but those I had absorbed over the years. That consumption would leave me with clarity.

I did not want to be with Vasily. I came to understand that I did love him, but not in the way I wish I had. The separation was painful nonetheless, and for some time, I considered whether I had made a mistake, even though in that gut of mine and in that heart I knew that I had not. And though I expected some form of grief at the end of that relationship, it did not prepare me for the kind that came with my father's departure.

On his last night, we had called the nurse from Divine Cup. The day-long slumber, the widening gaps between his breaths, their shallowness. He was close, she told us. I didn't want him in hospice because I didn't want him to be alone when it happened. He'd always feared Death and dying, yet as the day drew closer, he didn't seem to anymore. He wanted to talk to his sister, who was barely audible over the phone with her muffled cries. He didn't want a wake: he wasn't going to put on a show as a corpse. He wanted to be cremated. He wanted a memorial service, with pink flowers—roses, carnations, peonies if that was possible—and everyone wearing something pink. And he wanted a particular song played at the service, "Alma, Corazón y Vida," which the priest permitted even though the song wasn't even remotely religious.

He made us promise that when the time came, we'd prepare him for Death; that we'd make him presentable for his Maker. My father, in the end, was ready, as ready as anyone could be. He didn't seem scared.

But I was. And when he was home, I couldn't run away from it. I couldn't escape it. Death would come for him like it will one day come for me, for all of us. And I knew, sitting on that fire escape, as laughter joined the chorus of the night and the glow of the moon, that until then and despite death, life persists. I had to maneuver my way through it, in what form and in what way, I did not know. That was something my father didn't teach me in life. It is something I learn only with his passing and with time; with his memory still coursing through my center, in that very place where joy and sadness reside. And though I was afraid then—as I am now—of what tomorrow might look like, tomorrow would come. That, I must always remember.

And so when that morning came, and his toes bore blue, I acted with love in mind. I wiped down his body with my mother's agua Florida and lukewarm water, dressed him in freshly laundered pale blue pajamas, dabbed cologne behind his ears and along his collarbone, combed his silver-tinged black hair—one last time. My mother sat beside him, eyes swollen, reciting prayers and holding his hand.

Today, three years to the day he passed, we sit in the living room, facing his urn. Beside it is the bouquet of fresh pink roses and carnations I picked up on the way home. Laid down before it are a few of the peonies my mother had dried and saved from the day she got her bonus. My hand grips the lease I signed that afternoon. We saw just two apartments and decided on a two-bedroom in Jackson Heights. We were taking over the lease for a friend who had taken a job in California. The apartment is just a few blocks from the train station, and although it is more expensive than our current rent, the landlord was satisfied with my mother's proof of income and her steady job at DollaBills, and two letters—one from Sandeep about her raise and another from the new job I had in the works.

My mother sits quietly. The top half of her face is bloated in shades of pink that surround her amber eyes. The bottom half is pallid and sunken, her lips flaking from dehydration. When I scoot closer, she gets up and makes her way to the kitchen sink.

"I dreamed of Martín last night," she says, wiping her tears. She reaches for the faucet and lets a slow trickle run. It strikes me that she didn't say "your father." She said his name. There is something about saying it, hearing it, that always makes me feel like we're calling him back. Not his ghost, but his spirit.

The steady stream of water grows louder. I take a seat at the table. "What did you dream?"

Without turning, she points her head toward the front door behind me. "He came through there. He looked like he was before. You know. More hair. A healthy face. Not swollen from all the fluids or that look of a frail man. He wore a trench coat. Like he was a detective or trying to sell me a fake Rolex on Canal." She laughs. "I cried when I saw him. I was sitting there, where you are now. And I said, 'Amor, ¿qué estás haciendo aquí? No deberías estar aquí.' And he said, 'Mírame, Vieja, aquí estoy.' And he took off the coat, and you know what he had around his waist? A bomb. It covered his whole belly. Then he took it off. He said, 'Ya no me duele, Vieja. Ya no.'"

Her fingers reach to the slow drip. She lets the water trace her fingers. "I never told you this," she says, "but one morning, after we came home from the hospital, I asked if I could go with him. He'd suffered so much, Yoli. He didn't seem like the person he once was. It was just pieces of him left. At the time, I thought that's all that was left of me too. And so I told him we can go together. No more pain. No more suffering. He wouldn't be alone. *I* wouldn't be alone. He had so much medication. There was enough that we could go quietly. I could kiss him one last time and then we could wait for Death together. I thought that was something I could bear. I could bear letting him go if I was just moments behind him."

Her body leans against the edge of the sink. She tilts her face toward the gulping stream. The air in the room grows thinner. "He turned away from me, and I begged him to forgive me. How could I even say that to him? But how was I supposed to feel? I had lived almost my entire life with this man. We were supposed to go back to that store, back to Peru. To that river in his picture. We were supposed to be here, with *you*. Things I couldn't imagine doing without him. And you know what he did?" She pauses, not for me to answer, but for a breath. "He took my hand and said he was sorry. He was sorry that he hadn't always loved me the way I needed to be loved. Sorry that he couldn't love me still."

I resist the urge to go to her. My mother, always so distant, always reluctant to have the hard conversations with anyone, is having one with herself.

"I cried," she goes on, "and he said, 'Write this down, Paula. Write it.'" She wipes her face with some of that water. "'Perdóname si te fallé. Recuerda que siempre te quise.'"

My stomach sinks. The note. It wasn't my mother's petition after all. It was his.

"After he died, I left his words under the urn. It was his last note to me, so I keep it there, but I don't want his spirit to live with any kind of regret. The truth is that none of us are free from mistakes. I've failed you too, and I am sorry. But there is also love, and that is what I want to hold on to. Even Death can't take that. I carry that truth with me always."

Her face contracts as she brings her forefinger and thumb to her eyes, takes a deep breath, then brings the edge of her oversize pajama to her face. She muffles her cries.

"We are still here," she says. "I am still alive. We both are. These years have been hard, but the truth is, they haven't all been sorrow. This time is always the hardest. All the memories flood back. I'm still learning from it all and finding out things about myself that I never cared to know or wanted to know. There's something to that, I think. In the learning and unlearning. In facing who we are and realizing we are enough."

I let myself go to her and wrap my arm around her. She does not turn. The last time I held her like this was when my father's breath turned into a whisper. He left us that way, with a hum, the same way he lived his life, to a song only he could hear. After his diagnosis, I promised him that he'd never see me cry. I did then, at 11:21 A.M. on a bright summer morning, as a brown thrasher sang on the window ledge and the willow danced and the sun's fingers reached for him through the window.

I hold my mother and let myself cry like I did then, into her hair, relieved that even if he's still here, even if he can hear us, my tears are quiet and small, but out of me. This confession she lays out, with *Martín* on her lips, is not meant for me, not at all. My cry is for me. Hers are meant for the water.

AUTUMN

31

FLORES

THE FIRST DANCE I LEARN FROM LA CANTANTE IS LANDÓ. SATURDAY MORNINGS, I make my way to the dance studio she rents in Astoria, with my camera, a journal, and a ruffled skirt with red flowers. The students are young—the eldest is at most fifteen years old—but it is where La Cantante insists I need to be. At the beginning. Besides, she doesn't offer classes for adults in Astoria yet. For that, I'd have to go to Paterson. But if I want what I tapped into that day at the park, if I intend to seek out el duende or what resides inside, then I need to play, not perfect. And I am far from perfecting. Her choreography is hard for me to count out. My movements do not flow from one to the next. It is not about counting, she tells me, but the feeling. To flow with the music will take time. To move with that force guiding my spirit in all facets will take lifetimes.

In exchange for the lessons, I take her new head shots and will photograph two upcoming student shows. I have no aspiration to ever perform onstage. For the first time in my life, I am doing something simply for the pleasure it brings me, with no goal, no marker to measure my progress. The movements open up something deeper in me that I can't quantify. I *see* more, with and without a camera.

I have three weeks before I start my job at Silver Blue Ventures.

When I spoke with Nina that night of the storm, she'd already heard about what Eric had described as a "purging" at the Bowl.

"I'm embarrassed to ask," I started, but she didn't let me finish. She reminded me of the conversation we had that night after the summer party; that she's always in need of good people. The official offer to join the company came two weeks later, after several meetings with the CFO and her team. The role is a step up from my job at the Bowl, both in title and pay, and although I thought it would bring me some sense of retribution and satisfaction to now work at one of the Bowl's investors, it hasn't. Not quite. The job feels very much transitional, and that's what this particular point in my life—*our* life—feels like. Maybe every stage in life is, in some way, a transition. A movement we can learn from and hopefully build on. A constant state of flow with no end.

When my mother and I begin to pack for the move, we agree to keep only some of Pa's possessions. His chair. The alpaca blanket that he slept with, with its orange flowers bursting like sunsets. His favorite pink button-down shirt, with the ink stain on its breast pocket. A pair of scuffed burgundy shoes he wore on weekends. His maroon sweater and bomber jacket. We pack up the rest, along with some of our own clothes, and place them in bags destined for the Salvation Army. We sort through several kitchen items— mixers, plates, silverware, even some of Ma's mason jars—all of which we decide to leave on the sidewalk for whoever might make better use of them.

As I head downstairs with one box of pots and pans, I see Manny near the fence. Despite my objection, he takes the box from me and sets it next to the others. He stays in a squat, looks at the contents, his hands together as if in prayer.

"You're really leaving."

I take in a long breath as I sit cross-legged beside him, my chin resting on my knuckles. I can hardly believe it, either, but it feels right. "I'm ready," I say.

He smirks. "I never thought you'd leave again. You're as much a part of this block and this neighborhood as these trees, this concrete." He gestures west. "That river. Far back as I can remember, you and this place are like this." He interlocks his fingers.

"That's why it'll be good for me to go," I whisper. "New space, new neighborhood. Besides, it's not like I'm moving to another country, just the borough next door! I need change, you know? We need that sometimes, even when it's hard."

"I don't think it's hard for you to peace out." He chuckles. "You already left once. With your ex."

"This is different. It's harder. In some ways, it's easier to stay where you are—physically, emotionally—instead of taking the time to really figure it out."

"That's very deep, Yoli. Are you meditating now? Please tell me you're getting some yoga in."

"I *should*."

He sits down, his shoulder brushing mine. "I'm just not sure I'll ever leave. The only time I think I can is when, you know . . ." His voice trails off. I know. He can't say it because saying it calls it, as my mother would say.

"Not necessarily," I tell him. "You'll know when you're ready. And if you don't leave, well. This place isn't all that bad."

"Not at all! We got the flashy bars with the sixteen-dollar cocktails, the bougie C-Town with the ten-dollar strawberries, those fancy puppy bed-and-breakfasts." I laugh, and when a quiet moment settles between us, he clears his throat. "Do you think maybe now that, you know, we won't be neighbors and all, you'd consider going to the museum with me? If you need change to get to know yourself better . . ." I feel myself blush. "Maybe you can change your mind about spending some time with me."

I press my lips together. "Maybe."

"Yeah?"

"Yeah. Hit me up in a few weeks and we'll see."

"A few weeks?"

"I've got a surprise for my mom."

"Are you going to tell me?"

"Not before I tell her," I say.

"Are you taking her somewhere?" I put my finger on my lips. "Nice! Take some pictures, please."

"Oh, I will. Doesn't mean I'll show them to you."

"I'm not asking. Some things are just meant for us, I know that much," he says, and in that moment, I *see* Manuel. He turns to the mason jars, pairs them with their lids, and smiles. "Do you mind if I help myself?"

"No." I giggle, a sound so foreign that my instinct is to cover my mouth so he won't see the smile. Instead I drop my hand, unfazed if he does.

· · ·

"PERU?" MY MOTHER'S face goes pale as I show her the itinerary on my computer screen. She sits down next to me as if her legs might give.

"It's been so long," I say, "and there's so much to see. We can't possibly do it all in one trip, but there's no way we're going back without seeing Machu Picchu. So that's where we'll go first. We'll catch a flight to Cusco as soon as we land."

"*We?*"

"Yes, Ma! You and me. We can finally take that trip we were supposed to take back when Pa was alive. And we'll do the same when we go to Pucallpa. From Cusco to Lima, then straight onto a connecting flight to Pucallpa. I'd like to go to El Carmen, but maybe we'll save that for another trip. Anyway, we can spend a few days in Lima after we get back." I wait for a reaction to the plan thus far, but when she stays quiet, I propose something she might object to. "Maybe we can see my aunt? And I know it's not the family's anymore, but we could visit the store."

I pause, unsure if the shock will make way for joy or a hard no at even the prospect of going back. I prepared myself for both reactions—if it's joy, then wonderful. For the very first time in nearly two decades, we can return to a kind of home. This time, holding the memory of the person we both loved as we make our way to the places he wished he could have seen again. Even those he had only dreamed of seeing.

"Yoli, I just got this promotion," she reminds me. "It's like starting a new job. You can take time off before you start yours, but I can't."

"You can. I've already spoken to Sandeep." Before she can protest again, I pull up pictures of the hotels where we will be staying, point out the four-and-a-half-star reviews, the spacious courtyards, and even the balcony in our room in Pucallpa, which overlooks the pool. "We can go to Yarinacocha and visit San Francisco. Watch the sunset over the water while we're on the boat. The pictures will be incredible. Like Pa's." I can take a boat ride down that river for the very first time. If Ma resists, I'll make the trip without her. She may not be ready, but I am.

"It's been years." Her voice catches in her throat. "More than thirty years since I saw that river with your father. And then am I supposed to just forgive your aunt? Just walk into that store? Who knows what it is now."

"I'd like to see her again," I admit. "I think it might be good for me. She knew a whole other side of Pa. You have to let go of the anger too, Ma. And the store . . ." I close my laptop and turn to face her. "I was wrong. When I said that this apartment wasn't ours because we didn't own it. We loved here, we laughed here. We *lived* here. That store might not be yours on paper, but it is yours in every way that matters." I take her hand. "We're starting new chapters in our lives, Ma. It might be good to honor where it all started."

"Before closing those chapters," she whispers, her eyes distant.

"I'm not saying goodbye. Neither should you. But that was the last trip you took before coming here and starting this part of your journey. Whatever doubts or fear you had, you didn't let it hold you back. You turned it into something. I don't want us to forget. I want to learn to live with the grief. I want to make something beautiful out of it. We can tell that river whatever it is that's holding us back, and let it go. Or maybe—maybe—we can even tell it to each other."

"I have nothing to say to you that I haven't already said. Besides, I've never been good with words."

"You're good with writing," I say. "You're always leaving prayers on the altar. I'm not very good with the camera, Ma. But it wasn't until I picked it up and tried that I actually started to see things. Losing Pa taught me that. To pay closer attention. To see the world differently. Myself, differently."

She stands and walks to the altar and Pa's urn. They will be the last items we pack and take with us to the new apartment. Whether the urn will remain with us or not is something I've thought about too. We could place it in a cemetery nearby or scatter his ashes in the ocean, though whether Atlantic or Pacific, I'm not sure. Nor am I ready to bring it up to her just yet. One change at a time. But for now my mother takes a step closer to what I think is healing. She slides the urn gently, presses her index and middle fingers to her lips, and places the kiss over my father's name. She comes back to me and takes my hand. She sits a little taller.

"We'll go. And I promise you, hija, one day, I'll tell you." She turns my hand over and places the note she had tucked beneath my father's urn in the center of my palm. "We can start with this today," she says, holding my hand tighter, triggering a charge that flickers behind her eyes and sets my soul aglow.

Acknowledgments

THIS BOOK WOULD NOT HAVE BEEN POSSIBLE WITHOUT THE ENCOURAGEMENT I received from so many. I am eternally grateful to:

My agent and champion, Julia Kardon, Hannah Popal, and HG Literary.

My incredible editor, Sara Birmingham, and the wonderful team at Ecco for believing in this book.

Laura Pegram and Kweli's Art of the Short Story class, where the first pages of this novel took root.

Irina Akulenko, Jenn Baker, Emily Bang, Lizete Bautista, Jimena Caballero, Monica Carrillo Zegara, Veronica Frenning, Nitasha Mehta, Shanti Ragubir, Aleksandra Waxman, and Sarah Xie for their insight and clarity.

Andrea Bartz, Naima Coster, Angie Cruz, Patricia Engel, Angie Kim, Lisa Ko, Denne Michele Norris, Tracy O'Neill, Julia Phillips, Lilliam Rivera, Ivelisse Rodriguez, Etaf Rum, Ruchika Tomar, Da Fellows 2015, La Familia from Scratch, and my entire literary family for uplifting and sustaining our work and practice through challenging times.

The Homies and the BLS Detective Agency for their realness and friendship.

The matriarchs in my life, Zadith Rivero, Ewa Potocka, and Clotilde Isla, who teach me about family, resilience, and faith daily.

My father, Juan G. Rivero, whose spirit emerges in every Peruvian vals and every rose.

My brothers, John Rivero and Sixto Elias Rivero, and my sisters-in-law, Teresa Rivero and Laura Rivero. I am so lucky to have you.

My husband, Bartosz Potocki, and our children, Sebastian and Gabriel. I have loved you across lifetimes.